CRY CHAOS

and

Let Slip the Dogs of Tyranny

Jack Chase

ABOUT THE AUTHOR

Jack Chase is the author of three medical thrillers and the new political thriller *Cry Chaos and Let Slip the Dogs of Tyranny*. His novels have been published in multiple languages and sold throughout the world.

Jack Chase is board certified in internal medicine and infectious disease. His medical career has spanned the spectrum from clinical practice to basic research in molecular biology. He has served as director of clinical research for two multinational pharmaceutical corporations and as attending physician on the infectious disease services of a number of medical schools.

Jack is married to *New York Times* bestselling novelist Katherine Stone. They live in the Pacific Northwest.

Additional information about Jack Chase and his novels can be found at CryChaos.com or MedicalThriller.com.

Also by Jack Chase

FATAL ANALYSIS

MORTALITY RATE

THE MAGRUDER TRANSPLANT

Marx was fortunate to have been born eighty years before Walt Disney. Disney also promised a child's paradise and unlike Marx, delivered on his promise.

John Ralston Saul in *Voltaire's Bastards: The Dictatorship of Reason in the West*

Communism is not love. Communism is a hammer which we use to crush the enemy.

Mao Tse-tung

1

WHERE IS AMERICA?

Someone had painted those words on a sheet of plywood. The plywood was nailed to the front of a now-defunct bookstore, an opaque replacement for a now-defunct window. It had been quite a remarkable little store, operating at the same downtown location for decades. Victoria had always enjoyed browsing the shelves and hearing what new titles Helen and Jane were promoting. Operating an independent bookstore at a profit was a challenging proposition under any circumstances. The riots had rendered it impossible. Still, Helen had hung on as long as she could, often proclaiming that, if her beloved Jane were still alive, Jane would know just what to do.

Victoria knew that Helen had replaced the front display window at least twice, at enormous sacrifice, out of her personal savings—the bookstore's insurance policy specifically excluding damage caused by rioting. In the end, Helen, elderly and alone, saw that she had only one remaining option, surrender. She discounted everything in a last desperate effort to recover some value from her remaining stock, but, ultimately, most of her precious books were simply stolen. Thieves just walked in, grabbed as much as they could carry, then sauntered out, often with a smirk for Helen. Based on her many years in the book business, Helen said, she was suspicious that those people were not avid readers. The police said that the thieves would try to sell the books for whatever they could get. In the absence of ready buyers, the books would simply be abandoned to rot in some back alley. Naturally, no arrests were made.

Victoria glanced one last time at the sign.

WHERE IS AMERICA?

The words would soon be painted over. This was not a sentiment that was approved of by the authorities. Other graffiti, principally the work of rioters, was assiduously preserved on the surfaces of streets and on the sides of public buildings. Defacing these creations could result in serious repercussions—either at the hands of the law or the rioters, whichever happened to catch up with you first.

The once bustling downtown area was now desolate, its streets lined with derelict buildings—some still largely intact but long-since boarded up and abandoned; others simply reduced to charred rubble. The burned-out buildings reminded Victoria of the heavily bombed Kaiser Wilhelm Memorial Church on the Kurfürstendamm in Berlin. For decades, the blackened remains of the church's spire had been carefully preserved, a stark reminder of the horrors of war.

Even those few businesses still fighting the good fight and struggling to remain open had followed Helen's lead and refitted their windows with plywood. Now though, with the riots returning, Victoria no longer held any hope for the survival of the downtown area. Why did the government not care? Where *is* America?

Victoria returned her attention to the sidewalk, navigating as best she could around the denizens who slept there, keeping a sharp eye out to avoid stepping on anything unpleasant or dangerous. Hard experience had taught her not to make eye contact and not to respond to anyone who accosted her verbally. Victoria had parked her car in what she believed to be a relatively safe location, deciding that it was marginally safer to walk the last few blocks. She did not have a fancy car, but carjacking had become a constant worry, and she had been warned that her particular model was highly prized because it was so easy to sell. Victoria had decided that, on balance, if her car were to be stolen, she would prefer not to be in it. For most people, these kinds of considerations had become the fabric of everyday life, but Victoria was confident that no such concerns had entered her father's mind when he casually asked her to drop by the clinic for lunch.

Dad was a bit of a head-in-the-clouds type. A professor at the medical school, he had been a brilliant researcher, but his first loves were clinical practice and teaching. With students, he had the patience of Job; with faculty, he did not. Dad had a rigid sense of right and wrong and did not suffer fools lightly. There were constant battles with the administration over laboratory space, clinical trials that he regarded as unwarranted or unethical, the promotion of faculty he saw as unworthy, and on and on. The battles were interminable. In short, the medical students and residents loved him, the administration, not so much.

Fortunately, a solution was found and peace declared. The medical school would fund the downtown clinic that her father had been calling for, and her father would run it. The clinic would serve the economically disadvantaged and medically underserved. House staff and students would rotate through the clinic and get a taste of real medicine and real people. It was perfect. He had made it clear that he would love for Victoria to join him at the clinic, but she reminded him that she was still only an associate professor and had far too many pressing commitments at the medical school to even think of moving.

And then the riots came.

Dad was a lifelong liberal of the FDR variety, and Victoria had inherited the gene. Her father had marched for civil rights and equal opportunity, and Victoria doubted that he had ever voted for a Republican. But he simply did not accept that the riots were somehow the next step in the struggle for universal human rights. He regarded the riots as counterproductive and unlawful and could not understand how the government could encourage and support such lawlessness while turning its back on the victims, the most vulnerable of which were the financially destitute population that he was trying to care for. Defund the police? Who was that going to help? As it was, the devastation of the downtown corridor and the unremitting street crime had slowed to a trickle the formerly generous flow of donations from merchants that the clinic had depended on to augment its spare medical school funding.

Dad knew that leadership truly came from the top, and he had placed his hope in the idea that a new president, with a more liberal bent, would have the respect of the Left and therefore be able to lead it in a more productive direction. He had been desperately disappointed.

Victoria looked up, and, as though bidden by her own thoughts, new graffiti came into view on a building now just in front of her.

GRANDPA SHOULDN'T BE DRIVING THE CAR

And beside it, another, even more disconcerting.

IF GRANDPA ISN'T DRIVING, WHO IS?

Victoria turned a corner and suddenly found herself at the fringe of a swarm of police activity. There were twenty-five or thirty law enforcement officers of various stripes, most outfitted in what she would call SWAT gear. A dozen or more wore bulletproof vests imprinted with the initials FBI.

Helmeted and heavily armed, most carried what appeared to Victoria to be automatic weapons. In addition to a large number of generic-appearing police cars, there were two large armored, military-type vehicles. There was every appearance of well-armed troops prepared for battle. In the current climate, in which authorities refused to pursue all but the most extreme and egregious crimes, Victoria could hardly imagine what manner of criminal atrocity had prompted a response of this magnitude.

She needed to figure a way to circle around the horde of spectators blocking her route so that she could get to the clinic. She signaled a nearby policeman who appeared more dressed to help control the crowd than to engage in mortal combat, but as she did, she felt a tug on her shoulder. Turning, she saw a small man walking away, a vicious-looking box cutter in one hand and her shoulder bag in the other. He opened the bag, then, suddenly furious, threw it on the ground and began to walk back toward Victoria.

"Don't even think about it, Miguel." It was the cop, who had clearly witnessed the theft.

Miguel hesitated, then slowly turned and walked away.

The policeman retrieved Victoria's bag and handed it to her. "It's smart not to have much in your purse," he said, "but it's also a good idea to leave ten or twenty dollars in it. People like Miguel expect to get paid, and when they don't, things can get ugly. We've had some pretty brutal assaults."

Victoria was incredulous. "You know who he is?"

"We think so. When he first came to our attention, he had an arrest warrant that he'd been handed when he was apprehended crossing the border. As an arrest warrant, it was meaningless. The feds had no intention of ever enforcing it. Miguel used it for identification, which was precisely the purpose that the government had in mind when they gave it to him. He presented it like it was an American Express

Platinum Card. And why not? It gave him free travel to our fair city. It provides him food and healthcare and even a roof over his head."

"So, he doesn't need to steal."

"It's what he does, and, besides, he probably owes a lot of money to whichever cartel got him across the border. You hear about some family of six coming across and paying a cartel three or four thousand dollars apiece. They don't have that kind of money. They're indentured to the cartel until it's paid off. My guess, for most, it never gets paid off."

"Can't he be deported?" Victoria asked. But she knew better.

"Not once he's made it to our lovely sanctuary…"

A sudden burst of activity among the FBI agents drew their attention. The cop went back to supervising the abruptly energized crowd. Victoria studied the scene.

It looked like the FBI had got their man. He was mostly obscured from her view. A tall man; hands cuffed behind him. They had dressed him in a bulletproof vest, presumably out of fear that some vengeful victim of their prisoner might take a shot at him.

Then she could see the back of his head. White hair. That was a surprise. He appeared to be scanning the crowd. Then he turned, and she saw his face. Their eyes locked. He offered a faint smile and winked.

Oh, Dad, what have you done?

2

Victoria, watching in disbelief as her father disappeared into a waiting van, became abruptly aware of a man in the crowd who was staring at her. She turned her head, and he immediately averted his gaze. He was a big man, well over six-feet tall, and muscular. His tattooed biceps and forearms evidenced long hours spent in the weight room. The man held a large piece of cardboard, obviously a sign of some sort, but it was turned away from Victoria. As she watched, the increasingly agitated crowd—more of a mob, now, really—began to edge closer to the man. Someone bumped his arm causing the wording on the sign to come into Victoria's view.

LADY LIBERTY IS WEEPING

A ragtag group of young men and women, the sort Victoria had come to recognize as professional demonstrators and rioters, moved closer and began screaming at the man with the sign. As near as Victoria could tell, they were accusing him of being white. She noted that all but one of the professional screamers was also white. The screamers did not appear to be troubled by that evident irony.

An FBI agent in full SWAT gear hurried over and grabbed the sign. He tore it up and issued a stark warning, "You're about to be arrested for inciting a riot and obstructing a federal operation. My advice to you is to leave now, before that happens."

The now former-sign-holder said nothing. The FBI man turned and walked away.

But the screamers were not done. One grabbed the man's elbow, and what happened next occurred so quickly that Victoria could not be certain what she had seen—or, more accurately, what she hadn't seen. The screamer was suddenly on the ground, on his back, bleeding from his mouth. The man with the tattooed arms remained where he had been. Victoria thought he might have clocked the screamer with his right elbow. It reminded her of the time, many years ago, when a date had dragged her to a professional prize fight. Her date kept talking about the lightning jabs that one of the boxers was throwing. Victoria couldn't even see the punches. In her defense, neither could the other fighter.

The hostile mob, having now found a new focus for its fury, began to surround the tattooed man, screaming expletives, but taking care to stay just outside his reach. The man remained calm, stoic even, and appeared ready for whatever came next—albeit, perhaps not for the young woman who tried to spit on him. Her attempt turned out to be a tactical error, as she only managed to shower herself and her colleagues, resulting in their redirecting their expletives toward her.

Victoria saw the FBI man studying the scene. He appeared torn between wading into the melee or leaving the former sign-carrier to the wolves. At last he moved, shoving his way through the mob, then shepherding the tattooed man back through the crowd, the wary mob parting for the man with the tattoos in a way it hadn't for the FBI agent. She had no idea whether the sign carrier was being led to safety or arrest.

Victoria realized that she needed to get some distance between herself and the mob before someone figured out whose daughter she was. Her first thought was to make her way to the clinic to see what information she could glean, but when she moved around the periphery of the crowd to a point where she could see the entrance to the clinic, she found the area taped off and a host of law enforcement people shuffling in and out—in with empty evidence bags and out with bags stuffed with "evidence." They were also carting off computers, filing cabinets—virtually anything that was even remotely transportable. Victoria knew that the FBI's treasure trove of confiscated evidence would consist almost exclusively of patient data, and she wondered whether the government actually had a legal right to seize it. And how were patients supposed to receive proper care with all their medical records locked away in federal custody?

With their erstwhile target whisked away by the FBI, the mob quieted. Many simply drifted off, presumably to their next assignment—which raised the question of how had they known to show up for her father's arrest in the first place. Victoria, with no reason to linger among the residual looky-loos, began to retrace her steps, heading back toward her car while she formulated a plan.

All roads led through Brian. There was no question that he would know exactly what to do, but she suffered a brief moment of uncertainty, guilt really. She knew that he would expect her to come to him in a situation like this. He would be disappointed if she didn't. They would always be there for each other. Hadn't she recently told him that, should he contract syphilis and find himself in need of a spinal tap, he shouldn't hesitate to seek her out?

The reality was that neither of them had had a serious relationship since the divorce. They were still each other's best friend. Put more simply, they loved each other. They always would. Happily, there had been no third parties intruding into their marriage. Neither Brian nor Victoria had had a serious relationship *since* the divorce, much less during their marriage. No, the original sin that had doomed their marriage was tying the knot while Brian was in law school and she in medical school. At a time when their attention should have been sharply focused on each other, their minds were torn in separate directions. Unnurtured, their marriage had simply starved to death. When Tess came along, they both harbored great hope that the marriage might yet survive. You heard about couples staying together for the children. Fortunately, they quickly recognized that the toxic wasteland their relationship had become was no environment in which to raise a child. The key to saving their relationship was the dissolution of their marriage. Brian remained an active and devoted father, and he and Victoria were happier—and probably closer—than ever.

Victoria found her car unscathed, exactly where she had left it. She dialed her phone and quickly had Alice on the line. Alice had been with Brian's firm for something like three centuries. She was a gem. Alice knew the name of a new associate's first wife, which judge would be likely to rule most favorably on some arcane motion, and what was wrong with the plumbing on the 39th floor. Brian had inherited Alice when one of the firm's founding partners had passed away—in his corner office, of course. Brian had now worked with Alice longer than his marriage to Victoria had lasted.

Alice was all business when she answered the phone, but quickly reverted to her old-friend tone as soon as she heard Victoria's voice. Victoria told her that she needed to speak with Brian urgently, and that she was in the car headed for the office. Alice hoped that Tess was all right. Victoria assured her that Tess was fine, thank goodness. It was something else. Alice was glad to hear that, and said that she would let Brian know right away.

After saying good-bye, Victoria checked her watch, then called her own secretary to let her know that she was running late. As she pulled out of her parking place, Victoria saw a sign planted in the burned-out remains of what had once been a fashionable clothing store.

CHAOS IS NOT AN ACCIDENT – IT IS THE PLAN

—*3*—

Victoria rode the elevator to the 40th floor. When the door opened, there stood Alice, tall, dignified, elegant, with that glorious profusion of white hair—today, done in a French roll—and blue eyes that could be, in turn, stern or playful. Victoria had stopped asking herself how Alice knew things, *everything*, like when Victoria would be stepping off one of several elevators that surely opened at least a hundred times each day onto the 40th floor.

"Hi, Victoria. Brian has a client in his office, so I'll put you in a conference room."

They chatted idly as they walked down the carpeted hallway, with Alice, a seasoned veteran at protecting secrets, careful not to go anywhere near the question of why Victoria needed to see Brian so urgently. She opened a door and ushered Victoria into a long room with floor-to-ceiling windows that afforded a commanding view of the city. A conference table, surrounded by leather chairs, stretched nearly the length of the room. A serving table offered coffee, soft drinks, a variety of brands of bottled water, as well as cookies and other snacks.

"Make yourself comfortable," Alice said. "I'll tell Brian you're here." As she was closing the door, she leaned back into the room and said, "I'd be happy to bring you a latte if you prefer."

"Thanks, Alice. I'm fine."

Brian appeared more quickly than Victoria imagined he

could even cover the distance from his office—without even considering the additional time required to disengage himself from his client. He must have jogged, but nonetheless arrived with not a dark hair out of place. That was Brian. He was wearing one of her favorite suits, a medium gray with the blue repp tie. The suit matched his eyes. His face did not hide the concern he was feeling.

She stood and was quickly enveloped in loving arms. She rested her head on his chest, just above his heart.

"Alice said that Tess is okay."

"No, it's not Tess," Victoria said, reluctantly pulling herself away. "It's Dad."

"Oh, no."

Victoria understood that Brian immediately assumed that her father had developed some serious health problem. "No, Dad's fine. I mean, he's physically okay." Victoria took a deep breath. "He's been arrested."

"What!" Obviously, this was beyond Brian's perceived limits of reality. "Was it a traffic accident or something?"

"Frankly, Brian, I don't have the slightest idea why he was arrested. Dad invited me to lunch. When I arrived, half the FBI agents in the country were there to arrest him. They had machine guns or whatever they were, armored cars. They looked like they were going to war."

Then, something popped into Victoria's mind, something she'd been subliminally aware of, but, in the unreality of the moment, its significance had escaped her. "The media were there. How did they know?" Despite all the day's disturbing events, she found especially upsetting the thought that the arrest of her proud, accomplished father would be witnessed over and over again on TV.

"How the media knew is the easiest question of all," Brian said. "The Feds told them where to be and when to be there."

She watched as Brian went into attorney mode. Observing

him over the years, Victoria had learned that good attorneys approached legal questions the same way doctors solved medical problems. You do your best to discard emotion, gather the facts, then apply your knowledge and experience to find the answer.

"Where is your dad now?"

Victoria shook her head. "I have no idea. The FBI guys put him in a van and drove off." Victoria felt tears well up in her eyes. She had been all business until Brian entered the room. Now, she was struggling to hold herself together. Her father had been arrested! And she didn't have the slightest idea where they had taken him.

"Sit," Brian said. He took her shoulders in his hands and guided her back into her chair.

"I feel like I should have done *something*," Victoria said. "I just watched."

"There was absolutely nothing you could have done. Coming directly to me was exactly the right thing."

Brian reached into his coat and pulled out his phone. He began scrolling through his contacts.

"You know, it's not like the old days when I knew everybody. Ever since "Let 'Em Go" Larry was elected DA, all the experienced prosecutors have abandoned the sinking ship. Who wants to be a prosecutor when the DA won't let you prosecute anyone? Larry never met a perp he didn't like. So now the DA's office is filled with kids just out of law school who can't tell the bad guys from the victims—which is just fine with Larry.

"Same thing in the police department. A lot of the old stalwarts have moved on. They can't do their job. If they arrest somebody, they're more likely than the perp to face consequences. Cops can make more money in other states, or they can hire out privately to guard local businesses that are already drowning in taxes that are supposed to pay for law enforcement protection. What a mess."

Brian smiled. "Sorry. I'm just frustrated like everyone else. Let me make some calls and see what I can find out. I think Jim Michaels is still hanging around at the prosecutor's office, putting in his last few months before retirement."

It seemed like Brian was on the phone forever. He made several calls, finally getting Michaels on the line. Victoria could hear parts of Brian's side of the conversation. There were a lot of *I see's,* a couple of *when did that happen's,* and one resounding *Wow!* Brian closed his phone and sighed.

"Your dad was at the Capitol on January 6?"

"He was in Washington for a meeting of some kind. I had no idea he was at the Capitol."

"They're saying he was part of the so-called insurrection. For now, they've got him in a holding cell at the central lockup, but the Feds are going to transfer him to Washington where they're keeping all the January 6 prisoners."

"Not that hell hole where they hold them month-after-month, endlessly waiting for trial?"

"I'm afraid so."

"All the stories about that place. They don't even get decent food. A federal judge had to order a prisoner released because he was being denied proper medical care. Then they did an inspection and ordered something like 400 prisoners transferred out, but none of them were from the January 6 group. Apparently, the jail didn't meet minimum standards for some prisoners, but was plenty good enough for the 'insurrectionists.'"

"By all accounts," Brian said, "it's a very unpleasant place. I don't think that's an accident."

"Can I see him?" Victoria tried her best to keep the desperation out of her voice.

"Jim says no visitors until he gets to Washington. After that, it's anybody's guess. We've all heard stories...."

"Brian, we have to do something. At least we can get him an attorney."

"Jim says he already has one."

"Not some kid public defender?"

"No, somebody quite different. He arrived this afternoon in his own jet. Apparently, he's making quite a disturbance at the central lockup even as we speak."

"Well, who is it?"

"Hamilton Hobart IV, Esquire."

"Wow."

4

Victoria understood that her immediate challenge was to somehow find a way not to be consumed by her concern for her father. For now, she was unable to see him or even contact him in any way. She had little to offer but moral support, and even that, indirectly. Victoria had heard about people being caught up in the "system," and she was only just beginning to feel the sensation of abject helplessness that accompanied that process.

Fortunately, she had Brian. Her dad was in the legal system, Brian's world. Brian was on the case, and would use his contacts, pull in favors, and generally do whatever he could to help her dad and keep her informed. Meanwhile, Victoria had other responsibilities. She needed to check in at her laboratory at the medical school, then make it home before Nina dropped Tess off.

It was a bit of luck that she wasn't the attending physician in charge of the hospital's infectious disease clinical service this month. Being "on service" meant caring for patients and making rounds with a gaggle of infectious disease fellows, residents, medical students, pharmacists, and often sundry others from additional disciplines. The service saw patients in consultation, and the infectious disease problems of the patients they were asked to see were typically quite complex, often occurring against a background of some underlying immune suppressing process such as solid organ or bone marrow transplantation, cancer, HIV, and so forth. They also saw a fair number of patients with exotic infections associated with foreign travel. All in all, it was challenging and interesting work, but it at least doubled Victoria's already heavy workload. That was a strain.

Her laboratory responsibilities were a bit more flexible. Gone were the days Victoria had spent at the lab bench performing the hands-on portion of the research. Now she had technicians, fellows, and PhD post-docs to do that part of the work. Her role had become primarily supervisory. Victoria planned the research that was to be done and oversaw the writing of study protocols as well as the actual performance of the bench research. The one thing she hated was that, as the head of the lab, she was now the person in charge of finding funding for the lab's work. But, this thing she disliked most provided the flexibility a single mother needed. She could work on grant applications well into the middle of the night, *after* she'd spent a quality evening with Tess and had tucked her into bed. So, that dark funding cloud had a silver lining.

Victoria's first task was to extinguish the fires that invariably broke out in the lab during the course of a day. Next, she met with the entire laboratory staff, their regular Monday meeting, to discuss plans and problems. Then she was finally in her car headed for home. Good timing. She should arrive well ahead of Tess.

But when her house first came into view, Victoria's heart nearly stopped. Maybe she wasn't seeing what she thought she was seeing. Maybe that wasn't a little girl sitting on the front step, her head in her hands. Maybe the moon was made of green cheese. There was Tess, still wearing the face mask required by the school, sobbing into her tiny hands.

Victoria parked on the street to get more quickly to her daughter. At first, Tess didn't see her, then she came running.

"Mommy!"

She took Tess in her arms and hugged her tightly without saying anything. Tess held on like she would never let go.

Victoria felt herself on the brink of the emotional meltdown she'd been trying desperately to stave off all day. She could never have imagined that she could be so furious with Nina. What was Nina thinking! How could she possibly have left Tess alone like this? Victoria had long regarded her neighborhood as relatively safe, but so much had changed in the last few years. The house next door had been broken into. There were strange people wandering around the area at all hours. Here, as in most cities in the country, the time had long passed when a six-year-old child could be allowed to play, without adult supervision, in her own front yard.

Tess was beginning to feel heavy in her arms. Victoria slowly lowered her onto her feet and removed the silly mask from her face and took both her little hands in hers. The sobbing was over. She smiled at Tess, and Tess almost smiled back.

"I love you, Mommy."

"Oh, I love you, too, darling."

Victoria sensed that there was something more going on with Tess, more than just being abandoned to her own devices at the front door.

"Why aren't you playing with Jasmine?"

"She won't play with me anymore." The tears were back, and her small voice trembled.

"Don't be silly, Tess. Jasmine is your best friend. Did you two have an argument?"

Tess shook her head. "Jasmine won't play with me because I'm a racist." She pronounced it like "rackist."

Victoria couldn't believe what she was hearing. "Jasmine said that you were a racist?"

"Mrs. Smith said it."

Victoria tensed. She was beginning to understand where

this was going.

"Mrs. Smith said that you were a racist?"

Tess nodded. "First, she said like, you know, all the white kids are racist. Then she pointed right at me and said, '*You* are a racist.'"

"Do you know what 'racist' means, Tess?"

Tess nodded. "Hate."

"Do you hate anyone, Tess?"

She shook her head.

"Do you hate Jasmine?"

"I *love* Jasmine."

"So, you're not a racist."

"But Mrs. Smith said..."

"Teachers can be wrong, Tess, just like anyone else."

Victoria was suddenly acutely aware of the fact that she and Tess had been conducting their dialogue on a public sidewalk, in potential earshot of neighbors—probably not a good idea. She glanced around and saw no one, but noticed for the first time a very large black SUV parked down the street. She had not seen the car in the neighborhood before. It seemed out of place. The SUV's windows were heavily tinted. She had no idea who, if anyone, lurked inside.

"Let's get into the house," she said to Tess. "How would you like some cocoa?"

"Mommy, it's hot out today. It feels like summer."

"I know," she said, scooting Tess toward the door, "but I think it's just what we need. Don't you think you might be able to drink a cup?"

"Yes, please."

Victoria's phone began to ring as they walked through the door. It was Nina.

"Is Tess okay?"

"She'll be fine, but she's understandably confused about everything."

"Sounds like Mrs. Smith just figured out that all you honkies are a bunch of racists."

"That's what it sounds like to me."

"That woman is the whitest person I ever met. I could throttle her."

Victoria smiled. "Probably not the best plan."

"I'm so sorry, Victoria. Jasmine said that Tess was staying after school, and that you would pick her up. We've already had a discussion about that. The other thing is more complicated, but, of course, we'll be talking about that, too. For now, I think that the most important thing is to get the girls together as soon as possible and get this behind us. Then we can both go throttle Mrs. Smith."

"Let's not do it tonight, Nina. It's been such a hectic day. I think that tomorrow, when I take Tess and Jasmine to school, is soon enough. And we have to decide how to deal with Mrs. Smith. We simply can't allow her to do this to our children."

"Amen to that."

They chatted a while longer. Nina didn't mention Victoria's father, so she clearly hadn't heard that news. Victoria felt guilty about not sharing the information, but she was too exhausted to get into that today, and, besides, right now, Tess needed her full attention.

Victoria and Nina had been great friends for years. Ted, Nina's husband, had been a law school classmate of Brian, and now he and Brian were both partners at the same firm. Ted and Nina had been a couple since something like the second grade. They were married long before Brian met them. Ever since Victoria and Brian started dating, the two couples had spent a lot of time together. Then, when both almost simultaneously experienced unplanned pregnancies, and Jasmine and Tess came along, the closeness of the two families was sealed forever. Even after Victoria and Brian divorced, they continued to do things together, often with their daughters.

Nina had been an artist, a painter, from early childhood. She had majored in art in college, and early on her work had developed a narrow focus as she chronicled the black experience in America. She had become quite famous. Victoria had several of her paintings hanging in her house. She especially loved the one Nina had done of Jasmine and Tess. It was so beautiful, and hopeful.

Nina was so sophisticated and intellectual that people often assumed that she had been born with the proverbial silver spoon in her mouth. The truth was quite the opposite. Actually, it was Ted's family that was rolling in the big bucks. His father had developed some arcane but indispensable software that governments and global financial institutions used to zoom trillions of dollars around the world every day.

Victoria's thoughts returned to Tess, and then, suddenly, Oh, no, Tess! How was she going to tell Tess about her grandfather? It would be on the news. The kids at school would learn about it. They would probably tease Tess about it. What a mess. This was all far too much for a little girl to have to suffer through in a single day.

Victoria walked absent-mindedly to the living room window and gazed out at the street.

The black SUV was gone.

5

Over cocoa, Victoria began to prepare Tess for what was coming. She kept her tone even, almost casual.

"The police believe that your grandfather did something wrong."

Tess laughed. "Granddaddy would never do anything wrong!"

Victoria gave Tess her gentlest smile. "You and I know that, because we know him. The police don't know him as well as we do. Other people who don't know your grandfather may say mean things about him. I worry that some of the children in your school may say mean things to you about him."

"Is he in jail?"

"Yes, right now he is."

"How long will he be in jail?"

Victoria struggled to keep emotion out of her voice. "I don't know, sweetheart, for a little while."

Tess was studying the dregs of her cocoa at the bottom of her cup. She, of course, could not begin to comprehend the significance of her grandfather's being in custody, and thus was spared the anguish that racked Victoria.

"Mommy, can I have another cup of cocoa?"

"Aren't you afraid it will spoil your dinner?"

"It won't. I promise."

One more cup of cocoa, then a bath before supper. Tess could eat in her pajamas. Victoria was thinking that that sounded like a pretty attractive plan for herself, as well, but then Brian called.

"I just got a call from Ham Hobart."

Ham, Victoria thought. Best friends already.

"Your dad suggested that he call me. He would like to meet with us—tonight."

"So much for taking a hot bath and spending the evening in my pajamas."

"You're very sexy in your PJs," Brian said. Then, changing his tone, "How's Tess doing? Have you talked with her about your father?"

"Just briefly. Naturally, she doesn't really understand what I'm telling her. I think it's mostly just words for her. She has no sense of the reality the words represent. I warned her that the kids at school may say mean things. That will make it real. Right now, she's taking it all in stride, but I fear there are lots of tears ahead. Tomorrow is my day to take Tess and Jasmine to school. I'll talk to both of them then. I spoke with Nina this afternoon, and she didn't mention anything about Dad, so, clearly, she hadn't gotten the news. I didn't have the energy to get into it with her today." And this reminded Victoria about Mrs. Smith.

"There's one other thing we need to talk about, Brian. Not now. It's about school and Tess. It's just something we have to deal with."

Hamilton Hobart was supposed to arrive at 8:00. Brian would try to make it as close to that time as he could. Victoria and Tess had read a story together, and she'd tucked her daughter into bed with a lingering goodnight kiss on the cheek. Tess had finally started giggling and pulled away.

Then Victoria had nothing to do but wait. The sky was darkening as she kept an eye out for the attorney's arrival. In the distance, she saw a familiar orange glow. The rioters had found something new to set ablaze. They were bent on destroying the vital core of the city and clearly would continue their campaign of arson, assault, and looting so long as there were no consequences for their crimes. What was the point of that? Why didn't the authorities put a stop to it? Could you just do whatever you wanted so long as you pretended that you were acting in the name of some laudable cause? Could Victoria burn down a police station with impunity if she did it for world peace? This was insanity. It was the stuff of history's most horrific atrocities. Whether it was Nazis or Maoists, "revolutions" were always conducted in the name of something noble. They were always for The People. Horrendous crimes were committed. Resist the revolution and you were put in front of the firing squad— cancel culture in its harshest form. In the end, you could be certain that the one group that would never benefit from the revolution was The People.

So, who did benefit when rioters laid waste to these once beautiful, once productive cities? That was the question that needed to be asked—and answered. Who was profiting from the mayhem, financially or otherwise? You try to destroy a city, and its mayor calls it a "summer of love." What game were these politicians playing? The sign she'd seen earlier that day came back to mind. *Chaos is not an accident. It is the plan.*

There was movement down the street as a vehicle approached. The black SUV was back. Ominously, the driver pulled into a parking spot half a block away and doused his lights.

Victoria reached for her phone. Who could she call? Not the defunded police department that already had its hands full hosting the rioters. Brian? He would come in an instant, but he was miles away.

Another vehicle arrived. Another gargantuan, black SUV.

It parked closer to the house, just across the street. A light went on inside, and the driver stepped out into the street. He was a heavyset man, wearing a suit. He quickly disappeared behind the rear of the SUV as he walked around to the curb side.

At that moment, Victoria's attention was drawn away by motion at the other SUV. A dark form emerged and began moving rapidly down the center of the street toward the second car. Passing briefly under a street lamp, the form became a very large man dressed in a dark T-shirt and jeans.

She held her breath as this man, too, disappeared behind the second SUV. But then three men appeared, one bearing the slight, unmistakable silhouette of Hamilton Hobart. He was in animated conversation with the man in the T-shirt as they crossed the street toward the house.

Victoria opened the front door and stepped out onto the porch. She gave a welcoming wave, and Hobart replied with a warm, toothy smile. The second man stopped, leaving Hobart to proceed to the house alone. The attorney climbed the front steps nimbly for a man of his years.

"I'm Hamilton Hobart, Dr. Townsend," he said, offering his hand. "You might as well call me Ham. Everybody does."

So odd, Victoria thought, to hear that familiar, resonant voice engaged in casual conversation rather than the lofty, emotion-filled oratory she had heard so many times before.

"It's an honor, Mr. Hobart. I'm not sure I can manage the 'Ham.' Please call me Victoria."

As awed as she was to be standing beside Hamilton Hobart on her front porch, Victoria found herself distracted by the other man, still standing in the middle of the street. She had seen him before, but couldn't place him. Then she had it.

"The man in the street," she said, "he was in the crowd this morning when my father was arrested." She now clearly recognized the tattooed man who had been harassed by the crowd.

"That's Dennis. He works for me when I need him, if he's available."

"I worried that the crowd was going to tear him apart."

This brought another smile to Hobart's face. "I assure you, Victoria, the crowd was overmatched. Dennis has an extensive military background—special ops. He is extremely talented and very resourceful. I know that he went to Afghanistan to help extract American citizens and allies that our beloved country chose to abandon, and he's more recently back from Ukraine. I understand that he was quite helpful in Ukraine, although the details of what he did there are a bit sketchy. Sometimes, it's just as well not to know the details."

Victoria still wasn't convinced. "Today, though, he was just one man against an angry mob."

"Another thing that I've learned about Dennis, he's not always working alone, even when I think he is. He uses his own judgment to determine the resources that he requires. I find out later, when I get the bill."

"It saddens me," Victoria said, "to hear that a distinguished person like yourself requires the services of such a man."

"When you've been a civil rights lawyer for as long as I have, you cannot escape the knowledge that there are bad people out there, people who do not wish you well. Sometimes it's a man who can't read but can shoot the eyes out of a, well, a lawyer at three hundred yards. Other times it's the government. In either situation, Dennis can provide invaluable assistance.

"And there are other, unique situations, like this morning. Your father thought that it was important for you to witness his arrest. The problem was that the crowd might quickly become unruly and transform itself into an angry mob—as it has done so many times before. The solution was Dennis. And later, when Dennis was performing routine reconnaissance of your house, he noticed a little girl sitting all alone, crying, on the front steps. His first instinct was to go to her and comfort her, but, knowing that his presence often strikes fear in the hearts of grown men, he wisely understood that that approach might be counterproductive. So, he simply parked his car and maintained a silent, protective watch."

For maybe the hundredth time that day, Victoria found herself on the verge of tears. She turned toward Dennis and mouthed a "thank you."

He responded with a barely perceptible nod.

"Dennis is not overly emotional," Hobart said.

Then, realizing how long they'd been standing on the porch, Victoria opened the door. "Please, let's go inside. Would you like some coffee?"

"I would be grateful."

"Would Dennis…"

"Dennis will be more comfortable outside, where he can better keep an eye on things."

6

Hamilton Hobart couldn't have been much more than five and a half feet tall, but his nearly white hair stood another few inches from his head in all directions, imparting the illusion that he was taller. Victoria would have called his hairstyle an Afro, but she had no idea if that term had become unacceptable, and anyone using it, however naively, would be subject to immediate cancellation. Hobart appeared physically vigorous, despite his advanced years. His dark skin was punctuated by areas of vitiligo, a skin condition caused by loss of pigmentation, so that the involved areas were very light in color. She had once heard him comment on TV that the vitiligo was just some of his slave-owner ancestry showing through.

He stood near her in the kitchen, offering to help, as she prepared the coffee and tried to put together something for him to snack on.

"You have a lovely home," he said.

"Brian and I bought it soon after we were married. When we divorced, we both felt strongly that it would be best for Tess if she and I continued to live here. She shouldn't have to suffer the additional disruption of being uprooted and moved to a new house."

Settled in with their coffee, Victoria quickly learned that the attorney had a very special quality that few people possessed. He was able to concentrate his attention in a way that made the person he was talking to feel as though there were no other person and no other problem in his world. Nothing could pry his focus from the task at hand. It was an ability his clients must surely love.

"Now, Victoria," he said, "you must have many questions."

There was one thought she couldn't get out of her mind from the moment he'd planted it there. That seemed like a good place to start.

"You knew that Dad was going to be arrested today. He knew. That's why he invited me to lunch. That's why Dennis was there."

Hobart smiled. "Yes, we knew. We have friends, throughout government and law enforcement, with whom we share certain interests and goals. They are very helpful to us." He paused briefly before moving on to new ground. "I wanted to speak with you, Victoria, because I knew that you would have concerns, and your father and I both believe that, at this time, I am the one best positioned to provide the information that it is safe for you to have. The reason I speak this way is because my conversations with you are not privileged. That means that, at least in theory, the government has a right to discover anything we discuss. Obviously, you don't want to find yourself in a situation where you are forced to provide information to the government that might be harmful to your father's defense. It's also not a good idea for us to put you in a position that requires you to, let us say, misrepresent certain facts to the prosecution.

"Again, in theory, we could sidestep this problem by making you an official member of your father's legal team. However, this would instantly make the government very suspicious, and they would complain very loudly. A judge might allow them to pierce the privilege to find out what you were hiding. So, the only circumstance in which I might consider adding you to the legal team would be one in which I was absolutely confident that you had no information harmful to your father, and I wanted to misdirect the prosecution, causing them to expend myriad resources drilling what would, inevitably, turn out to be a dry hole. At the end of that road, one thing is certain. The government would be convinced that you were lying to them—you surely know something incriminating, otherwise, why would we have put you on the legal team in the first place?

"Welcome to the world of legal intrigue." He gave her a weary smile. "Of course, we could put Brian on the team, and we might actually do that at some time, but that doesn't solve the basic problem of our needing to limit the information that we provide to you. Brian would have to be just as cautious as I do about disclosing information related to your father's case."

That raised another question that Victoria had wondered about. "Do you know Brian?"

"Only by reputation. We spoke for the first time this afternoon."

They sipped their coffee before moving on to the heart of the matter.

"To the extent that you can tell me," Victoria said, "what did my father do that has gotten him into so much trouble?"

"That part is easy. He did nothing—nothing illegal. He was present on the Capitol grounds on January 6, but he committed no crimes."

"What is the government claiming he did?"

"They have filed the usual litany of charges—entering a restricted area of the Capitol grounds, disorderly conduct, and, more seriously, assault on a federal officer. The main reason that I wanted to come here this evening is to tell you, face to face, that your father is innocent of each of these charges. As you know, it is the government's obligation to prove guilt, not ours to prove innocence. But, in this case, we are prepared to *prove* that your father is innocent.

"For a while now, and especially since January 6, your father has been increasingly outspoken about the problems this nation is facing. He has associated with others who have similar concerns. This is how he came to the government's attention, and why, only now, so many months after the incident at the Capitol, he has been charged. Let me assure you again, he has committed no crimes, and he will be vindicated."

They heard a key working the lock on the front door and turned to see Brian letting himself in. For a short while after the divorce, Brian had gone through the ritual of knocking and waiting for Victoria to let him in. That silly formality had been dispensed with very quickly.

"Don't get up," Brian said as he crossed the room, but Hobart was quickly on his feet. The two shook hands, and Brian formally introduced himself, then turned to Victoria and kissed her lightly on the cheek.

Hamilton Hobart shook his head in wonder. "You two have the most compatible divorce I've ever witnessed."

"Sorry I'm late," Brian said, settling in beside Victoria on the sofa. "Couldn't get away. What have I missed?"

"Just going over some of the basics," Hobart said. "There are some additional nuts and bolts that Victoria needs to hear, so that she understands what will transpire. Your father will have what's called an initial appearance tomorrow. That has to happen within twenty-four hours of his arrest, and must be held here, before he's transferred to Washington. Additional procedures that will be held here are a preliminary hearing and hearings for removal and detention."

Brian groaned.

"I believe that we have to anticipate, Brian, that the government will claim that Victoria's father is both dangerous and a flight risk. They've done that with so many of the others arrested for their alleged conduct on January 6. We could fight all of this, even the basic charges. We might even win something, but my belief is that the better route is to keep our evidence to ourselves for now and save it for later, when we can begin to test the government's case. I've discussed this with Victoria's father, and he agrees."

"I just hate to think how long he's going to have to be in custody," Brian said. "I heard about a case where the Feds spent six weeks just transporting a prisoner to Washington. No one even knew where he was."

"They will play their games," Hobart said. "That's what they do. But there's some good news here. We will demand our right to a speedy trial. We're ready to proceed, and the government better not claim they're not—after all the time they've had. No judge can permit that."

"How did you come to represent my father?" Victoria was beginning to sense that there was much more going on here than met the eye.

"I knew your father back in the old days. We marched together; protested together. We weren't really close, just fellow combatants in the same cause. Then, more recently, we discovered that we were once again fellow travelers, in a new cause."

"Is that something you can talk about?" Victoria had no way of knowing the exact boundaries of what Hobart could share. Where did her father's case end and the rest of the world begin?

"In the earliest days of the fight for civil rights," Hobart said, "everything was framed in racism. It was all about the suppression of black people. That suppression was accomplished through many means, ranging from simple daily harassment to murder. Black people had to be very careful about what they said and how they said it. A black man's eyes dare not stray to a white woman.

"As a young lawyer, I was especially outraged by what was done under the color of law. Not only was it nearly impossible to get a fair trial in front of a white jury, but there was also an enormous disparity in the application of justice. A young black woman might face significant consequences for sitting in the wrong seat on a bus, but a white man could beat a black man with impunity. If you were black, you lived in a totalitarian state with no claim on basic human rights. It was an evil world.

"What I see now, and what your father sees as well, is some of these old methods being applied to new purposes. The enemy is no longer a person of a different color. He is a person of a different political persuasion. It's not subtle. Rioters of one political persuasion are permitted to burn and loot and assault with minimal consequences. They leave ruined cities in their wake, rife with crime, and what is the government's response? Defund the police. Prominent politicians openly support the destruction of those cities. They cheer the rioters on.

"Now, let's examine another case. On January 6 at the Capitol there was indeed a riot, but, under any objective examination, it was trivial compared to the destruction and violence that had taken place before in cities across our nation. Indeed, it would not be unreasonable for the Capitol rioters to have believed that they, like those who preceded them in the cities, would be allowed to riot with impunity. Such was not the case. The full force of the federal government was thrown at them. Hundreds were charged. Many have been incarcerated for months pending trial. And what of the unarmed woman shot and killed in the Capitol by a policeman on that day? Or, another woman seen clearly on video being beaten by police as she lay motionless on the ground? She, too, died. I ask you to imagine the political and judicial responses that would have ensued had those deaths occurred in a different context. Our nation's recent history is chock-full of such responses—nonstop outrage from politicians and the media, riots in the street. But as to the January 6 deaths, what do we hear? Silence. 'Crickets,' in the current vernacular.

"There is much more to be said about the events of January 6, and, in the future, you will be hearing from me at great length on that subject. For now, the hour is late, and we have all experienced a long, exhausting day. Let me just say, in a very narrow response to your question, Victoria, it is this disparate application of justice that brought your father and me together once again. I have seen this throughout my career, but the racial civil rights disparity is generally much improved, compared with my earliest experience. Over recent years, however, a new menace has arisen—the politicization of the legal process, especially at the Department of Justice, to such an extent that crimes committed by persons of one political persuasion are completely ignored, while even the flimsiest allegations against the other side are pursued, sometimes for years, until finally not even the most shameless, or witless, prosecutor is willing to appear before a judge and pretend that they are true. Examples of such conduct are legion.

"This politicization of the legal process must end, now. It is repugnant to the Constitution. This is not justice. This is tyranny!"

With these last words, Hobart's indignation rose, as did his voice. It was a reminder of his legendary courtroom eloquence.

"I'm afraid I let my passion get the better of me," he said. "I am an old man. This will likely be my last battle. I believe it is an important one. Now, what further questions can I answer for you before we say goodnight?"

"When can I see my father?" It seemed such a mundane request in the wake of Hobart's words.

"That may be a bit difficult. Your father understood this. That's the main reason he wanted to be certain that you saw him earlier today. These first hearings will be brief and their timing unpredictable. I would suggest you save your visits to court until the case moves to Washington. Meanwhile, I'll try to arrange for you to see him before he's removed, but I can't promise that I will be successful."

There was some idle chatter before they said their final good-byes. Victoria thanked Hobart profusely for what he was doing for her father. When they opened the front door, they found Dennis and the other man standing in the street at the driver's side of the SUV, both facing the house. Had they been there all evening, or had they known exactly when Hobart would appear?

After seeing the attorney and his entourage off, Brian and Victoria walked back inside. They fell into each other's arms, and Victoria let go the tears she'd been fighting all day. Finally, the tears abated, and she was able to speak.

"Can you stay?"

"Of course."

7

Some mornings, Jasmine could be incredibly slow—slow to get out of bed, slow to get dressed, slow to eat her breakfast. It was almost as though, the more they needed to hurry, the slower Jasmine became.

Ted had left early to meet with a client before court, so it was just Nina and Jasmine. Nina tried to get them organized while Jasmine played with her breakfast. It was exasperating, but she knew that her daughter was far too young to be deliberately passive-aggressive.

"Eat your breakfast, Jasmine. We need to leave early so I can have a talk with Dr. Townsend."

Ted and Nina had been getting ready for bed with the evening news in the background when they first heard of the arrest of Victoria's father. It was shocking, absolutely inexplicable. Why hadn't Victoria mentioned it? Poor Victoria. She shouldn't have to deal with that alone.

Nina finally got Jasmine into the car, and they made the short drive to Victoria's, luckily finding a parking place right in front of the house. She let Jasmine ring the doorbell. As soon as Victoria opened the door, Nina knew that something was very wrong.

Ordinarily, Victoria opened the door widely and made a fuss over Jasmine. Today, Victoria's greeting was curt, her demeanor cautious. She opened the door only partially and stood in a way that prevented Nina from entering.

"Victoria, what's wrong?"

Completely oblivious to the adult drama, Jasmine suddenly squirmed past Victoria and darted inside.

"Jasmine!" But it was too late.

They heard Jasmine's cheerful voice coming from the interior of the house.

"Hi, Tess. Hi, Mr. Townsend."

Nina cocked her head and arched an eyebrow, then she pushed past Victoria and stepped inside. Brian was sitting at a table, eating breakfast.

"Well, looky here. Mr. Townsend's come all the way out here just to enjoy one of Victoria's famous breakfasts!"

Brian, trying his best not to look sheepish, "Hi, Nina."

"Let's see what epicurean delights Victoria has whipped up for her ex. Brian, are those corn flakes you're eating? Not getting any corn flakes at that fancy downtown loft you live in?"

"Are you done, Nina?"

"Not near, Brian. Not near."

She looked around. The little girls were off playing upstairs. So much for yesterday's racial crisis. Victoria had taken a seat at the end of the table.

"I remember you as a man who always loved the way Victoria served his corn flakes. You remember that time we went camping? I believe it was before you and Victoria were married."

Victoria had her forearms on the table. She lowered her head onto her arms. She and Brian had heard this routine before.

"Ted and I were in a tent close by. We were a married couple, you understand. All of a sudden, there was this noise. We thought a bear had wandered into our camp. Turns out, it was just Brian enjoying his corn flakes. He had three bowls that morning. Ted counted."

"Are you done, yet, Nina?"

"Not quite. You know, Ted and I have an understanding—which means that I've clearly explained the situation to him. If he moves out, finds a fancy place downtown, he better not drop back home, from time to time, thinking he's gonna find a nice big bowl of corn flakes waiting for him. No, if Ted moves out, he knows he's going to have to find himself some Cap'n Crunch somewhere. No more corn flakes for that man."

Brian was laughing. "Is that it, Nina?"

"I think that's all I have for now. Thank you, you've been a wonderful audience. Remember, I'll be here all week, and please don't forget to try our world-famous margaritas." She gave a little bow and sat down next to Victoria, touching her on the arm. "How are you holding up?"

"Okay, I guess, everything considered."

"You could have told me."

"I was just too tired to get into it, and, besides, there's really not much to tell. If you've watched the news, you know about as much as we do."

"Have you talked to your dad?"

"No. I'm not sure when I'll be able to talk to him. I did see him yesterday at the arrest."

Out of the corner of her eye, Victoria caught a sharp, warning look from Brian. Be careful. Don't say too much.

"Coincidentally, Dad had asked me to lunch yesterday. I actually saw him as he was taken away. It was from a distance, but we managed to make eye contact. I'll have to be content with that for now."

The little girls came trotting down the stairs, giggling about something. Best friends again.

"I guess we didn't really have to worry about Tess and Jasmine," Nina said.

"Not until they get more poison served to them at school. Actually, Brian has some thoughts about the, uh," Victoria saw that the little girls were now paying close attention to what she was saying, "CRT problem at school."

"Mommy, it's c-a-t, and we don't have one at school."

Victoria smiled. "That's right, sweetheart." Turning back to Nina, she said, "You figure very prominently in Brian's plan."

"Does it involve cereal?"

"If it does, Brian didn't tell me. Anyway, Brian wants to look into some things, and then he'll get back to us."

"Sounds like a plan," Nina said. "Why don't you let me run the girls to school? That way, if Brian wants another bowl of corn flakes before he goes to the office..."

"Enough!" Brian said. "Why don't we talk about the swimming pool incident instead."

"I can't believe Ted told you about that."

"He was quite proud of himself."

"Okay, time to go to school," Nina said.

They gathered their daughters' school supplies and herded the girls to the door.

"You know," Nina said softly, "your dad's going to need a really good lawyer. The feds are really playing hardball on all of this January 6 stuff."

"We think he has one."

"Really? So soon? Who?"

"Hamilton Hobart."

"Wow."

— 8 —

Victoria and Nina were in the car, headed for their daughters' school. Nina had an appointment to meet with Mrs. Smith, the infamous first-grade teacher. They had brought with them a large portfolio that contained images of some of Nina's most famous works.

Brian's plan was simple. Sue the teacher, the principal, the school, the school board—anyone who could possibly be implicated—for defamation of character. The legal issue was very straightforward. Could you really get away with publicly calling a six-year-old girl a racist with the sole evidence being that she was white? He seriously doubted that the school district could summon the audacity to even attempt to defend such a proposition.

Brian said that the suit would include a "prayer" for monetary damages. Experience had taught him that this was the best way to capture the attention of the school board, and, more importantly, stoke taxpayers' interest in what was going on at the schools they were paying for. He thought that a request for relief in the amount of ten million dollars would adequately serve both needs. The school board had loudly proclaimed that the schools were not teaching this nonsense. The suit would make clear that that was a lie, and it would also let parents know exactly what kind of garbage was being forced down their children's throats every day.

Too few parents these days were able to find the time to follow as closely as they should what their kids were being taught at school. They depended heavily on what their children told them. That's why a major tenet of these school racism and gender identification programs was, Children, whatever you do, don't tell your parents what's going on.

The school boards were a similar problem. In general, no one knew much about the people running for school board positions. No one much cared—especially if they had no children in the public schools. Leftist activists understood this. They depended on it. Public apathy allowed them, with minimal cost and effort, to elect their slate of favored candidates, clearing the way for the grooming of a generation of brainwashed Americans to grow up and support their views. The school board elections were analogous to the elections for the local district attorney. If you didn't pay attention, you ended up with "Let 'Em Go" Larry.

And certainly, there was no possibility that these leftist views, once firmly implanted in grade school, would be challenged later if a child should go on to college. College was merely the final stage of the grooming program—one last chance to make certain that no young mind escaped full indoctrination.

Arriving at the school, Victoria was transported back to her own childhood. Physically, it was not much changed from when she had attended. But, back then, it had appeared large and new. Now it seemed small and old. When Victoria was in school, she was able to walk back and forth with her friends. That was often the best part of her school day. But Tess and Jasmine would never know that simple joy. It had become far too dangerous for children to walk to the school without adult supervision, even before the "homeless" encampment first appeared and began its ugly sprawl.

Why the camp was allowed to remain, and grow, literally on school property, was mystifying. Children could no longer use the playground due to the presence of discarded drug paraphernalia, human waste, and the very real possibility that they would be assaulted. One of the nuttier members of the city council had extolled the virtues of the children having their horizons expanded by exposure to a different culture. That exposure, Victoria thought, provided the opportunity for grade school children to watch adults engage in a number of activities ending in the letters "ate." None of these words was "educate."

Victoria was also troubled by the euphemism "homeless." Lumping all of these people under that term would be analogous to her combining all of her infectious disease patients under the heading "febrile." Homelessness, like fever, was merely a symptom. Housing was no more a solution to their real underlying problems than aspirin was for Victoria's patients with fever. It mattered whether the underlying problem was drug addiction or mental illness, just as it mattered whether a patient's underlying illness was meningitis or pneumonia. These people deserved help, and labeling them as homeless—and expending public funds to support and perpetuate that status—deflected attention and resources away from the solutions that their primary, underlying problems so desperately required. The current approach consigned them to miserable lives on the street, their futures abbreviated and finally obliterated by the ravages of crime, weather, and disease. If a patient came to you with sepsis, and all you did was treat his fever with aspirin, he wasn't going to do well. No one would regard that kind of medical care as compassionate, and no one should regard current liberal policies toward the homeless as compassionate.

"Earth to Victoria."

Nina's words brought her out of her reverie.

"Sorry," Victoria said. "I was just worrying about the homeless camp. It's filled with all kinds of risks for the kids, and it's just so unnecessary. Why don't the authorities do something about it? I really believe in public education. We could have put Tess in a private school. In many ways, that would have been so much easier, but Brian and I both wanted this for Tess. We believed that it was important. But I have to admit, I'm beginning to waver."

"You know that Ted and I feel the same way," Nina said, "but I've got a performance to put on. I'd better get started before I lose my nerve."

"Good luck."

Nina grabbed her portfolio and headed for the school. Inside, an aging security guard directed her down a long, empty hallway to Mrs. Smith's classroom. Nina knocked lightly and received no response. She cautiously opened the door and saw a young woman, probably in her late twenties or early thirties, doing paperwork at the far end of the room. She had short-cropped, blond hair and large, serious eyeglasses. She studiously ignored the fact that another person had entered her classroom.

"Mrs. Smith?"

"May I help you?" The message was clear. She was an important person and regarded Nina's intrusion as insubordinate.

Since Nina had called and spoken to the teacher only yesterday to make an appointment to meet with her, she deduced that the teacher was either absurdly pretentious or dumber than a sack of hammers. Of course, those were not mutually exclusive conditions. Nina remained patient.

"I'm Nina Bass, Jasmine's mother."

"Oh, yes, you called. Something about some artwork. Have a seat." Mrs. Smith remained firmly planted behind her desk.

Looking around, Nina saw only chairs designed for first graders. Nina was slender, but she was also just two inches short of six feet in height. Those little chairs were not going to work. Mrs. Smith was watching her closely. Perhaps this was a test of Nina's problem-solving abilities.

"Why don't I just stand," Nina said. "That way I can show you some of my work and explain what I hope to do."

There was an audible sigh from Mrs. Smith, but her expression turned to panic when Nina plopped her portfolio on the teacher's desk. Probably to do with the sanctity of her desk, or perhaps the violation of her personal space.

Nina opened the portfolio and began slowly turning through the work for Mrs. Smith to see. The teacher viewed the images with evident distaste, then suddenly brightened.

"You know," Mrs. Smith said, "some of these aren't half-bad. You might even be able to sell that one."

Nina continued to turn through the work, waiting for her opportunity.

"Wait a minute," Mrs. Smith said. "I've seen that one before." Her tone was accusatory.

"It's in the Black History Museum," Nina said.

"That's right. It's hanging facing the front door. Everyone sees it as soon as they walk in. Why would you be showing me something that's in the museum?"

Nina was confused. Then she understood.

"I'm the artist. It's called 'Women at Work.'" Nina decided that further clarification might be required. She spoke slowly. "I painted it."

"How did it end up in the museum?"

"I donated it."

"Oh." Her tone said, *that* explains it.

"After my first show at the Guggenheim," Nina said, "many years ago, I let Sotheby's auction off some of my work—just a few things that I was willing to part with. The painting they were most eager to get for the auction was 'Women at Work.' You wouldn't believe what they said it would bring, even back then. But I just didn't want it to end up hidden in some foreign collector's private gallery. This was a painting I wanted people to see. I hoped that they would be moved by it, that it would broaden their understanding of the black experience. So, instead of selling it, I donated it to the museum. Over the years, I've donated quite a few pieces to museums around the world."

Mrs. Smith remained seated, open-mouthed but thankfully silent. The moment had come for Nina to act—literally.

"Jasmine has told me so many things about what you're doing here for racial equity. I had the idea that I might create a work of art that's in the spirit of what you're trying to accomplish—something tangible for the children to see."

"One of your paintings, just for the classroom?" Despite their previous phone conversation, Mrs. Smith was only now beginning to grasp the enormity of such a thing, and what it might mean for her career.

"Absolutely. So, if you don't mind, I'd like to shoot some video of your classroom with my phone. When I get back to my studio, the video will help me create a work that is not only powerful, but also just right for this environment."

"Please do!"

Nina made an elaborate show of wandering around the room with her phone, then returned to the teacher's desk to begin what she'd truly come here to do. Brian had said that one thing was critical. Mrs. Smith needed to consent to being recorded, and that the consent itself must be recorded.

"Now, Mrs. Smith, I really want to hear from you about what you're accomplishing here in terms of racial equity. I'm terrible at taking notes, and my memory isn't what it used to be, and I need to have your thoughts in mind as I create my painting for the class, so I hope you don't mind if I just keep the camera running so I can have an accurate account of your words to refer to."

"Of course not," she said.

Bingo!

"So," Nina said, "why don't you just tell me, as best you can, how you're fighting the battle against racism."

"Well, it's not complicated. We want to turn these kids into anti-racist activists, but first they have to be decolonized. You have to wash all that natural white supremacy and hatred right out of their brains. They don't even know it's there until you point it out to them."

"But they're so young. It must be very difficult."

"No." Mrs. Smith was becoming excited now. "First grade, even kindergarten, is the best time. Their brains are really malleable. They're very susceptible to external influence. We just have to make sure that influence comes from us, not from their parents."

"Are you all alone in this, or are other teachers doing the same thing?"

"Everybody is *supposed* to be doing it. There are a few resisters, but they get a lot of pressure from the administration. There's a third-grade teacher who won't take part. I'm pretty confident that she won't be back next year."

"So, you are getting support from the administration," Nina said.

"Oh yes. We've had formal training. They bring in outside people for lectures and special small-group sessions." She started to giggle. "One of the lecturers had a slide that really said it all. The slide said 'Burn Stuff Down.' Only it didn't say 'stuff' if you know what I mean."

Nina nodded knowingly. She knew exactly what Mrs. Smith meant.

"And that gets right to the meat of it. You have to burn all that crap out of these kids' minds and replace it with correct thinking. It's actually quite similar to what they're doing downtown. You get rid of the old buildings, the statues, all of that false history and start over."

"In practice then," Nina said, "this is full-on critical race theory that you're teaching."

"Of course! We're not supposed to call it that, but *absolutely* it is."

"Do the children respond? How do you find the time?"

"They mostly respond. Once you get the hang of it, you can saturate almost everything you teach with anti-racist messages."

"And it doesn't get in the way of their other lessons?"

"Maybe, some, but you have to have priorities. This early age is the critical time to wash all that hatred out of their minds. They can pick up the reading and writing, the other basics, anytime. There's a new world order coming, and my job is to prepare these kids for it. It's not about being able to read and solve math problems, it's about social responsibility and racial equity. If a child can do the math but doesn't have the right answers when asked about social issues—which are much more important—then that child is not going to do well in my class or in the new world that's almost here. I'm not going to pass on to the next grade a white child who doesn't understand that he or she is a white supremacist."

"Jasmine said that you called out one girl in particular recently for being racist. Pointed right at her."

"The Townsend child," Mrs. Smith said, "a classic case of white supremacy. Her parents are teaching her at home. How is that fair? A lot of families can't do that. We thought that doing away with homework would even things up, but some of these white families go ahead and teach at home anyway. These kids have math and reading skills way above grade level. They ought to make that against the law. I mean it."

Then the teacher was suddenly more animated. "Her father was just arrested for being a white supremacist. It was on the news. Very dangerous guy. They had to bring out the

SWAT team to capture him. He was the leader of that group that tried to burn down the Capitol and kill everybody in it back on January 6. I can't believe that I have to put up with having his daughter in my class. She shouldn't be allowed around the other kids."

"Just because she happens to be his granddaughter—"

"Daughter," Mrs. Smith said.

"I'm sorry. Just because she happens to be his daughter doesn't mean that she's guilty of anything."

"But that's the point. That's what critical race theory is teaching us. All white people are racist, but this little girl is just so hopelessly infected, she's going to need a lot of special attention—probably throughout her entire life. Businesses and government are catching on to this and providing reeducation and extra training for those who need it. If they don't shape up, they're out of a job."

Nina was working very hard to maintain her composure. It took all the restraint she could muster not to scream at this sanctimonious twit. She repacked her portfolio and carefully zipped it closed.

"I think I've heard everything I need to, Mrs. Smith."

"When will I be hearing your plans?"

"Oh, I suspect you'll be hearing from my people soon."

Her people. Mrs. Smith was very impressed.

Nina hesitated, then went off script, just for fun.

"You know," Nina said, "another thing I've been thinking about—another project you might be interested in—is renaming the school. I would love to see it named after my civil rights role model, Senator Elizabeth Warren. Her life is such a magnificent example.

"The woman proudly proclaimed her Native American heritage despite knowing that, living in this racist country, identifying as a Native American would bar any opportunity for advancement. Imagine all the hours she must have spent in isolation, completely ignored and denigrated at Harvard, eating all by herself in a far corner of the faculty dining room, all because of her Native American heritage. Think how awful that must have been. No hope of faculty advancement. No chance for a political career. All because of her heritage.

"And here's the kicker. You may not agree, and I know that Senator Warren, that beacon of all that is righteous and virtuous, would never have done this, but I've often thought to myself, if Senator Warren had not been so guided by her strong moral sense, she might never have mentioned her heritage at all. I believe—and, again, you may not agree with this—that if the senator had never mentioned her Native American heritage, it's just possible that she could have passed for white and avoided all that terrible racial discrimination that she has suffered under for so many years. But no, she shouted her racial heritage from the rooftops knowing full well the personal hardship that would result. That kind of bravery certainly needs to be recognized and rewarded."

Nina departed, leaving Mrs. Smith to ponder the renaming of the school for the great American civil rights icon.

Victoria was growing restless. What was taking Nina so long? She hoped there hadn't been a problem. She glanced in the mirror and saw that her hair was a mess. She had a habit of running her hands through it while she was thinking. She needed a better mirror. That was as good an excuse as any to get out of the car and stretch her legs.

Inside the school, she saw Nina coming toward her from way down the hallway. Nina made an okay sign with her thumb and first finger, presumably indicating that all had gone well. Victoria would have to remind her that that particular sign was a secret signal used by white extremists to indicate something or other.

She found the girls' restroom and was amazed by how low the counter was. It had been much higher when Victoria was a little girl.

She pulled her brush out of her purse and began to repair her hair. Looking in the mirror, she noticed for the first time that the door to the stall directly behind her was open. A massively obese man with a long beard was seated there, his shirt open, his pants down, just a few feet from where she was standing.

"What you lookin' at, bitch? I'm a little girl."

Victoria grabbed her purse and headed out the door, nearly running into Nina.

"Let's get out of here," Victoria said, "fast."

"I just want to make a quick restroom stop first."

"Not a good idea." She took Nina's hand and pulled her toward the entrance. "Our daughters cannot spend another day at this school."

"I was just going to say the same thing."

They were quickly in the car and on their way. Victoria noticed a sign someone had planted on the school lawn near the exit from the parking lot.

PARDON OUR DUST

YOUR CHILD'S EDUCATION IS STILL IN THE

DEMOLITION PHASE

9

Before she left home this morning, Victoria had sent an email to Tess and Jasmine's school principal and copied the superintendent of schools and various school board members. She had hesitated, given the load of bricks they were about to drop on the school—in the form of their defamation suit—but any doubts she had were quickly overwhelmed by her concern for the children and her desire to protect them from imminent harm. In the email, she dispassionately described what had happened in the school bathroom the previous afternoon, expressing, as a physician and mother, her fear of the very real risk this man's presence posed for students and staff. She expressed confidence that the school, now made aware of the problem, would move quickly to correct it. She included her contact information at the medical school, should they need anything further from her. Victoria did not mention that Tess would not be returning to the school, ever.

Nina had offered to have the girls at her house today. Such generosity was typical of her friend, but Victoria recognized that it was completely unfair to shift the burden to Nina just because her studio was in her home. Nina had work to do. The girls were a joy, but they were also a major distraction. And they needed to be in school. Tess and Jasmine could be with Nina today, but they needed to find another solution—soon.

Victoria had settled into her work in the lab, and the noon hour was fast approaching, when she got a call from the ER. The infectious disease team was tied up with a couple of patients in one of the ICUs, and there was a critically ill patient in the ER who urgently needed ID evaluation and antibiotic recommendations. Would it be possible for Victoria to come down and see her? Of course.

What Victoria found in the ER was yet another tragic, heart-rending manifestation of the nation's seemingly endless epidemic of illicit drug use. Two children had overdosed. The 16-year-old boy was already in cardiac arrest when they found him. Resuscitation efforts were unsuccessful. He was known to the hospital because of his sickle cell disease which had been treated there since early childhood. He had endured multiple, painful sickle cell crises, and it was likely that he had turned to drugs to alleviate that pain. He had been living on the street for an unknown period of time.

The girl was thought to be fourteen or fifteen. Her identity was unknown. She had been intubated in the field and was now breathing on a respirator. She was unresponsive and in heart failure. She had a temperature of 103, but, at this time, was maintaining her blood pressure on her own. Examining her, Victoria found weakness on her right side, evidence of embolic phenomena in her extremities, and, on listening to her heart, a smorgasbord of heart murmurs. The child's arms showed scars from previous intravenous drug use. She was very thin and almost certainly malnourished.

Victoria told the ER team that she had little doubt that the child had bacterial endocarditis, infection of the valves of her heart. Based on her examination, Victoria was confident that the aortic and mitral valves were involved—and possibly the tricuspid valve, although that was almost impossible to diagnose at the bedside given the patient's overall clinical condition. It was possible that the child had congenital heart disease, and that previously abnormal valves had become infected, but it was more likely that she had infected previously normal heart valves through intravenous drug use.

The most likely infecting organism was staph, but, in this setting, the list of potential causative bacteria was lengthy. More than one organism might be involved. Antibiotic coverage needed to be broad.

It appeared that emboli from her infected heart valves had traveled to her extremities and brain. Other likely targets included her liver and kidneys. Abscesses could occur in any of these locations, including the brain.

Victoria detailed her antibiotic recommendations, and, after ascertaining that appropriate cultures had already been obtained, said that antibiotic treatment should begin immediately. She was told that the cardiology team was "on their way." Victoria recommended that the cardiovascular surgeons see the patient in the ER as well. Especially because of her aortic valve insufficiency, the child's clinical condition might deteriorate rapidly. The surgeons would probably want to admit her to their ICU.

If their patient could be stabilized, it was likely that one or more heart valves would need to be replaced. This was a difficult prospect because artificial heart valves were especially prone to becoming infected. If this young girl survived, and returned to using intravenous drugs—not an unlikely possibility—she would surely, sooner or later, infect her new valves. That was a hopeless cycle that would, inevitably, lead to her death.

Victoria told the team that a spinal tap might be necessary, but that they should obtain an MRI of her brain first. If the child did have an abscess in her brain, her intracranial pressure would likely be elevated. If a spinal tap were performed and fluid removed, there was high risk that the increased pressure above would force the brainstem downward in a fatal herniation.

Her phone announced that yet another text message had arrived. This one was the second in the last half hour from

Arthur Johnson, the chairman of the department of medicine. He wanted to meet with Victoria as soon as possible. This type of urgency generally meant some horrific funding snafu that needed to be sorted out immediately. She did not envy the chairman his job. His brilliant hematology career was now supplanted by concerns about funding, headcounts, and hiring and firing. Medicine had been replaced by politics, and this had made him miserable. It was widely rumored that he was looking for a way out.

Victoria wrote a note in the young girl's chart, then headed upstairs to see if Johnson was available. His secretary was not in the outer office, but his inner office door was open, and she peaked in to find him eating at his desk. His mouth full, he waved her in and pointed to a chair which she slumped into gratefully.

"Sorry I didn't get back to you sooner, Art. I'm not on service, but the ID team was tied up, so I went to the ER for an emergency consultation. Tragic case. Fourteen-year-old girl, IV drug use, endocarditis of multiple valves, congestive failure, unresponsive to painful stimuli, probable brain abscess. Heartbreaking."

Johnson tried to appear sympathetic while he continued to chew and swallow as fast as he could. Victoria thought that he must have half a sandwich in his mouth.

"I just don't understand," Victoria said, "why the government isn't doing more to stop the flow of drugs into the country. It seems like every night there's a news story about border patrol agents arresting someone crossing the border with enough fentanyl to kill everyone in the United States ten times over. And there seems to be broad agreement that the quantity of drugs seized is only a tiny fraction of what actually comes into the country.

"There's no secret about what's going on. The raw chemicals are manufactured in China and shipped to Mexico where the cartels transform the chemicals into the desired drugs and smuggle them into the United States, raking in billions of dollars. And they say that the cartels make nearly as many billions smuggling people across the border, and the chaos that creates occupies customs and border control agents to such an extent that they don't have the resources to intercept drug shipments. It's a win-win for the cartels.

"And when the cartels deliver all these people to our country—as many as two million entering illegally in the last year—our government says 'thank you very much' and provides a lovely taxpayer-funded concierge service that whisks these folks, often in the dead of night, to secret locations throughout the country. Do you see how this works, Art? The United States government actively assists Mexican drug cartels as they make billions of dollars smuggling people into the country, which in turn makes much easier the cartel's drug-smuggling operation—which the CDC estimates killed one hundred thousand Americans last year alone. Fifty-eight thousand Americans died in all our years in Vietnam, and there was rioting in the streets. One hundred thousand die of drug overdoses in a single year, and you hardly hear a peep.

"Who wants this, Art? The American people? Of course not, but someone does. Someone on this side of the border is profiting big-time from this humanitarian disaster. I'm beginning to understand that it's important to learn who that is."

"You're beginning to sound like your father," Johnson said, finally able to speak.

"Actually, I've never heard my father say anything like that. Have you?"

"No, I guess not. But we do need to talk about your father. That's one of the reasons I asked to see you." He hesitated briefly, as though trying to gather his thoughts. "I've tried to contact your dad, but haven't had any luck. No one seems to even know where he is, not even his attorney—or at least his lawyer's office said that they couldn't provide me any information."

"I don't know where he is either, Art. It's terrifying. They're supposedly transporting him to Washington, but his lawyer says sometimes that takes weeks. It's a game they play. His lawyer calls it pre-trial punishment. He says that they're especially likely to pull this kind of stuff when they think they won't get a conviction. They try to exact their pound of flesh before the acquittal. We're learning that we don't have the type of government most of us thought we had, aren't we?"

"Be that as it may," Johnson said, "we have a couple of serious problems we can't ignore. One is that, without your father, there's nobody in charge of the clinic. And no one I've talked to seems very interested in taking that on, especially now that the riots appear headed in that direction. It looks like it's only a matter of time, and probably a very short time, before the clinic would have to be closed anyway. It's simply too dangerous to keep it open."

"So, because the city refuses to control the rioters, the people that the rioters once claimed to be supporting are going to lose access to healthcare."

"People have a right to protest, Victoria."

"That's a straw man, Art, and you know it. No one denies the right of people to protest. But when did they get the right to burn down cities and assault police officers?" As soon as she said it, Victoria realized that the truth was that *some* people had the right to protest, just like *some* people had the right to enter the United States illegally. She decided it was probably best not to open that can of worms with Johnson.

"Nonetheless," Johnson said, "I have to make a decision about your father."

"What does that mean?"

"Well, obviously, he can't stay on at the medical school. The board of regents certainly will not allow that."

"He hasn't been convicted of anything, Art."

"Maybe not, but he was *there*. He's not denying that is he?"

"If you mean the Capitol, I honestly don't know. I hadn't heard that visiting the Capitol was a crime."

"I mean, it's more than that. What about the white supremacy? The racism!"

"What on earth are you talking about?"

"You should see what people are saying on the bias reporting tool. Lots of complaints—hundreds—accusing your father of racist and white supremacist attitudes. Medical students are saying that they don't feel safe going to class. They're asking for exemptions from tests. We're planning additional safe places for medical students to go to. We're setting up support groups with counselors to help them through this."

"The bias reporting tool, Art? You mean the Nazi snitch tool, the one set up by the medical so the Hitler Youth can snitch on their parents and teachers? Like lots of stuff on the internet, those reports are almost one hundred percent anonymous. That's the whole point of the tool, to let students and staff report microaggressions and bullying and allegations of bias anonymously so they can't be retaliated against. The problem is, you have no idea whether a hundred people have complained or one person has complained a hundred times. You don't know if a complainer is a medical student or the plumber that my dad reported to the Better Business Bureau who's trying to get revenge. Absolutely anyone can access the tool and make up anything they want. Tell me, Art, do you have one single incident that has been confirmed in which my father behaved in a manner that could even be described as racially insensitive?"

"Not yet."

"Not yet! You've known my dad for decades. You know that he doesn't have a racist bone in his body."

"It's not my decision. It's out of my hands. It's in the newspapers. It's on TV. It's all over social media. The medical school just cannot have ties to a person with this kind of reputation. If your father simply retires, I think I can still preserve his status as professor emeritus. I can't even promise that. But, if he's fired, he leaves with nothing. I'm not even certain about his pension."

Johnson had red hair, or at least used to have. He was very pale-complected and tended to turn red in the face when angry or embarrassed. He was currently glowing crimson. Victoria hoped it was because he was deeply ashamed.

"There's something else, isn't there, Art?"

"I'm afraid so. I've had an email from the school board."

"The school board? What can that possibly have to do with my father?"

"It's not about your father. It's about you. Here, let me just read it. It was addressed to the dean. He sent it to me." He searched his desk and pulled a sheet of paper out from under the remains of his sandwich.

"'We have just received the attached email from Dr. Victoria Townsend who is, we understand, a member of your faculty. Frankly, we were shocked to receive such a hate-filled transphobic screed from a person purported to be a physician.

"'For the record, Jennifer Beaulieu is a valued member of our community. We fully support her decision to undergo transition to the gender of her choice and will do everything we can to make her transition safe and satisfying.

"'We feel that exposing students to Jennifer Beaulieu is an excellent way to broaden their cultural horizons and help them toward a fuller understanding of gender issues.

"'Again, we were dismayed to receive such an email from a member of your faculty and are forwarding it to you for prompt corrective action.'"

Victoria could hardly contain herself. "'Transphobic' is just one of the words that the Left has made up to vilify their opponents and stifle criticism of their worldview. If you disagree with them, you're a bigot. It is not transphobic for a mother to worry about a three-hundred-pound man using the girls' bathroom at her daughter's elementary school! What was it Mark Twain said, first God made idiots, but that was just for practice—then he made school boards."

Johnson interrupted her. "I caution you not to say anything more. The administration and board of regents takes these matters very seriously. If you're cooperative, we can deal with this quickly and quietly. You'll meet with a human resources counselor. You'll have to attend a few reeducation classes and undergo a period of intense reflection, maybe make a public apology—or at least something in writing to the dean—and then all will be forgotten as long as there are no subsequent incidents or other episodes that turn up from your past."

"Reeducation? Public apology? How quickly we've traveled from Nazi Germany to Chairman Mao's Cultural Revolution. Do you think I'll have to stand in the Quad with a sign around my neck?"

"Please don't say anything more, Victoria."

Victoria looked around the room. "They're not listening to us, are they? It hasn't come to that yet, has it, Art? This is still America."

"Please, Victoria," he begged, "I have to tell them what you say!"

To his credit, Johnson looked like he was about to break into tears.

Victoria left without another word. She took an elevator down to the ground floor and went outside in search of fresh air in hope of regaining her composure before going up to her lab. There was a flagpole in front of the building where Old Glory proudly waved in a gentle breeze. Victoria briefly considered lowering the flag to half-mast in memory of the country she loved.

Half a dozen protestors had gathered on the grass a short distance from where Victoria stood. Each held a small sign. Students and faculty walked back and forth in front of the protestors, oblivious to whether the signs were mocking or supporting their woke agenda.

CONFORMITY IS DIVERSITY

TRUTH IS FICTION

FICTION IS TRUTH

MEN ARE WOMEN

WOMEN ARE MEN

FACTS ARE DISINFORMATION

10

When she finally found a minute, Victoria called Brian to bring him up to date on her meeting with Arthur Johnson. Brian had the ability to quickly shed emotion and become coldly analytic. He tended to see things through a legal lens and always cut immediately to the chase. Regarding Johnson's plan to force her father to resign, Brian simply said, "They can't get away with that—not if your father isn't convicted of anything. Hamilton Hobart would make them pay millions."

The Jennifer Beaulieu problem, he said, was more complex. He thought that Johnson was probably right, that if Victoria cooperated and agreed to submit to the university's proposed Maoist reeducation process, the issue would be handled quietly and all would be forgiven. Victoria said that she would not go gentle into that good night, which did not surprise Brian. He said he needed more information.

They agreed to get together to continue their discussion later that evening and decided to have dinner at Hussein's, their daughter's favorite. Mr. Hussein always made a fuss over Tess and had two daughters, not yet old enough to go to school, that Tess liked. The days were growing longer, and Brian thought it was safe to go to Hussein's as long as they could come and go in daylight.

After wrapping things up for the day in the lab, Victoria dropped by the ER to find out which ICU they'd sent her patient to. She wanted to check on the little girl and make certain that the infectious disease team was following her.

Dave Langdon, the head nurse, was reviewing charts at the main desk.

"Hi, Dave."

"Hi," he said. He looked exhausted.

"Tough day?"

"The worst."

"I wanted to check to see where they sent the young girl with the endocarditis and heart failure."

Langdon shook his head. "She didn't make it."

"Oh, no."

"The MRI did show the brain abscess that you anticipated, but it was on the wrong side. It wasn't the abscess that was causing her neurologic deficit. She had a very large tumor. The neurosurgeons said that it was most likely a primary brain tumor—not metastatic—but that it was clearly unresectable. When she came back from the MRI, her heart failure began to worsen dramatically. Under the circumstances, the decision was made not to intervene any further. She only survived another hour or so."

"Life is so unfair," Victoria said.

Langdon nodded.

"Thanks, Dave. Hope you're about to go home and get some rest."

"It'll be a while. We haven't even had report yet."

Victoria imagined those two kids somehow finding each other. Both were on their own, both in pain—one from sickle cell disease, the other from her brain tumor. They found solace in the drugs that eased their pain and, hopefully, in each other. Society had failed them. Permitting months of endless rioting had hindered the delivery of social services and tied the hands of defunded, undermanned law enforcement agencies. This was an environment in which the needs of children like these went untended. She couldn't say that these deficiencies had caused the children's deaths, but they certainly hadn't helped. And did anyone believe that allowing two million people per year to illegally enter the country across the southern border was going to do anything but further strain the delivery of healthcare and other social services?

Brian picked up Victoria and Tess at home so that the three of them could drive to Hussein's together. Tess was excited to be going out with both parents for the first time in quite a while.

Someone at Brian's firm had told him that Hussein's was still open, but, as they approached the restaurant, they began to fear that that wasn't true. Like every other business on the block, Hussein's windows and front door were covered with plywood. The only indication that the restaurant might be open was the lighted neon sign over the door. It advertised Hussein's Café Americain—a whimsical nod to Rick's café in the movie *Casablanca*. When they pulled up in front of the restaurant, they discovered that someone had inscribed Voltaire's grim warning on the plywood.

THOSE WHO CAN MAKE YOU BELIEVE ABSURDITIES

CAN MAKE YOU COMMIT ATROCITIES

Brian got out and tried the door. It was locked, but as he was returning to the car, the door opened and Hussein appeared. He was a small, dark man with a short, carefully trimmed beard.

"Please come in. There's not very much on the menu, but you are welcome." Then he noticed the passengers in the car and brightened considerably. "Hello, Mrs., and little princess. So good to see you."

Hussein ushered Victoria and Tess into the restaurant while Brian parked the car. When Brian returned, he found the door locked once again. Hussein responded promptly to his knock.

"I have to keep it locked," he said. Then, speaking softly so the ladies couldn't hear, "They defile the outside of my building. Each morning I wash the sidewalk and the side of the building. Sometimes I have to do this more than once a day. If the door is not locked, they do the same thing inside. And they won't leave. I call the police, but the police don't come."

"I'm sorry, Mr. Hussein," Brian said. "It is such a difficult time."

"Why do the authorities not stop it? Why do they allow this beautiful city to be ruined? I try to understand, but cannot. The one thing that I am certain of, what I learned in my country before I came here, this is happening because the rulers want it to happen. First, they create the chaos, then they apply their remedy. First comes the Reichstag fire, then Hitler's tyrannies. The remedy is always worse than what came before. The ordinary people always lose—money, property, liberty, whatever they have left to lose—and the rulers get richer and ever more powerful. The cycle ends when the people have finally lost everything. The rulers always go too far. The great Alexander Solzhenitsyn wrote, 'You only have power so long as you don't take *everything* away from them. But when you've robbed a man of *everything* he's no longer in your power—he's free again.' I carried his words always in my mind before I came here. Now, I'm remembering them again."

It was easy to forget that Hussein was an intellectual. Recognition dawned in Brian's mind.

"I see that you're also a fan of Voltaire."

Hussein smiled. "Yes, that is my work. Others write on my plywood, why shouldn't I?"

Brian took a seat at the table with Tess and Victoria.

There was no one else in the restaurant. It was a small, family-run place. There was nothing fussy about the restaurant. The food wasn't fancy, just delicious, with generous portions. Before the riots, it would have been packed at this time of day. It was the kind of place that locals knew about and tried to keep secret.

Hussein did not have his usual menus to present to them. "I am sorry that I have little to offer. With so few customers and prices rising so quickly, it's a problem that is difficult to solve. I cannot afford to buy expensive food with no customers to eat it. I used to feed my family with what was left over, but they have gone to stay with my brother, away from the city. It is safer for them there. I miss them. I'm glad to have you here, especially the little princess—because I know that I have what she wants for supper."

"Grilled cheese!" Tess said.

"I also have tomato soup with some special ingredients that is simmering on the stove."

"That sounds wonderful," Victoria said. "Why don't we all have grilled cheese and tomato soup."

When Hussein disappeared into the kitchen, Brian told Victoria that he had discovered some interesting things. They could discuss them later when there were no little ears around.

"I know you're talking about me," Tess said.

They invited Mr. Hussein to join them while they had their supper. He said that he had already eaten, but would be honored to sit with them.

"I imagine," he said, "that you will be the last customers at Hussein's Café Americain. It is a hopeless situation.

"You know that I was an economist before I came here. I taught at the university. I knew that that life was over when I emigrated, but I could still apply my knowledge of economics and business in my new home. A lot of planning went into the decision. What type of business did we want to have? Then, when my wife and I decided to run a restaurant, there were all the questions of what type, where, and so forth. We thought that we had planned for everything, but we never expected this." He gestured with his hand to indicate what was going on outside in the city.

"Did you know that I bought the building? The restaurant was doing so well, it was the natural next step. There is a nice apartment upstairs, a place for us to live. Now what can I do? Property values have fallen so much, I couldn't sell the building for enough to pay off my mortgage. No one wants to invest in this part of town. It may never come back to anywhere near where it was before. It's all very sad and so unnecessary. Why are they doing this to us?

"Nine years I spent before I was allowed to come to America to become a citizen. Nine years. Now, they just walk across the border. Millions every year, I am told. Who will take care of these people? It is not according to the law. Why does no one stop it?"

"Some say that the Democratic party wants the immigrants because they believe that they will eventually vote for them, that they want to change the demographic of the electorate," Victoria said. "But it seems like a long wait—for the immigrants to finally become citizens and for their children to reach voting age."

"If they're required to become citizens in order to vote," Brian said.

"Actually," Hussein said, "the Democrats benefit immediately. There are 435 members of the House of Representatives, and each state's share is determined by its population. The bigger your population, the larger the proportion of the 435 seats your state receives. The population numbers come from the census, and both citizens and noncitizens are counted. I learned all of this when I was studying for my citizenship test. So, I did some arithmetic. At this time, there is one representative for every 770,000 residents. So, if a state like California has four or five million noncitizen residents, it gets five or six additional representatives based on those noncitizens. That way, each congressman from California represents just 660,000 or so actual citizens. That gives each California voter more power than voters in other states. That gives the Democrats more power."

"I did not know that," Victoria said. "Did you?"

Brian shook his head. "I'm guessing that, in addition to the problem of packing states with illegal immigrants to increase the number of representatives they get, it's a lot easier to cheat when you're counting for the census than it is when you're counting ballots."

"I remember," Hussein said, "that one of the first things that Obama did when he got into office was bring the census into the White House and put it under the control of his own chief of staff. Why do you suppose he did that? And the Census Bureau has admitted that, in the 2020 census, they undercounted the populations of six states and overcounted in eight states. Not surprisingly, all but one of the undercounted states voted for Trump in the last election, and all but one of the overcounted states voted for Biden. Of course, the Census Bureau is very sorry for the mistake, but unfortunately, until the 2030 census, the Democrat-controlled states will have more members of Congress and more votes in the Electoral College than they're entitled to, and the Republican-controlled states will have fewer. Nothing nefarious going on, just bad luck for the Republicans. Do they really believe that the public is stupid enough to believe that this happened by accident?"

They moved on to other topics. Hussein said that his wife and little girls were doing well. He would join them soon.

His brother owned a farm. They would survive.

The food was remarkable, as always. It was hard to believe that Hussein was not a trained chef. He was able to transform tomato soup and a grilled cheese sandwich into something truly special.

They continued talking for a while after they'd eaten, but Tess was nodding off to sleep. Brian went to get the car, and, when he returned, Hussein joined them on the sidewalk to say good-bye. Brian handed him his business card.

"I'm not sure if I can be of any help," Brian said, "but feel free to call me if there's anything you want to discuss. I'll be happy to do whatever I can."

Hussein had tears in his eyes as they pulled away. Their departure marked, for him, the end of yet another dream.

Tess instantly fell asleep in the backseat, providing the opportunity her parents needed to discuss adult issues.

"I'm afraid that I don't have any news of your father," Brian said. "The feds have him somewhere. They say he's being transferred to Washington. Ham Hobart is applying whatever pressure he can, demanding access to his client, but, in the end, there's apparently very little he can do until your dad is in Washington."

"Makes you proud to be an American," Victoria said.

"I've been looking into who would be best to handle the defamation suit against the school. Obviously, as a party to the suit, it shouldn't be me, and I really think it's best to go outside my firm. Anyway, there's an overwhelming consensus among the lawyers I've talked to that Ida Silverstein is the person we want. She has a public interest law firm and has handled lots of high-profile cases. I spoke with her briefly, and she's very enthusiastic about representing us. She couldn't believe that we have the teacher on video admitting that she called Tess a racist. I explained that we're not after a big financial settlement, that what we really want is to get them to stop filling children's heads with this racist nonsense. She agrees with the strategy of seeking a large monetary settlement to use as leverage against the school to force them to stop preaching critical race theory. She may even want to go higher than ten million dollars. If you agree, we'll need to set up a meeting with her to talk strategy and sign some papers and so forth."

"Whatever you think, Brian. You're the expert."

"The last item on my list," Brian said, "is Jennifer Beaulieu, formerly known as Jerome Robert Brown. Unfortunately, it's worse than we thought.

"Brown had multiple arrests as a juvenile, including convictions for sexual assault. This is all hidden from public view because he was a juvenile, but I've spoken with attorneys and police officers who were involved at the time. Brown was very well known to law enforcement. He was incarcerated as a juvenile and released when he reached the age of eighteen so that he could continue his life of crime as an adult.

"As an adult, he has had multiple arrests, including for sexual assault. Police believe that he's a sexual predator and probably a pedophile. His only conviction as an adult was for strong arm robbery. He was sent to prison and quickly decided to identify as female. He demanded to be transferred to the women's prison, and, of course, the department of corrections complied.

"Not surprisingly, in the women's prison, he engaged in all manner of sordid activities, some of them alleged to be nonconsensual. He was separated from the general prison population, and, when the COVID pandemic hit, the department of corrections saw an easy solution to their problem and released him forthwith. Needless to say, he's never taken any affirmative steps to become female, other than occasionally wearing women's clothes."

"'This world is a comedy to those that think, a tragedy to those that feel,'" Victoria said. "I think it was Walpole who said that."

"Truly awful, isn't it? Anyway, that's how the department of corrections' problem became our problem, and how Jerome Brown became Jennifer Beaulieu. I've been organizing a letter in my head, summarizing all of this. I'll get copies tomorrow to the school board, the principal, all the relevant parties. I'll send a letter to Arthur Johnson as well. Your problem at the medical school should quickly disappear."

"I know who you're talking about." It was Tess, unexpectedly awake in the back seat.

"You do?" Victoria said.

"You're talking about Jennifer. She's funny. She has a beard. It tickles when she kisses you."

11

Leonard Lutz was a happy young man. On top of the world. He was out of the city, on a warm spring day, testing the limits of his new Porsche 911 Turbo on winding, backcountry roads. 572 horsepower. 0-60 in 2.7 seconds. Top speed 199 miles per hour—on the track, the ad had cautioned. Over $200,000 to get the setup he wanted. Cash was no problem. A powerful man should have a powerful car.

The Porsche ad had offered a powerful suggestion— *Carpe secundum.* Not the hackneyed *carpe diem. Carpe secundum!* Seize the second! That would be his motto from now on. This would be the new guiding force of his life.

Lutz ran the Toward a Fairer America Project, a dark money siphon that funded, well, essentially whatever Adam Michaelson wanted funded. TFAP was a 501(c) organization, which meant it didn't have to disclose its donors' names or any other sources of money. It seldom gave money directly to ultimate beneficiaries, but rather "donated" to other dark money groups, typically also controlled by Adam Michaelson. The money, millions and millions of dollars, sloshed around, back and forth between the groups, until it was virtually impossible for either the IRS or some intrepid investigative reporter to sort out its origins. Of course, since TFAP was a weapon of the Left, neither the IRS nor investigative reporters cared where the money came from. All they wanted was to keep the cash flowing to the causes they supported.

There were so many of these dark money pools these days that the toughest problem when you launched one was creating a noble-enough sounding name that hadn't already been taken. Leonard loved that he had come up with Toward a Fairer America. It was beautiful! Who could be against that?

Lutz reluctantly braked the Porsche as he approached the painstakingly inconspicuous, unmarked turnoff that was the entry onto the Michaelson estate. The first guardhouse was invisible from the road. Beyond that, there were two additional guardhouses and a full ten-minute drive before he would finally arrive at Adam Michaelson's home. The architecture of the guardhouses previewed the solid stone, fortress-like structure of the main house.

An armed guard motioned for him to roll down his window. "May I help you?"

"I'm here to have dinner with Mr. Michaelson."

"Name, please."

"You know who I am."

"May I see some identification, please."

The guards were rigidly formal, but infallibly polite. Leonard hated being treated like he was dropping off laundry. Couldn't they see the car he was driving? He tried to tamp down his anger as he handed over his driver's license.

"One moment, sir." He disappeared into the building to make a phone call and confirm that Lutz was expected. The guard finally returned, after several minutes, deliberately dawdling to prolong Leonard's wait. He handed back the license.

"Thank you, sir. Enjoy your dinner."

Leonard's only response, the screaming of his tires as he launched the Porsche toward the next guardhouse. His route wound through dense woods that, to the unwary, suggested isolation. But Lutz knew that he was not alone. Armed guards patrolled the forest, accompanied by enormous, eager security dogs straining at their leashes. There was, in addition, a complex electronic surveillance system that further protected the vast estate. If you wanted to access the main house without an invitation, sneaking in was not an option. You had to bring an army.

At last he broke out of the woods, and the main house appeared suddenly before him. Lawns and gardens extended a few hundred yards in all directions from the building. The elegant grounds were certain to wow any visitor, but they also served a practical purpose. The final approach to the house was over open ground—one last obstacle for anyone attempting clandestine entry—and, from the point of view of the security people, there was a clear, 360° field of fire.

The house itself was massive, rising three stories. Someone had said it was thirty thousand square feet. Lutz had no idea. The stone walls must have been at least a foot and a half thick. Security personnel had access to the roof. They mostly stayed out of sight, but he had seen them up there from time to time, carrying high-powered rifles, keeping watch with binoculars.

Lutz reluctantly surrendered his Porsche to the attendant waiting at the front of the house. The car would disappear for now, then magically reappear the moment he was ready to leave. As he climbed the steps to the front entry, the door opened, and George appeared, dressed, as always, in a dark suit. George was in his mid-sixties, lean and balding. He had worked for Michaelson since the beginning of time.

"Good evening, Mr. Lutz."

On his first visits, Leonard had been perplexed by the interior of the house. It was simply overwhelming, and seemed calculatedly so. Only as he began to think of it, not as a home, but as an exclusive, boutique hotel, did it begin to make sense. The cavernous vestibule that opened beyond the main door was simply a lobby. Seating areas were scattered around for more private conversation. There was a massive fireplace that you could actually stand in. But the feature that was designed to capture everyone's attention was the view across the lobby to the main terrace. The terrace overlooked lawns and gardens and the forested valley beyond. It was especially magnificent on a clement evening like today's when the glass separating the lobby from the terrace could be opened and the outdoors brought in.

In short, the house was not designed for Michaelson, but for his visitors—global industrialists, artists, scholars, heads of state. It was a place where the president of France could spend a few days and feel secure and comfortable, as he reportedly had.

"I'm afraid that Mr. Michaelson has been delayed," George said. "I expect him to arrive within the hour."

This was a commonplace occurrence working with Michaelson. Lutz found such rudeness increasingly annoying.

"May I offer you a cocktail, or, perhaps, champagne?"

"Champagne, please. Thank you, George." When Michaelson was serving, you always went with the wine. It was certain to be some obscure, ancient vintage that Leonard knew he would likely never be offered again in his lifetime.

"You will be dining on the terrace this evening," George said. He led the way to the terrace where a bottle of champagne was already waiting on ice. George opened and poured the champagne, and then said, "Ah."

Lutz was momentarily bemused by the "ah," then he, too, heard the helicopter. The helipad was only a short distance from the house. He saw the helicopter land and Michaelson and Thomas Fielding emerge. It would be a while yet before they made it to the terrace. Plenty of time for Lutz to have at least one more glass of champagne. It was exquisite.

The popular press generally estimated that Michaelson was worth in the neighborhood of $200 billion. Leonard had been around long enough to understand that Michaelson's wealth was, at minimum, twice that amount. He had so many holdings in so many countries with so many shell corporations that the man himself could probably only guess at his own wealth.

When people described Michaelson, they usually started with "philanthropist." Leonard had come to learn that Michaelson's was a philanthropy of a very special kind—the profitable kind. It was what Leonard admired most about the man.

Michaelson's philanthropy was always cloaked in liberalism, his professed desire merely to aid the oppressed, the downtrodden, the poor. Those who opposed his views were simply greedy bigots who cared nothing for the common man. Michaelson warned of the strongman on the white horse who would sweep in and seize power, then confiscate the nation's wealth and subjugate its people. And while everyone's attention was diverted to the search for this nonexistent strongman on the Right, the Left went happily about increasing the power and control exercised by its own strongman—government. The elite Left's ambitions were, of course, not confined to a single nation. They imagined themselves ruling the entire world under their new false god, globalism. They dreamed also of the near limitless wealth and power that would surely inure to them as members of this global ruling class.

In support of this global goal, Michaelson had a long history of conspicuous donations outside the United States, especially in Eastern Europe and Africa. In a given country, he might give either to the ruling power or the opposition, depending on which leaned further Left. He aggressively funded   universities   and   myriad   nongovernmental organizations in support of his schemes. Michaelson's efforts gave him enormous political influence and access to invaluable insider information, both of which were utilized for financial gain. Michaelson's "philanthropy" sometimes brought him very tangible benefits such as mining or drilling rights. At other times, his gains were more subtly acquired, for example by utilizing his insider's knowledge to place large bets for or against a nation's currency.

Michaelson understood instinctually the inextricable entanglement of political power and financial gain, and, from the beginning of his career, he had pursued both with equal ruthlessness. For a man whose wealth and power not only could, but frequently did, influence the course of nations, it was remarkable how his influence filtered down to the lowest levels of government. In the United States, through his dark money 501(c)s and their financial support of layers of political action committees and racial justice groups, he influenced politics at the grassroots level.

Early on he had understood the enormous financial benefits that could be gained, at trivial cost, by controlling local elections. He could buy a thousand district attorneys for the cost of one president. A state's senior election officer was typically its secretary of state. If you controlled that office, you could exercise enormous power over the conduct, and consequently the outcome, of state elections. No one paid much attention to candidates for secretary of state. It was another office that was cheap to buy.

Even down to the level of local school boards, Michaelson had his people involved. School boards selected texts and determined curricula. They influenced what books could be found on the shelves of school libraries. With a proper social education, young minds could be taught to think in ways that would profit Michaelson and his fellow elites. Social education. That was the essence of modern schooling. Michaelson was in this for the long term. He was a patient man.

Leonard Lutz understood Michaelson's game. Leonard paid close attention, always eager to learn. But Leonard was also eager to cut himself in for a piece of the pie. He was learning to read Michaelson, to understand what Michaelson was up to. By paying attention to where his boss was giving money away, Leonard was sometimes able to guess how Michaelson was planning to make money on the flipside of his philanthropic coin. There was an opportunity to make money by either acting ahead of the boss or riding his coattails. It was risky, in more ways than one, but Leonard had played his hand cautiously. He had made money—big money—and wanted more. In fact, he had recently seen through Michaelson's latest scheme. Leonard planned to cash in, then be done with Michaelson forever. Michaelson might be a patient man. Leonard was not.

At last, the big man appeared. Actually, not such a big man. Maybe six feet tall, a bit overweight. He was sixty-five years old with steel-gray hair and steel-gray eyes. Michaelson's suit probably cost more than Leonard's car. Okay, that might be a slight exaggeration. You'd have to throw in the shoes and tie. With Michaelson there was always this aura of wealth and power. Leonard wondered if he would sense that if he had no idea who Michaelson was.

As always, Michaelson had Thomas Fielding in tow. Fielding was the lawyer, the consigliere. He made things happen. Fielding was a tall, thin, austere man. About Michaelson's age, he still had jet-black hair. His eyes were brown and his skin had an olive, almost jaundiced hue. Legend had it that he and Michaelson had started as partners. Somewhere along the line, Fielding had become an employee. Lutz regarded him as inconsequential, probably only worth a few hundred million dollars—a billion tops.

"Sorry we're late," Michaelson said. "I had to give a speech at the United Nations. Afterward, a couple of ambassadors from the Middle East wanted to go over some issues. It went on and on."

Michaelson's involvement in the Middle East tended to center around two things. One was oil. The other was the fact that he was a raging antisemite. He had learned to express his antisemitism largely in terms of support for pro-Palestinian causes. He also shared the current administration's enthusiasm for a nuclear-armed Iran.

"I see that you've found the champagne," Michaelson said. "I think I'll wait and have wine with dinner. George has promised something truly special. How about you, Thomas?"

Michaelson always offered alcohol to Fielding. Fielding always declined. Leonard hadn't figured that one out, yet.

Predinner, there was a brief discussion about the Toward a Fairer America Project. Leonard gave Michaelson a brief financial overview—where money was coming from and where it was going. Fielding listened, taking mental notes. He had a prodigious memory. You had to be careful. A casual remark that turned out to be inaccurate could come back to haunt you.

It wasn't until they'd eaten and the plates had been cleared that Michaelson got down to serious business. Leonard was sipping cognac.

"You know, things are progressing nicely. Better than I expected, even," Michaelson said. "Who would have thought that we could have, at this point, half the people in the country believing that whether you're male or female has nothing to do with biology? It's a choice you make. Or that white people come out of the womb racist? Hard to believe people are that gullible.

"I often think of it like those Nigerian email scams that are all over the internet. They're preposterous on their face. You know, 'I am the widow of His Excellency So-and-So who left me $2 billion in solid gold bars—but I have no cash. I need $10,000 to transport the gold out of the country. If you would kindly provide that amount, I will split the gold with you.' If you don't already know it's fake, they fill the email with errors in spelling and grammar, so you'd have to be even more unbelievably stupid to fall for it. I asked an FBI agent about it, and he said, 'That's the point. The scammers know that if you're dumb enough to reply to that kind of email, they can probably take you for every penny you've got. They're not looking for smart people. They're looking for rubes.' I thought about that, and decided we're on the right track. If you can convince them that men can get pregnant, they're ready to believe anything." He shook his head.

"So, Leonard, I want you to tackle a new problem. Cost it out and get me a proposal. Let me know which groups money should go to, and how much it's going to cost. What I want you to do, I want you to convince people that they're supposed to walk on their hands. I want to be really aggressive about this. Eighteen months from now, when I walk down the street, I want to see at least twenty-five percent of people walking on their hands."

Michaelson stopped and stared at Leonard, waiting for a response. Then he broke into a big belly laugh. Even Fielding cracked a smile.

"I wonder if we could do it," Michaelson said. "I bet we'd have some takers, especially on the college campuses. Be great to see those sociology professors and all those woke students walking around on their hands. I learned many years ago that it's hard to lose money betting on stupidity.

"Seriously, though, there is a problem we do need to discuss. Things have quieted down in the cities. There hasn't been anything you could call a real riot in months. It's all degenerated into random shootings and looting. In the end that's counterproductive, in the absence of rioting. We need an incident, a spark. Get your people on it. Keep an eye out. Summer's coming. The timing couldn't be better. As soon as we have the right incident, then we fire up our people in the news media and social media, get the outrage really going. Then we give a lot of money to the people we know can be counted on to take it to the streets. Like last time, only a whole lot bigger."

Leonard smiled for the first time in the entire evening. Now you're talking. This is what he had been waiting for. He threw back his cognac and said, "Yes, sir."

"I really feel that this is the moment," Michaelson said. "Who knows when such an opportunity will come our way again. We've got our people in key decision-making positions in the White House, Congress, the Pentagon, the courts—throughout the federal bureaucracy—and the Oval Office is vacant."

"The president is an empty suit," Lutz said.

"No," Michaelson said, "he's rather less than that. To paraphrase Orwell, I wouldn't dignify the president by calling him an empty suit. He is simply a hole in the air.

"Do you know when I first became certain that our goal was in reach? It was on Election Day—not after the vote count was reported, for obvious reasons. In the first place, the tallies weren't even reported on Election Day. In the second place, we knew who was counting the votes, so the result was never in doubt. No, I knew that this would be our moment when I saw the president step before a group of supporters in Philadelphia, with a megaphone in his hand, put his arm around his granddaughter and say, 'This is my son, Beau Biden, who a lot of you helped elect to the senate in Delaware.' On the day that he was elected president, he confused his granddaughter with his son, a son who, by the way, had been dead for four years and had never been elected senator from anywhere. What a moment! You can still find the video on the internet, I'm told. No matter how hard we try, it's difficult to get rid of every copy.

"At this moment, the government is ours. We control nearly everything. But, we have to act quickly, before the public wakes up and says, 'Wait a minute. Who is running the country?'"

Michaelson stood. "Remember, Leonard, the cities are dry tinder right now. All we need is a match, and we need it now."

Michaelson gave his watch a studied glance. "Well, I have an early meeting at the White House tomorrow. It was good to see you, Leonard. Thank you for coming."

Leonard understood that he was being dismissed. He rose, made his good-byes, and headed for the door. He was excited. Michaelson had confirmed the scheme. Leonard was about to make a really big score.

As soon as Lutz was out of earshot, Michaelson turned to Fielding. "He drinks too much. He's in no condition to drive. Put him in a limo and have somebody drive his car to his house." Michaelson paused then added, "Leonard is starting to worry me. He's up to something. He thinks he knows something."

"I saw that, too," Fielding said.

"Have Dennis look into it, see what's going on."

12

"You look tired, old friend." Hamilton Hobart had warned his client that his time in the D.C. Jail—formally known as the Correctional Treatment Facility—would be grueling, especially for a man of 70. The strong, fit man who had entered incarceration now appeared gaunt and exhausted. He was slightly unkempt and perhaps a little stooped, but the bright blue eyes remained alert, telling Hobart that, though his body may have been weakened, his mind remained keen.

"Are they treating you okay?"

"Better than most. I have no right to complain." He even managed a smile.

They were standing in a courtroom in the Prettyman Building which housed the United States District Court for the District of Columbia. This was where the case, *United States of America vs. Alexander Walker,* would be tried. A grand jury had issued a three-count indictment. The defendant was charged with Entering and Remaining in a Restricted Building or Grounds, Disorderly and Disruptive Conduct in a Restricted Building or Grounds, and Assaulting, Resisting, or Impeding Certain Officers. If convicted, Alex Walker could potentially be sentenced to spend the next twenty years of his life in prison. This harsh possibility was intended to strike fear into the heart of the defendant and force him into a plea bargain—to accept the certainty of a much shorter sentence instead of going to trial and rolling the dice. If a defendant, claiming to be innocent, refused to accept the proffered plea agreement and was subsequently convicted, prosecutors typically retaliated with requests for brutally long sentences. More often than not, judges complied. These extorted plea bargains rather effortlessly added cases to the prosecutors' "win" columns and magically cleared judges' dockets.

Hamilton Hobart had made it clear that his client would, under no circumstances, accept a plea bargain. Alexander Walker was innocent and looked forward to absolute vindication in a court of law. Furthermore, his client asserted his right to a speedy trial. Which was why they were here today. The government was dawdling.

"Please, Alex, have a seat. We can talk here, quietly, without being overheard."

They huddled together at the defendant's table, awaiting the arrival of the judge. It was a rare opportunity to exchange information. Access to his client at the jail was frequently denied, and, when Hobart was finally allowed to see Alex, they had to assume that everything they said was listened to, if not recorded.

"This hearing shouldn't take too long," Hobart said.

Alex Walker smiled for a second time. "Take as long as you like. This is infinitely more pleasant than the jail."

"Victoria sends her love. I keep her up to date, as much as I can."

"Please tell her not to worry. I'm fine."

"Of course," Hobart said.

His gaze traveled the wood-paneled courtroom. Still no judge. There would be time to fill his client in on what to expect at the hearing. "The judge we've drawn is Abraham Tevis Jones—often sarcastically referred to, behind his back, as Honest Abe. He's a bit of a mixed bag. He attended Harvard, where he was trained not to think. He is reflexively liberal, but the single most important issue in Abraham Tevis

Jones' world is Abraham Tevis Jones. In all things, Judge Jones, first and foremost, looks out for Judge Jones. I've found it useful to bear this in mind.

"The judge and I are actually poker buddies, of a sort. He enjoys being entertained by my stories, and I enjoy taking his money. The trick to beating him at poker is to get him laughing. I know I've dialed in the proper amount of levity when I see bourbon coming out of his nose.

"On the bench, Judge Jones can be fierce and overbearing. He can be tyrannical in his support of Leftist causes, such as the prosecution of cases like yours. But, he's aware of this image and hates to be taken for granted by prosecutors. If he senses this, or feels that he is being disrespected, he can become vindictive. All this aside, he is a very intelligent man—and very unpredictable.

"The prosecutor assigned to your case is a newly-minted Assistant U.S. Attorney who has virtually no trial experience. He was assigned because they expect you to eventually accept a plea bargain and because the government has failed to understand the significance of this case. By the time they realize the magnitude of their mistake, it will be too late. Also, the young man has a couple of vulnerabilities that we may usefully exploit."

The judge suddenly appeared and instantly dominated the courtroom. Standing behind the bench he presented a massive form, tall and wide. He was a black man of about sixty with a receding hairline and clumped, black hair. His visage was somewhere between dour and cross. It would be easy to imagine that he'd just received some terrible news.

After the usual courtroom formalities and Judge Jones' attending to other business at the bench for several minutes, the discovery hearing began.

"Now, Mr. Hobart, I have read your motion and am shocked to hear that the defense believes that the government is, at the very least, slow in producing—and possibly even withholding—potentially exculpatory evidence. We'll hear from you first." The judge's words dripped with sarcasm and impatience.

"Thank you, Your Honor," Hobart said, rising to his feet, "but, as urgent as these discovery matters are, I feel that it is appropriate that we take just a moment to properly recognize the recent achievement of this young man who represents the government in this case. I speak of none other than Mr. Irving M. Schitzfuke."

The name was a minefield, even without the unfortunate initials, and Hobart was careful to mispronounce it without straying into vulgarity. Schitzfuke, for his part, had the appearance of a deer caught in headlights—a very young, very skinny, utterly bewildered deer.

"I have only just learned," Hobart said, "that Mr. Schitzfuke recently traveled to the great state of Arkansas, where he took, and also passed, the state's extremely challenging bar exam. In so doing, he followed the route first traveled by the woman universally acknowledged as the most brilliant lawyer in the world, our beloved former First Lady, Mrs. Hillary Clinton. So, Your Honor, I hope you will join me in congratulating and welcoming to the bar Mr. I.M. Schitzfuke."

Each time he spoke the unhappy name, Hobart mispronounced it in a different, ever more creative manner. Schitzfuke glowed red.

"Hear, hear," the judge said, his mouth covered and tears in his eyes.

The more subtle barb, certainly not missed by the judge or Mr. Schitzfuke, was that Irving, like Hillary, had first failed the bar exam in Washington, D.C. and then gone to Arkansas in search of a more favorable testing climate. Hobart's comments were deliberately calculated to unnerve and distract Schitzfuke. To the uninitiated, this harassment might have seemed unnecessary, even cruel. It was not. Hobart's client deserved every advantage his lawyer could gain him. "Cruel" wasn't a little teasing. "Cruel" was indicting a man for political reasons for a crime he didn't commit and then fabricating and withholding evidence. Hobart wanted to throw Schitzfuke off balance, and he had certainly accomplished that. The young attorney was in way over his head, and things were about to get much worse.

"Just one additional matter, Your Honor." Hobart wanted to keep things rolling while the judge was still in a light-hearted mood.

"This is a discovery hearing, Mr. Hobart." But the judge's tone indicated that he would be delighted to view any further entertainment that the defense had on its program.

"If you would indulge me for just a few moments longer, Your Honor. You see, I fear that the bland wording of the government's indictment might lead one to misunderstand the magnitude of the crime that is alleged. Just how seriously the government judged this alleged crime to be was evident from the very beginning. They did not contact his attorney so that he could be quietly produced for arrest. Under normal circumstances, one might have expected that approach for the arrest of a man who is an internationally renowned professor of medicine at one of the nation's finest medical schools, a man who has lived at the same address for over thirty years. No, the government took a different tack. They gathered an assault force armed with automatic weapons. They had armored vehicles. For all we know, there were helicopter gunships or even B-2 bombers hovering above in case things really got out of hand.

"This armed force stormed Dr. Walker's clinic, where, for many years, he has provided medical care for the underprivileged of his city. Officers broke into an examining room where he was in the process of evaluating a scantily clad, middle-aged, female patient. The woman, who spoke very little English, assumed, for whatever reason, that she was the focus of this military invasion. To her credit, she resisted valiantly. She launched a furious counterassault, physically attacking several of the officers and, apparently, causing some significant injuries. In the end, she was successfully subdued, handcuffed, and herself placed under arrest. I understand that the government would very much like to make her one of the very few persons residing illegally in our country who is actually deported, but they face a very steep uphill battle due to the difficult fact that she was arrested in a sanctuary city."

By this time, Judge Jones was once again hiding his mouth and wiping away tears. Everyone within earshot had stopped whatever they were supposed to be doing in order not to miss a word of Hobart's monologue—and Hobart had yet to deliver his punchline. Poor Schitzfuke had no idea how to deal with the situation.

"Just one more moment, Your Honor, as I return to my initial concern about the indictment. Despite the government's manifest concern regarding the grave threat Dr. Walker represents to the community, demonstrated by the manner of his arrest and their demand that he remain in custody prior to trial, the indictment reads rather innocently. Take, for example, the first count, Entering and Remaining in a Restricted Building or Grounds. That sheds very little light on the heinous nature of the alleged underlying crime. Dr. Walker was on the Capitol grounds that day. We don't dispute that. Millions of people visit those grounds every year. But that's not why we're here. That's not why his clinic was invaded. That's not why he has been held in jail all these weeks awaiting trial. The answer to why we are here lies in two innocent-sounding words hiding in open view, 'restricted' and 'grounds.' The defendant was on the Capitol grounds. I have already said that we do not dispute that, but the government alleges a crime so hideous they dare not say its name. If the allegation is to be believed, not only was Dr. Walker on the grounds, but also," Hobart paused several seconds for effect, then, "HE STEPPED ON THE GRASS!"

The courtroom erupted. The dazed Schitzfuke looked like he might cry.

Judge Jones banged his gavel, said something that sounded like "five minutes," and fled the bench.

13

It was more like fifteen minutes before the judge had composed himself enough to feel that he might safely return to the bench. He now had a fixed scowl on his face so that there could be no doubt that the fun was over.

"I am not opposed," he said to those in the courtroom, "to a little levity from time to time in my court. It can lift spirits in the face of what can be very stressful proceedings, and a little humor is generally innocuous—especially if there is no jury present. Having said that, it's time for us all to focus seriously on the questions at hand."

Schitzfuke indicated that he wanted to be heard.

"Mr. Schitzfuke," the judge said.

Only, he didn't say Schitzfuke.

Gasps were heard throughout the courtroom.

His Honor had stumbled into the absolute mother of all possible mispronunciations. The one that had to be avoided at all costs. He absolutely, unequivocally said it. Both syllables!

This time, though, the judge was not amused. He threw an angry look at Hobart for getting him into this mess, then did something that Hobart had never, ever seen him do. He apologized.

"I hope that the Government," Judge Jones said, nimbly avoiding the potential hazard of a second disastrous mispronunciation, "will accept the Court's sincere apology. The name is difficult to pronounce, and the Court would greatly appreciate your providing a phonetic spelling so that such mistakes will not, in the future, be repeated."

Schitzfuke, in an obvious huff, hastily scratched something on a piece of paper and, without a word, approached the bench and, more or less, threw the paper onto the judge's desk. The judge glanced down to read what had been produced.

"The Court notes," he said, "that the Government has provided the normal spelling of the name, not the phonetic spelling that was requested." Schitzfuke's action was straight-up, in-your-face disrespect, if not full-on contempt of court. Jones was manifestly furious.

Hamilton Hobart sat motionless, his left arm held across his chest to support his right elbow, his right fist clenched and held in front of his mouth. Only moments ago, Schitzfuke had been in a position that lawyers dream of but seldom experience. The judge was not only angry at opposing counsel, but was also personally embarrassed by his treatment of Schitzfuke. It was the type of situation that a judge typically would bend over backward to correct, to make it clear that he had made a mistake and bore Schitzfuke no personal malice. The judge might, for example, grant a motion that had previously had little likelihood of a favorable ruling. An experienced attorney would immediately recognize this possibility of a future favor and carefully consider how and when he might best capitalize on it. The proud, callow Schitzfuke had thrown all that away in a fit of indignation. In the same instant, Hobart had been released from the doghouse and returned to the catbird seat. Such are the vagaries of the practice of law.

"I believe," Judge Jones said, "that the Government wishes to be heard." Perhaps Schitzfuke had just received his favor. The judge would ignore his impertinence without further comment.

"Your Honor, although Mr. Hobart may attempt to make

light of the first count of the indictment, I assure the Court that we take it very seriously. That said, I would draw your attention to the remaining counts, one of which relates to the defendant's assault of an agent of the Federal Bureau of Investigation."

"The Court is familiar with the indictment. Perhaps we should move on to the purpose of this hearing. Mr. Hobart."

Hobart rose to his feet. "Thank you, Your Honor. Mr. Schitzfuke"—Hobart pronounced the name flawlessly—"however accidentally, has raised an issue that is at the heart of Dr. Walker's defense. We will show that, as Dr. Walker's criticism of the government rose, and he became a more outspoken critic, persons within the government began to look for a way to silence him. Dr. Walker's attendance at a rally in Washington on January 6 provided the opportunity they sought. Of course, the defendant was only one of many ensnared on that fateful day, but his is the case that we are dealing with today. After attending the rally, Dr. Walker, like thousands of others, walked over to the Capitol. Prior to his arrival, all signs and barricades related to the so-called "restricted area"—that portion of the Capitol grounds that Dr. Walker is alleged to have entered onto—had been removed. Nonetheless, the defendant remained on the walkway."

"Mr. Hobart," the judge said, "you are trying the Court's patience. What is the discovery issue here?"

"Your Honor, my client did not enter the restricted area of his own accord. He was pushed. He was pushed by a person in the employ of the Federal Bureau of Investigation. Furthermore, that person deliberately shoved Dr. Walker into an FBI agent who was standing just off the walkway, thus paving the way for the assault and disorderly conduct charges. We will also show that the FBI agent who claims to have been assaulted by the defendant was not the person that Dr. Walker was pushed into. The discovery issue is quite straightforward. The government refuses to identify the federal agents and others being paid by the government who were present that day. It also refuses to provide video of the incident. All we have is an affidavit sworn by an FBI agent, a person who we will show was not involved in the incident."

Schitzfuke was on his feet. Judge Jones cautioned him, with a hand gesture, to remain silent.

"These are very serious charges, Mr. Hobart."

"Indeed, they are, Your Honor. Indeed, they are. May I approach?"

Hobart delivered a sheaf of papers to the bench, then returned to his place behind the defense table.

"This is our initial potential witness list, Your Honor. It has previously been provided to the Government. Most of the names are persons that we have not yet even interviewed. In addition to the persons named, there are others listed only by description and their location on the Capitol grounds that day. Many of these individuals, we have good reason to believe, were either undercover federal agents or others working at the behest or employ of the government. We have demanded that the Government identify those persons working in its employ or on its behalf, and, in the alternative, if one of the persons on the list was not so employed, the government should simply say so."

Hobart noted that, as expected, Judge Jones had not gotten beyond the first page of names. That was because the first name on the list was a person well known to His Honor. Fortuitously, the name Cheryl Agutter fell at the very top of the alphabetical listing—although Hobart had dropped a man named Adams from the list to modestly improve the hand that fate had dealt. Hobart had, himself, not previously heard of Cheryl Agutter, and he was quite confident that Schitzfuke hadn't the slightest idea who she was. It was the ever-resourceful Dennis and his team who had identified her and discovered her significance. She was a refined person of impeccable reputation. She was highly educated and held an important position at the Department of State. It was unclear why she was at the Capitol that day—perhaps on official business. There was no evidence that she had done anything the least bit suspicious, much less unlawful. Her importance lay in the fact that she was not Mrs. Abraham Jones, a well-respected and talented woman in her own right. Cheryl Agutter was the judge's girlfriend.

It was expected, and hoped, that Judge Jones would see the appearance of her name on the list as mere coincidence. Their relationship was so closely guarded that the judge would be unlikely to suspect that Hobart had any knowledge of it. Still, the situation was a can of worms. The vast majority of the people whose names appeared on the list would never see the inside of the courtroom. However, should Agutter be called as a witness, the judge would at least have to identify her as some sort of acquaintance. Who knew where that might lead?

Judge Jones turned once again to Schitzfuke. "What does the Government have to say?"

"First of all, Mr. Hobart's claim of a government conspiracy to entrap his client is preposterous. The best evidence of that is the fact that the FBI was totally unaware of his identity. After scuffling with the FBI agent, Dr. Walker fled the scene. Months passed before the defendant was finally identified so that he could be charged.

"Regarding the discovery issue, it is the Government's duty to protect the identities of agents and others working under cover. This is necessary to protect the integrity of investigations, to avoid tainting future prosecutions, and to safeguard the very lives of those involved. In many cases, this confidentiality is a matter of national security. These names simply cannot be made public. Your Honor has all this information in our response to the defense motion.

"Finally, Your Honor, I want to personally express outrage that defense counsel would suggest that the Government has presented evidence in this case that it knows to be false. Integrity is at the heart of what the Department of Justice does. Does counsel truly believe that we would manufacture data to obtain the conviction of an innocent man?"

"Mr. Hobart."

"Thank you, Your Honor. We will show that the reason for the delay in indicting Dr. Walker was not that he was unknown. Quite the contrary. The Government feared that his prominence rendered their scheme far too risky. But, as time passed, and Dr. Walker's role as a leader of the resistance to the current administration grew, it was decided that the possibility of silencing him was worth the risk.

"I would further add that the defendant did not flee the scene, as the Government claims. Dr. Walker simply disentangled himself from the agent, apologized, and went on about his way.

"As to Mr. Schitzfuke's outrage, recent history has taught hard lessons as to what the Department of Justice is willing to do, especially when political considerations are involved. It was on the eve of the 2020 elections that the DOJ revealed the so-called plot to kidnap the governor of Michigan. It turns out that there were more government agents and paid informants in that episode than there were conspirators. Juries have refused to convict each and every one of the accused that the government has brought to trial in that case. It is widely believed that that government operation was merely a dress rehearsal for the January 6 debacle that ensnared my client.

"Then we have the Russia hoax which hung over the previous president for the duration of his presidency. A senior FBI attorney admitted—admitted, Your Honor—to deliberately falsifying a document that was presented to the FISA court, an act designed to perpetuate the hoax.

"A recent deputy director of the FBI was fired for repeatedly lying under oath in relation to another investigation with political overtones. And one final example, if I may, we have the specter of the attorney general of the United States, the attorney general, holding a clandestine meeting on an airport runway with a former president of the United States whose wife was, at that very moment, under active investigation by the Department of Justice. Sadly, there are many, many such examples of bad faith and outright crimes committed by those who we rely on to honestly deliver justice in this country.

"Mr. Schitzfuke can spare us his outrage. Do I *believe* that the Department of Justice would manufacture evidence to convict an innocent man? No. I *expect* it!"

"Mr. Hobart, please address your other discovery issue."

"Yes, Your Honor, the matter of the video. It is widely reported that authorities have in their possession no less than 14,000 hours of video taken in and about the Capitol on January 6. The defense seeks the release of this video in its entirety so that it can be searched for exculpatory evidence."

"What is the Government's position?"

"This video has been carefully scrutinized for any evidence that might be remotely exculpatory. None was found. Specifically, no video evidence was found of the incident for which his client was charged. We have, however, offered a great deal of video to Mr. Hobart for his review. Much of the remaining video, however, cannot be provided because it is classified."

"Your Honor," Hobart said, "leaving aside the silly proposition that the government would need to classify even a single second of video taken of a crowd gathered outside the Capitol in broad daylight, I would like to ask exactly who *scrutinized* the 14,000 hours of video. Was it Mr. Schitzfuke?"

"Of course not."

"Ah," Hobart said, "'of course not.' Might we know who did, in fact, examine the video?"

Schitzfuke was growing tense once again. "I do not know."

"Your Honor, do you believe that this video was 'scrutinized'—to use Mr. Schitzfuke's word—with our witness list in mind? Once again, in the words of Mr. Schitzfuke, 'Of course not.' Your Honor, fairness requires that the defense have the opportunity to examine this video in its entirety."

The judge had heard enough. "I have your motion, Mr. Hobart, and the Government's response. You will receive my decision promptly. In the meantime, you have made some very serious allegations here today, and the Court expects to see evidence that supports them."

"Yes, Your Honor, but you see how difficult it is when the Government claims that they have no video of the alleged crime. It is only by the grace of God that we have access to other video which we believe shows Dr. Walker during every second of his time on the Capitol grounds that day, including the incident in question."

Schitzfuke's head snapped around so quickly he nearly lost his balance. "Your Honor, the Government has a right to see this video."

"And I'm certain the Government will," the judge said with a smile returning to his face, "but the way this works is, the Government turns over its evidence first, then the defense."

"This is entrapment!" Schitzfuke was beside himself.

With this, Judge Abraham Tevis Jones began to laugh out

loud. Tears returned to his eyes and his shoulders began to shake. "We're adjourned," he said.

Hamilton Hobart turned to his client. "At long last, Mr. Schitzfuke has gotten something right."

Alex Walker said nothing, but he did manage a broad, contented smile.

Hobart watched as his client was escorted from the courtroom, then hurried to catch Schitzfuke before he departed.

"We have not formally met," Hobart said, offering his hand.

Schitzfuke ignored the gesture.

"I'm not surprised that you are angry with me," Hobart said. "I'm trying to make amends. If you will permit me, I will tell you how you can save your job."

Schitzfuke maintained his sullen silence.

"You need to understand," Hobart said, "that everything I said today in the courtroom is true, and that I can prove it. Our video shows all. You also need to understand that your boss, or your boss's boss, or someone even higher up—whoever hatched this scheme to frame Dr. Walker—also knows that everything I said today is true, because that person is the one who planned this farce. The problem is, that person doesn't know, yet, what I said. Which is where you come in. You don't have to believe me. All you have to do is make certain my words get passed up the chain of command. When those words reach the right ears, this case will end.

"If you fail to pass my words along, I will be airing our video in Judge Jones' court. I will also be calling your bosses into court to testify. They will be humiliated and their perfidy will be revealed to the entire world. I do not pretend to know what will happen to them. These days, it seems that you can get away with just about anything at the Department of

Justice. For all I know, they will be promoted.

"There is, however, one thing that I am certain of—you will be fired and find yourself headed back to Arkansas. You will be found guilty of the crime of not warning your bosses that their treachery was about to be proven in a court of law.

"Have a nice day, Mr. Schitzfuke."

14

"Those who cast the votes decide nothing. Those who count the votes decide everything." —Joseph Stalin

"It's no longer about who gets to vote…it's about who gets to count the vote." —Joseph Biden

The quotes were in an email that Ted Bass, Nina's husband, had sent him. Biden had let the unfiltered thought escape his mouth in Atlanta on January 11, 2022. It must have given his handlers chest pain after all the work they'd done to prevent anyone from even discussing the possibility of foul play in the counting of the votes that resulted in Biden's election. The newspapers and talking heads on TV had condemned any suggestions of election irregularities as lies and disinformation. Make such an accusation on the Left-controlled social media, and you were banned for life. Democrats in Congress even tried to make it illegal to spread election "disinformation." So much effort, and now Old Joe just comes out, unbidden, and spills the beans.

The phone on Brian's desk buzzed. It was Alice.

"Harsh wants to speak with you in his office right away."

"Harsh" was Dewitt Marvin Harshman, also known as Dewey. He was the firm's managing partner, and the single person—in the entire firm—who Brian strived hardest to avoid. Brian couldn't count the number of times he'd waited for the next elevator to avoid spending thirty claustrophobic seconds with Harsh. The man was arrogant, obnoxious, insufferable, and one of the most powerful partners in the firm.

Harsh had played football in college and apparently was good enough that he would have made the team even if his father hadn't paid for the stadium. He had made it through law school—no record of how many buildings his father had built there—and then joined Brian's firm decades ago, long before it had achieved its current prestige and prominence. Not surprisingly, Harsh's personality made him a disaster in the courtroom. He evinced equal contempt for the judge and the jury, who, in turn, quickly learned to loathe, and—which is much worse—distrust the man.

Harshman family money and connections brought millions of dollars' worth of business to the firm each year, so firing him was not an option. Someone came up with the idea of making Harsh managing partner as a means of keeping him out of the courtroom. Harsh thought they had crowned him king.

If Brian had needed a reminder of Harshman's odious character, he received it as soon as he walked into the managing partner's office.

"He's on the phone, Mr. Townsend," his secretary said. "It's a very important call. He'll be with you as soon as he's done."

What a petty, little man. This was one of his favorite power games. He would summon you to discuss something urgent, then make you cool your heels in the outer office for fifteen minutes while he tended to something more important than your lowly self.

"He can see you now," his secretary said, putting down her phone. Her eyes were red. She looked like she'd been crying. She often looked like she'd been crying. In addition to his other fine qualities, Harsh was a misogynist and a sadistic bully.

"Hi, Dewey, how are you?" Brian knew that Dewey preferred "Harsh." It sounded so menacing.

Harsh didn't say anything or even glance up for several moments. He was totally preoccupied with the manifestly important paperwork on his desk. Probably his lunch menu.

"I'm afraid this is serious," Harsh said when at last he deigned to recognize Brian's arrival.

For emphasis, Harsh rose and walked over to the floor-to-ceiling window that flanked the sitting area of his office. He gazed out the window, at nothing in particular, deep in thought.

It was the moment Brian had yearned for. Harsh had forgotten to cut back on his eating when he cut back on his exercising. He was an enormous, bald, bowling ball. Brian had long since calculated that, by hitting Harsh at just the right angle, he could propel him into the window. Dewey's weight would do the rest. He would make quite an impression on the pavement below. The problem had always been, how to get a man of his size, against his will, to the window without attracting undue attention. Alas, Dewey, his deep contemplation at an end, returned to his desk. The moment was lost.

"This suit that you and your wife have filed against the school board is attracting a lot of attention," Dewey said. "How's that going?"

"Former wife."

"Pardon?"

"Victoria is my former wife. We're divorced."

"Whatever. How's the suit going?"

"Very well, I think," Brian said. "Ida is in the process of taking depositions from everyone involved."

"I was going to ask you. Of all the firms you could have picked to handle this, why did you go to a couple of…"

Dewey caught himself just in time.

"I believe that the word you're looking for is 'lesbians.' We chose them because Ida and her wife are very, very good at what they do. Victoria and I are also growing personally very fond of both of them. They're nice people."

"I wasn't going to say 'lesbian.'"

"Of course, you weren't," Brian said. That brought a little color to Dewey's cheeks—an auspicious sign.

"Your suit against the board is racist to its core," Dewey said, his voice rising. "It smacks of white supremacism. That term is actually appearing on TV and in newspapers in the same sentence as the name of this law firm. The Executive Committee has determined that this suit reflects badly on our firm and undermines everything we stand for. They are demanding that you drop it, that you walk away. Now."

"If you and the like-minded members of the Executive Committee had IQs above room temperature, you'd understand that calling people racist is just the latest tactic the Left uses to stifle dissent. If you disagree with them, about anything, you're a racist. They expect you to cower and cave when they call you that. Most people do. It's a slimy ploy—racist to its core, as you would say—but it's effective."

"It's not just you." Dewey was growing loud and livid. "It's your whole damn family. Your father-in-law is a white supremacist and an insurrectionist. Your wife is not only party to this racist lawsuit, but we've also learned that she has written some transphobic screed to the school board that they're about to go public with."

"Former father-in-law. Former wife."

"That's it. There's no reasoning with you. The Executive Committee demands your resignation, immediately!" Dewey was furious. His face was red. His body was shaking.

"The executive committee can demand whatever they

want. I'm not resigning." Brian had Dewey almost where he wanted him, just one more little nudge. "I like it here. If it weren't for you and a couple of other deadwoods on the executive committee, this would actually be a pleasant place to work."

"That's it! You're fired, effective immediately!"

Bingo.

"Dewey, are you familiar with the term 'defenestration'?"

Dewey was bewildered. "I think it's a polo term, right?"

"Close," Brian said, "dressage."

Dewey was breathing hard. Brian had just one more item to tick off his list.

"Since my firing is effective immediately, I better go down and pack my files."

"Those files belong to this firm. If you take so much as one of them, you'll be prosecuted for theft. You'll end up in prison, which is just where you belong."

"Oh, my," Brian said.

Dewey picked up the phone and buzzed his secretary. "Hannah, get me Security!"

Bingo.

15

Brian managed to get back to his office ahead of the security forces. Alice was at her desk.

"Tragic news, Alice. Harsh just fired me."

Alice rose with a broad smile and offered her hand. "Congratulations!"

"Security should be arriving en masse at any moment."

"Oh, that reminds me," Alice said. "I found a portable hard drive that had somehow been overlooked. It was way at the back of one of your desk drawers under some papers. I put it in my purse."

"Thanks, Alice. It should be safe there."

Friends on the Executive Committee had warned Brian of what was coming, that he was about to be ousted. They said they were just one vote short of stopping it. This was only the latest manifestation, his friends said, of the troubles within the firm. It had simply grown too big with too many factions and fiefdoms and too much backstabbing. The firm, as currently constituted, would not survive. Everyone knew that. It was just a matter of how they split up the pie. The firm's demise would come soon, but not soon enough for Brian.

For his part, Brian realized he felt very little rancor. This was not a personal action taken by the partners against him— with the possible exception of Dewey Harshman. Everyone knew that Brian was the firm's rainmaker. His departure would only hasten the firm's demise. Getting rid of Brian was simply a lifestyle choice made by a handful of wealthy senior partners whose lives floated above and seldom touched the real world. They rode their limousines each day back and forth from their homes in distant suburbs taking no notice of the decay of the city that had made them rich or the disintegration of the society that had made possible their luxurious, comfortable lives. Woke politics were in vogue, so they, and their uber-wealthy friends, supported woke politics. After all, it had nothing to do with them in any real way. Woke politics was all about the rules by which the hoi polloi, the little people, would be governed. That's the way socialism always worked. It was designed to be great for politicians and titans of business, not so great for the masses whose job it was to feed and clothe the politicians and titans of business. There was a name for this kind of arrangement. It was called fascism. The current flock of fascists had big ambitions. Not content merely to ruin single countries, their aim encompassed the entire world. They fancied themselves to be globalists.

The problem for the woke partners was that woke politics did not even tolerate discussion, much less dissent. You either agreed with their policies, or you were evil. If you didn't agree with their ideas on race, for example, you were a racist. If you were a racist, you had no business expressing your ideas in the public square, the space now occupied almost entirely by the big-tech social media companies. Under the new woke politics, politicians—from presidents to former presidents and on down—now spoke openly about the need to prevent the spread of disinformation, a term that applied to statements, however factual, that the politicians either disagreed with or, for whatever personal reasons, desired to suppress. Until very recently, the vast majority of Americans would have understood that such suppression of ideas was abhorrent to the very concept of our democracy and would have shunned, and openly mocked, those attempting to steer the country in the direction of speech and thought control.

The herding of people like Brian's partners into the woke fold was greatly abetted by the activities of the nation's universities. There, intellectuals—best thought of as individuals who thought about things but had no skin in the game—drove woke ideology into the minds of children and set a tone. If you agreed with them, you were smart and sophisticated. If you disagreed, or even questioned, you were uninformed or stupid—or likely both.

Cowardly "elites," like Brian's woke partners, adopted woke ideology the way they adopted other social manners. They would no more say that the determination of sex was a matter of biology rather than personal choice than they would use the wrong spoon during the soup course at one of their fancy dinners. It just wasn't done if you wanted to travel in certain circles. They faced a simple choice. They could either pursue the woke agenda and continue to attend all the best cocktail parties and enjoy the false patina of intelligence and sophistication, or follow Brian down a road that led to social ostracization and professional oblivion.

Put simply, the partners feared that Brian's violation of woke protocols might taint them and their firm. On the other hand, getting rid of Brian buttressed their woke credentials. Problem solved. The partners were oblivious to the fact that, if allowed to follow its natural course, the woke revolution would eventually come for them as well. For the moment, they were useful idiots, pawns of the revolution receiving a temporary reprieve. Allowed to progress, this revolution would end up eating its own. They always did.

Brian's office phone buzzed twice, Alice's signal that the cavalry had arrived. When Brian emerged from his office, he was confronted by Fred Bascomb and two of his uniformed security underlings.

"I have orders to secure the office and everything in it, Mr. Townsend."

"Call me Brian, Fred. We've had that conversation before. I know you're just doing your job. You'll that find everything is in order."

"I'm afraid I'll also have to search you, Mr. Townsend."

Brian shook his head. "You know you can't do that."

"I have very specific orders," Fred said.

"I'm sure you do, but that doesn't make it legal. Here's how that would go down. If you try to search me, I will resist—simply because I will not tolerate that violation of my civil rights. Neither of us wants a scuffle right here in the office. That would be embarrassing for both of us. I would also sue. There might even be criminal charges.

"The other thing is, I, of course, know who gave you the order to search me. We also both know that, if things get messy, Harsh will leave you dangling in the breeze. He'll deny that he gave you any such order. So, Fred, if you don't have a signed order and a couple of very reliable witnesses, as your friend, I would strongly recommend that you not wander out, all by yourself, on that extremely rickety limb."

Fred folded immediately. Brian probably hadn't told him anything he didn't already know.

"Well," Fred said, "I'm also supposed to escort you out of the building."

"Fred, I would be delighted to have you walk with me to the front door. I'll even let you have a look in my briefcase if you like, but first I have to have a word with some of the other partners to let them know about some cases they'll have to pick up."

"Harsh, I mean, Mr. Harshman said 'forthwith.'"

"Fred, you and I both know that Dewey doesn't have a clue what 'forthwith' means."

That brought a smile to Fred's face.

"Alice," Brian said, "I'll be back in about a half hour."

Brian started to leave, then turned. "Fred, I promise I won't leave the building without you."

Ted's office was just a few steps down the hall. His secretary threw Brian a big grin when he walked in.

"He's been sticking his head out every five minutes, asking if I've seen you. Go right in."

Ted greeted him with, "So, how did it go?"

"Smoothly, I think," Brian said. "The thing I'm most proud of is that I didn't throw Dewey out the window. That required considerable restraint. Fred and his team are in my office right now, searching and securing everything."

"So you did manage to get yourself fired."

"Dewey fired me on the spot. I told him I was going to go back to the office right away to pack up all my files. He, of course, immediately called security. He told them to lock down my office and march me off the premises 'forthwith.'"

"Not a chance Harsh knows what 'forthwith' means," Ted said.

"Exactly what I told Fred. But, of course, the point is, when the other partners hear what happened and all hell rains down on Dewey, he can't, having summoned security, claim he didn't fire me—which he might have tried had I not goaded him into calling Fred."

When Brian first learned that he was going to be asked to resign, his first thought was that he had to make certain that he was fired. There were all kinds of rules, spelled out in documents that Brian had been required to sign, that were designed to prevent attorneys from leaving the firm and taking their clients with them. The rules applied only if you departed on your own accord. If you were fired, those rules didn't apply.

The other problem, if Brian was going to continue to

represent his clients after he left the firm, he needed his clients' files. The firm would eventually have to cough them up, but negotiations could drag on for months. Brian needed the files now. Alice had come up with the solution. Why not just send copies of the files to the clients and ask them to archive them until further notice? Nothing even suspicious, much less legally questionable in that. In the end, those files belonged to the clients. If, as expected, the clients followed Brian, he would merely retrieve the files from them. If the client remained at the firm, all relevant files would still be in the hands of the firm and its clients, and Brian wouldn't have access to them.

Ted had produced a bottle of champagne and was preparing to pop the cork.

"Let me make a call first," Brian said.

It took a minute for Alice to pick up.

"Sorry to leave you with all that to deal with," Brian said. "How are things going?"

"All is well. They're here, but, between you and me, I don't think they're sure why they're here. Not really much for them to do."

"Can you slip down to Ted's office for a few minutes?"

"I'm on my way."

Alice arrived with her purse and immediately produced the portable hard drive she'd found.

"I don't know what you boys would do without me," she said as she placed the drive on Ted's desk.

"I have no idea what's on that hard drive," Brian said. "Frankly, I have no memory of it. Maybe one of the computer techs used it to transfer files or install software or something. Would you mind smuggling it out of the building, Ted?"

"No problem," Ted said as he began pouring the champagne. "What should we drink to?"

"To the law firm Townsend and Bass, of course," Brian said.

"To Bass and Townsend," Ted said.

Alice said, "To freedom." And they drank to that.

Ted and Brian had talked for years about starting their own firm. They began to plan more seriously when Brian discovered that Ida Silverstein had unused space that would ideally suit a small firm. Having a place to go suddenly made it all seem possible. When Brian learned that he was going to be asked to resign, the timeline became fixed. As of today, Brian had successfully extricated himself from the firm. Alice would merely retire after decades of faithful service, then quickly unretire. The only problem was Ted. They were unable to come up with an offense serious enough to get him fired that would not also get him disbarred.

"It is easier," Ted had said, "for a camel to pass through the eye of a needle than for a law firm to fire a black attorney."

In the end, they decided that Brian and Alice would go ahead and start the new firm, and Ted would hang around here until the old firm dissolved. That could be in a few weeks, at most a few months. Then he would join them.

"What do you think of Hannah Montgomery, Dewey Harshman's secretary?" Brian asked Alice.

"I think she's terrific," Alice said. "Her only problem is her boss."

"If everyone agrees, maybe we should think about poaching her when the time comes. What do you think, Ted?"

"I think she'd be great."

Brian glanced at his watch. "I'd better get going. I promised Fred Bascomb we'd go for a walk. Then I'm seriously thinking about taking the afternoon off."

16

OBAMA LED FROM BEHIND

BIDEN IS LEADING FROM HIS BEHIND

Just two pickets in front of the medical school today as Victoria drove by. They had obviously coordinated their messages. They were young men, probably undergraduates. Victoria was seeing more and more of this sort of thing. It appeared that, at some level, a resistance was developing.

She found a parking place, then groaned softly to herself as she saw the chief of medicine approaching her.

"Victoria, could I have a word?"

"Good morning, Art."

"I'm afraid that the school has decided that your father cannot remain on the faculty in any capacity."

"You're firing him?"

"That sounds harsh, but I guess it comes to that. His clinic had to be closed anyway, due to all the unrest in that part of town. My problem is, I need to send him official notification, and I don't know how to get it to him."

"Just send it to his attorney. He's the one who'll be handling the lawsuit that Dad will file against the medical school for firing him. I don't have the address with me, but you can just check the internet for Hamilton Hobart in Washington, D.C. He has a website."

"They're saying that Hobart has lost a step or two."

"Of course they are. That's what 'they' do. An attorney can defend a murderer, and that's just fine. That's the American way. Everyone's entitled to a defense. But, defend someone of the wrong political persuasion and they vilify and denigrate the attorney. Why? Because they want to suppress opposing political voices. If you oppose them, you aren't entitled to an attorney. And they're also sending a message—loud and clear—to any other attorney who might consider representing someone like my father. They're saying you better not do it if you value your reputation. We will ruin you.

"It's not just your right to an attorney, they're attacking freedom of speech, Art, if you haven't noticed. My father is in jail, not because of something he did, but because of things he said. If you don't have freedom of speech, you don't have America. Remember what Salman Rushdie said. 'Free speech is the whole thing, the whole ballgame. Free speech is life itself.' From my point of view, it's pretty hard to argue with that."

"Human Resources says you're not cooperating," Art said, refusing to be drawn in.

"You mean because I won't attend their Maoist reeducation camp? Because I won't denounce myself as a counter-revolutionary and submit to indoctrination? I protected my six-year-old daughter from a pedophile. I'm not going to apologize for that. I'd do it again in a heartbeat."

"It's because of that note you sent to the school board," Art said.

"You're right, Art. I didn't *do* anything. I just said something that those who want to be our rulers didn't want me to say. Thank God I wasn't at a school board meeting when I said it. That Department of Justice task force that they launched to silence terrorist parents who have the temerity to speak up at school board meetings would have nabbed me on the spot. I'd be in jail right next to my father. Of course, I don't know if the Department of Homeland Security's Disinformation Board has set its sights on me.

"What do you think? Is it a good idea for the Department of Homeland Security to set up a board to monitor speech and be on the lookout for thought crimes? Does the United States need a Ministry of Truth?"

Arthur Johnson apparently had no opinion on the matter. He maintained his silence and continued to stare blankly at Victoria.

Victoria tried to control the rising sense of disgust she was feeling, doing her best to keep any sign of it out of her voice and off her face. "I will say one thing, Art. Because I've suddenly found myself thrown into the middle of this 'trans' issue, I have been giving it quite a lot of thought. I want to understand it as best I can. I don't claim to be an expert, but I've come up with three potential categories for people who consider themselves 'trans.' The first, and by far the easiest to deal with, is someone like this Jennifer Beaulieu character. He's a fraud. He's running a scam. He needs to be dealt with by the legal system, and no one, including the school board, should be abetting his scam.

"Next, I understand that there are people who are genetically and anatomically one sex who *believe* they are the other. That's called a delusion. When I was in medical school, I had a patient who simultaneously believed that he was the King of Egypt and the president of the world syndicate. No one suggested that the proper care of this man included getting him on an airplane headed for Cairo. No one said, let's call the mob and let them know that their leader is in the hospital. Everyone understood that these were delusions that were a manifestation of his underlying disease, schizophrenia. If his psychiatric disease could be successfully treated, his delusions would disappear. And please don't tell me that I'm saying that people who profess to be trans are schizophrenic. I'm not saying that at all. What I am saying is that, if they have a delusion, I believe that the medically responsible approach is to try to determine and treat the cause of the delusion, not to pretend that the delusion is a manifestation of reality.

"The third category I've come up with is people who are genetically and anatomically of one sex who *want* to express their sexuality in a different way. This is where individual choice comes in. Within very broad limitations for health and safety, I don't have a problem with choice. I do have a problem with scammers, and, as a physician, I feel that it is my ethical responsibility to help people recover from their delusions, not support them. And for the record, I also believe that someone, say a high school senior who is genetically and anatomically male and chooses to identify as female, should not be allowed to share a restroom with little girls or a locker room with female teammates—for reasons that are obvious to anyone with an IQ above room temperature."

"This is very dangerous talk, Victoria." Arthur Johnson appeared genuinely concerned.

"Help me, Art. Where am I wrong in this?"

"I didn't say you were wrong. I said this is dangerous talk. The administration will not permit it. You must either cooperate with Human Resources and adjust your thinking or resign. I'm afraid it's that simple."

"I don't like to say this, but I have offers, Art—several. Excellent medical schools have offered full professorships, lab funding, much more than I have here. I've enjoyed working here, but, if you force me, I'll leave."

"I don't doubt for a second that you've had offers, Victoria. You're brilliant. You're an extremely productive researcher, and you're probably the best and most popular clinician we have. But I'm very confident that the schools that made those offers are unaware of the fact that you have been accused of being transphobic. Universities are of one mind on this. Until and unless this issue is resolved, no medical school will hire you."

"Art, I don't have a closed mind on this. Like I said, I don't claim to be an expert. I'm dealing with this the same way I deal with any medical issue. I'm happy to read and learn and discuss it with colleagues—just like we're doing now. What I won't do, I won't go down to Human Resources and be told what to think. Don't you see how wrong that is?"

Arthur put his hands on her shoulders. "Victoria, I am not your enemy. I am your friend. I'm trying to help you through this. You're approaching it like it's a medical problem. It's not. It's a political problem. I don't mean that there are not important medical issues involved. What I'm saying is that 99 percent—probably much more—of this is political. This transgender issue only directly affects a minuscule fraction of the population, but we're hearing about it so much because large political groups are advancing it to achieve other objectives. It's like COVID. Politics completely drowned out the medical data, such as it was. Every talking head on television was suddenly an expert telling us what the 'science' said. These people knew nothing about science. Their only experience with the subject was a class they took in seventh grade called, you guessed it, 'Science.' They knew nothing about COVID, but they knew a lot about politics and how to influence the public.

"The politicians were pretty much the same, and the public began to see through them. They no longer trusted their leaders. They began to believe that all the COVID regulations were merely a thinly disguised mechanism for controlling the population. I really believed that that was all nonsense until I began to pay attention to how they were managing the data. It was purely political. Data that served their political ends was made public, other data was concealed. I no longer trusted them.

"One thing that especially bothered me was the way opinion leaders talked about the origin of the epidemic. I'm not talking about the big public brouhaha into whether the virus originated in a lab. That's not unimportant, but the Chinese have buried the evidence so deep no one is ever going to find it. But we do know some very, very important things that hardly ever get discussed. The Chinese government knew that they had an epidemic that was spreading rapidly from person to person—and they lied about it. They said there was no person-to-person transmission. At the same time, they *prevented* travel within China while *allowing* Chinese citizens to leave China and spread COVID throughout the world. Fifteen million people died as a result, and hardly anyone ever mentions it. It's like a bank robber goes into a bank and shoots ten people, and all the press and politicians want to talk about is where the gun came from. I'm thinking, He shot ten people! What does it matter where the gun came from?

"Which brings me back to the control issue that I thought was nonsense. Once again, I looked to China. In 2022, I see them locking down a city of fifteen million people over just a handful of COVID cases. And, in China, locked down really means locked down. These people could not leave their homes. Sometimes the doors to their apartments were literally locked from the outside by the government. People were hungry. You could hear them screaming. It didn't make sense. So, like you, I put on my medical hat and came up with some possibilities. Perhaps they had a lot more cases— and a lot more deaths—than they were admitting. They were simply lying again. Or, maybe, they were dealing with a new virus that scared them to death. That was another possibility.

Then I began to think, maybe this isn't a medical issue at all. Maybe it's all political. It's about controlling the population to serve some political objective. I don't know enough about the inner workings of Chinese politics to even guess what their goal might be, but it made me take a hard second look at what was going on here. I now believe it is likely that, with the COVID restrictions, our government was testing the limits of what the population would accept in terms of control. Nothing else makes sense. There was absolutely *no* medical data to support what they were doing. Much of it was just silly. I was especially concerned about young school children remaining masked without any conceivable benefit. What were they up to?"

"They are really focused on our children, aren't they?" Victoria said. "When you look at it closely, it's these very young kids that they're trying to brainwash with all this sexual identity nonsense and the racism embedded in critical race theory and all this 'America is evil' tripe, trying to obliterate our country's history. They want to start with a blank slate and create a generation of automatons, accustomed to being controlled and censored. It's terrifying."

"It doesn't have to be," Art said. "I know you thought I was naïve and unaware of what's going on. As you can see, I'm paying close attention. I think that I'm politically astute, and, what's more, I'm a survivor. That's how I got where I am.

"Like I said, Victoria, I'm your friend, and I'm trying to help you. I want *you* to be a survivor. Big changes are coming, and people who try to resist them are going to get hurt very badly. I don't want that to happen to you. If you get with the program now, and cooperate, you'll do fine. If you don't, if you continue to resist, things are about to get extremely difficult for you. It's up to you. That's the last thing I have to say on this matter."

Arthur turned and headed toward the medical school. Victoria waited, stunned by the warning she'd just been given, then followed Arthur Johnson at a distance. Two lonely sign carriers were in the Quadrangle, their messages stark.

CENSORSHIP IS FREEDOM

CHAOS FIRST – REVOLUTION TO FOLLOW

17

Hamilton Hobart was back in the familiar courtroom waiting for Judge Jones to appear. Waiting for his client as well, for that matter. The parties had been given short notice that the judge wanted to see them. Hobart knew that the jail might use that as an excuse not to produce Alex Walker. Schitzfuke was at the other table looking nervous and unhappy and refusing to make eye contact. Hobart hoped that was a good sign.

Then, Alex Walker was brought in and at least that worry was over. His client looked stooped and exhausted. He had clearly lost weight. Hobart hurried him into a chair.

"What's up?" Walker asked.

"Apparently the judge is ready to rule on our request for discovery, but Schitzfuke said he wanted to be heard first. The clerk said that the request infuriated the judge, but, for some reason, he relented. My guess is that Judge Jones is still feeling guilty about his misadventure trying to pronounce Schitzfuke's name. That's why he's leaning over backward to accommodate the Government."

The judge finally arrived and dealt with some unrelated matters at the bench before turning to the issue at hand.

"The Court understands that Mr. Snag... that the Government wishes to be heard." He shot a vicious look at Hobart who quickly covered his mouth, and his smile, behind his hand.

The clerk had told Hobart that the Judge was referring to

Schitzfuke as "Snagglepuss" in chambers. He had apparently decided that using the cartoon character's name was safer than attempting the actual name.

"Yes, Your Honor," Schitzfuke said rising from his chair. "The Government is willing to dismiss all charges so long as the defendant agrees to return to his home and not return to the Washington, D.C. area for one year."

The judge appeared surprised. Hobart was less so.

"Mr. Hobart," the judge said.

"Your Honor, I am confused. I thought that we were here to discuss discovery issues, but it appears that Mr. Schitzfuke wants to plea bargain. The Government cannot prove its case and is willing to dismiss all charges, but having failed, it wants to tarnish my client with a condition that suggests that Dr. Walker's presence in this city creates some kind of danger—that the city must be protected from my client.

"We reject that notion, Your Honor, and, as Mr. Schitzfuke has been told many times, we will reject any plea bargain offered. We will accept nothing less than Dr. Walker's absolute vindication."

His bluff had been called, and Schitzfuke had nowhere to hide. He looked defeated and humiliated.

"The Government moves to dismiss all charges," Schitzfuke said.

"That motion is allowed. Anything further, Mr. Hobart?"

"Indeed there is, Your Honor. We have here a spectacle of a distinguished physician and scientist, a man of world renown who has not the slightest blemish on the record of his life, who was taken in handcuffs and at gunpoint from his clinic where he had, for many years, tended to the medical needs of the economically disadvantaged members of his community. To make certain that his humiliation was complete, federal agents notified the press of what was about to happen and assembled a mob of political activists to exhibit faux outrage as Dr. Walker was dragged into custody. The doctor was then transported from one federal holding facility to another for a period of weeks, during which time his legal counsel was denied access. Finally, he has endured, at length, the horrors of our local jail. Now comes the Government to announce that it does not even have a case sufficient to bring to trial. Of course they don't! Dr. Walker is innocent of these charges, and the Government knows full well that we were prepared to go beyond the requirements of a successful defense. We were prepared to *prove* that Dr. Walker is innocent.

"Your Honor, it would be unfair to allow the defendant to leave this courtroom today with any possibility that these malicious charges might be reinstated, to have hanging over his head the possibility that, at any moment, this circus might be repeated. We therefore move that these charges be dismissed with prejudice."

Judge Jones appeared to be thoughtfully considering the request. Hobart knew that it would not have escaped the judge's mind that granting the motion would forever erase the embarrassing possibility that his girlfriend would appear in his courtroom.

"The motion is granted. All counts are hereby dismissed with prejudice. Anything further?"

"If you could indulge me in just one other matter, Your Honor," Hobart said. "My client is elderly, and his time in jail has taken a significant toll, both mentally and physically. We request that he be released immediately from custody without having to return to the jail for the formal discharge procedure. He has suffered enough. He deserves to walk out of this court a free man."

"Granted," the judge said. "The defendant is released from custody and is free to leave. We are adjourned." He banged his gavel, and it was over.

Hobart threw his arm around his client's shoulder. "Good to have this part behind us. Now, we need to get you into a good hotel suite and let you rest. You could use a good meal, perhaps a little libation, and then we'll talk about what comes next."

Hobart looked up and saw the judge motioning to him. As he approached, the judge signaled for him to come closer.

"Tell me, Ham," the judge said, "just between us, do you really have all that on video?"

"Just between us, Abe?"

"Of course."

Hobart looked about conspiratorially, then said, "Absolutely."

Victoria was rushing around the house trying to get dinner ready, throwing clothes in the washer, straightening the mess that she and Tess had left behind when they hurried off that morning. The phone kept ringing. It was the landline which no one ever called on. She was trying to ignore it, but finally relented.

"Hello."

"Hi, sweetheart."

"Dad! How are you!"

"I'm feeling pretty good, Victoria. I'm free."

"Free? What do you mean?"

"Out of jail. Lying on a bed in a fancy hotel. All charges have been dismissed with prejudice—meaning the Government can't come back and charge me again. I'm free."

"When are you coming home?"

"It'll probably be a few days yet. There are some things that Ham and I have to attend to here before I can leave."

"Are you okay? I mean, this can't have been easy for you."

"I'm tired, that's all. A few good nights' sleep is all I need. And I'm expecting that room service will be a big step up from jail food."

"I'm sure I can't imagine how awful jail was. I'm so sorry you had to go through all that."

"It was unavoidable—the necessary first step."

"So," Victoria said, "you're admitting what I've suspected all along. You guys are up to something. This was no accident."

"No, it was no accident. Ham and I have friends in Washington—at the FBI, the Department of Justice, other places—people who are concerned about what is happening in our country. They tipped us off that a big crackdown was planned for January 6. We expected abuses. In our wildest imagination we didn't think that two people would die at the hands of federal officers. We were also warned that my activities had come to the attention of certain people at the FBI, and that I might be targeted. So, I made myself available and was careful not to do anything unlawful. Ham had people video every minute that I was on the Capitol grounds. The video, incidentally, captured a lot of activity that had nothing to do with me that is pretty interesting.

"Anyway, as time went on, I began to think maybe they wouldn't come for me after all. They knew that they would have to use fabricated evidence to convict. They have lots of experience with that, but there was also risk for them. Ham and I decided that I should become more vocal, a little more of a thorn in the side of the government in an effort to provoke a response. That seemed to work. That got me arrested."

"I don't get that," Victoria said. "Why on earth would you *want* to get arrested?"

"We wanted a clear, unequivocal demonstration that some in the federal government are willing to fabricate evidence and file false charges in order to suppress voices that disagree with their plans for this country. Essentially, we entrapped them. We caught them red-handed. In court, Ham described what they had done and revealed that we had video of the whole thing. That forced them to drop the charges. They couldn't very well risk going to trial, then have us prove, in open court, the serious crimes they had committed. The Government had to cut its losses and hope it would all go away. It won't."

"What are you planning now? Why can't you come home?"

"The short answer is that Ham and I, and a bunch of others, are fighting back. Someone has to. We can't just let these people steal our country. They're subverting everything America stands for. If you belong to a favored group, if you're furthering their aims, you can riot in the streets, burn down government buildings, assault police officers, and cause billions of dollars in damage, and, not only will there be no consequences, you will be openly supported and encouraged by political leaders. If you're someone like me, and you oppose them, it seems like there's nothing they won't do to stop you. Look what they did to me, and I'm only one of many examples of what is, at the very least, unequal application of the law. In my case, of course, much more sinister even than that.

"They're deliberately creating chaos. Look at what they're doing to our city. Violent offenders are released without bail. Looting isn't prosecuted. Violent crimes are pled down to misdemeanors or not prosecuted at all. These policies have led to a staggering increase in crime and brutality. Little children are, literally, being shot dead in gang wars, and, at the same time, police funding has been drastically cut. Meanwhile, our streets are taken over by the mentally ill and the drug addicted—with huge consequences for public health and safety. Businesses can't function in this environment. The core of the city has been destroyed and may never recover.

"And there's more chaos at the border, which they've opened to virtually anyone, from any nation in the world, who wants to enter the country. It has been predicted that by the end of this administration, fully twenty percent of the people living in the United States will be here illegally. A country that does that to itself can't survive. It's no longer a country. I could go on and on. With one hand, they're taking our country from us, with the other, they're handing over whatever's left of America to foreigners.

"Things are moving quickly, spiraling out of control. That's their plan. Once the chaos reaches a certain level, and the public is screaming for relief, they'll crack down, and all our remaining democratic institutions will disappear. We have to resist, and I've agreed to help. My arrest has given me more prominence and credibility. That was part of our plan. I'm going to take an even more visible role as a leader of this resistance. There's a rally here tomorrow. I will be the featured speaker."

"Then will you finally come home to us? Tess has been asking for you."

"In a couple of days. There's also a lawsuit I need to deal with before I leave."

"I know. I'm sorry, Dad."

"What do you mean, you're sorry?"

"You know, about what happened at the medical school."

"What happened at the medical school?"

"They're letting you go, Dad, because of the arrest. I thought you knew. Art Johnson asked me who to send the official notification to. I sort of offhandedly said to send it to Mr. Hobart because I assumed that he would soon be suing the medical school on your behalf. I'm sorry they did this to you, Dad. I presume they'll retract the termination, now that the charges against you have been dropped."

"I wouldn't be too sure of that, Victoria. These days, the authorities seem more worried about what you say than what you do. Walk out of a store with $500 worth of merchandise you didn't pay for, and nothing happens. Describe someone using the wrong pronoun, and you lose your job.

"I'll talk to Ham about what I should do. If he's received something from the medical school, he may have decided to let me enjoy being out of jail for a couple of days before telling me."

"I'm confused, Dad. What lawsuit were you talking about?"

"We're suing the FBI and Department of Justice for false arrest. I think Ham called it 'a politically motivated, malicious prosecution.' He wants to file for an enormous amount of money—tens of millions of dollars. Apparently, what you do first is file a claim with the government. If they don't pay, you sue. Ham says they can't go to court and have their crimes exposed for all to see, so they'll have to settle. It'll probably take forever, but it's a good way to keep our cause in the public eye."

"Be careful, Dad. These are dangerous people. You've already seen firsthand what they're capable of."

"Don't worry. I'll be fine. Is Tess around? I'd love to say hi."

"She's over at Nina and Ted's, playing with Jasmine. She'll be so sorry to have missed you."

"Please tell her that I love her and that I will see her soon. Love to you, too."

"Please be careful, Dad."

"I will."

18

The day promised to be a very busy one for Victoria. For starters, it was her day to take the girls to their new school, which, fortunately, Tess and Jasmine loved. Victoria and Nina had not experienced a moment's hesitation at pulling their girls out of the public school. It had to be done. Their biggest concern was not for their daughters' leaving, but for the children who were left behind in that poisonous environment. Something had to be done to protect them. Victoria and Nina had discussed the problem, but, so far, had not come up with a practicable solution.

The girls' new school was close-by and sponsored by a local church. Their teacher seemed excellent—intelligent and involved—and there was none of the toxic wokeness that infected the public school. The school was happy to take on new children at irregular times. The girls' class was small. Best of all, in the view of Tess and Jasmine, was the presence of Walter. Walter was a giant Newfoundland dog that must have weighed close to 200 pounds. He loved the kids, and the kids loved him.

After dropping off the girls, Victoria headed to the medical school. Recent, relatively minor rioting and looting had damaged several small businesses nearby. Storefront glass was now replaced with plywood in several of the buildings. A now-closed auto parts store bore a new message painted on its plywood.

CHAOS IS THE GATEWAY TO TYRANNY

Victoria wondered again about the people who placed these signs. Who were they? How many of them were there? Was there some kind of resistance movement being organized?

She spent the morning in her lab. There were some exciting new lymphocyte findings to review. If confirmed, the data would provide important new understanding of the function of this type of white blood cell. This was the kind of discovery that made laboratory research so alluring.

Her afternoon was blocked off for rounds with the infectious disease team. Victoria was the attending physician in charge of the infectious disease consulting service this month. Her team consisted of an infectious disease fellow, a resident, an intern, three medical students, and a pharmacist. The fellow, Diane Chau, was her second-in-command. Diane was now in the third and final year of her infectious disease training. Prior to becoming a fellow, she had completed four years of college, four years of medical school, and three years of training in internal medicine. She was board certified in internal medicine. She was also brilliant.

Diane Chau would one day be a professor at a leading medical school. Importantly, her career path would be determined by her success in the research laboratory, not by her clinical skills. All of the infectious disease fellows had research projects that continued even when they were assigned to the clinical consultation service. This created a constant tension. Their careers—and their research supervisors—demanded they be in the lab. Their patients needed them in the hospital. Diane was not the first fellow that Victoria had had on her service who had a tendency to shirk her clinical responsibilities in order to spend more time in the lab. This behavior was understandable, but unacceptable.

Rounds began in a conference room just down the hall

from Victoria's laboratory. This allowed everyone to sit comfortably around a table while they first reviewed the progress of the patients they had been following, then discussed the new patients they had been asked to see that day. When all of this had been accomplished, they would begin the walking portion of their daily rounds, and the entire team would visit each patient at the bedside. Today, each medical student had a new patient to present. The last turned out to be the most interesting.

The final patient was a 27-year-old female, Olivia Diaz. She and her husband had just immigrated from Mexico. She reported no significant previous medical issues except for recurrent urinary tract infections. These infections had from time to time made her quite ill, but, previously, her symptoms had always responded quickly to medication. Her husband had brought her to the ER this morning with concern that she had once again developed a urinary tract infection. Because she appeared quite ill and her ability to keep oral antibiotics down was uncertain, the ER doctors had decided to admit her.

While listening to a case being presented, Victoria usually developed a mental picture of the patient. This was based on the information provided by the presenter and on Victoria's knowledge of the disease that had been diagnosed. Typically, on arriving at the patient's bedside, the image that she had formed was confirmed. Occasionally, as in this case, the patient before her was quite different from the one she had imagined. This young woman was desperately ill. She was, at the moment they arrived, experiencing a shaking chill, and her gown and bed clothes were soaking wet. She complained of headache and pain in her abdomen and in her arms and legs. On examination, Victoria thought that the young woman's eyes looked slightly jaundiced. She also had an enlarged spleen.

This presentation suggested a specific disease process to Victoria, one that she thought Diane Chau should have considered.

"Where is she from?"

"Mexico," the medical student said.

"What part of Mexico?"

No one seemed to know.

"Are any family or friends available for us to talk to?"

"There's a husband who's been in the waiting area. He was kind of jumpy and sweaty when I talked to him. I think he's probably on something—some kind of stimulant."

The husband was still in the waiting area, and they were able to find a quiet place down the hallway where they could speak privately. The young man appeared to be about the same age as his wife. He *was* sweating profusely.

Victoria introduced herself. The young man's name was Gabriel Diaz.

"How is Olivia? Is she going to be okay?" He spoke excellent English.

"Your wife is quite ill," Victoria said. "We're still not certain what's wrong with her."

"She has a urinary infection," he said.

"Maybe," Victoria said. "How long have you been sick?"

Gabriel seemed surprised by the question. "A couple of days."

"What do you think you have?" It was an old clinician's trick. What was the diagnosis the last time you felt this way? It was especially helpful when you were evaluating a patient from a foreign country who might have contracted some exotic, local disease.

"Malaria, I suppose," he said. "I've had it before. It's not too bad. You take some medicine. It goes away."

"Where do you live in Mexico? Which state?"

"Chiapas."

"Have you traveled outside of Mexico in the last month or so?"

"Just to Guatemala to visit friends."

"I think you're probably correct in thinking that you have malaria, Mr. Diaz," Victoria said, "but it may be a different type from the one you've had before. I think it's likely that your wife has malaria as well. The problem is, you may have been infected in Guatemala. In Chiapas, the malaria is caused by a malarial parasite called vivax. It tends to cause less serious disease. In Guatemala, it is possible to contract a different malarial parasite called falciparum. It more frequently causes very serious disease. We need to do some blood tests to be certain.

"You should be evaluated to see why you're sick. It may be malaria, but it could be something else. If you like, we can do that for you."

He shrugged. "Of course. Thank you."

"Why don't you go back to the waiting area? Someone from our team will come back to get you in a few minutes to supervise your evaluation. If you do have malaria, it's likely that you will be able to take pills, so you won't have to be in the hospital."

Victoria explained to the team that there were only two states in Mexico that currently had malaria—Chiapas and Chihuahua. In both states, 100% of reported cases were vivax. Falciparum was present in Guatemala. There had been no malaria in Guatemala that had been reported to be resistant to chloroquine, an important antimalarial drug. She also explained to the team that their female patient likely had severe falciparum malaria and was at risk for complications in her lungs, kidneys, and brain. They needed to immediately obtain blood specimens to examine for malarial parasites. If the blood smears were positive, therapy should be started as soon as possible.

"I'll call Bud Small and ask him about the case. He may have some thoughts on management. If he has time, I'd like him to see the patient and make recommendations. You should just go ahead and implement whatever he suggests. You don't need to run it by me."

"I'm not sure that's necessary," Diane Chau said. "I think we can handle this."

"Diane," Victoria said, "How many cases of malaria have you managed?"

"I don't know, two or three."

"I've managed a few hundred myself. With that kind of experience, I don't typically ask for help. But our patient is severely ill and at some risk of dying, in part because her diagnosis—if she has malaria—has been delayed. Bud Small is one of the world's leading experts on malaria. Every time I talk to him about the disease, I learn something new. In medicine, what you know is important. Often, understanding what you don't know is infinitely more important."

Victoria wasn't happy that Diane had missed the diagnosis. She was furious that Diane wanted to go "cowboy" and manage the patient on her own. She would have to have a talk with Diane, but not now.

The first thing was to get the blood smears and find out what they were dealing with. In the old days, Victoria would have made the smears herself. Now, for medical-legal reasons, the smears had to be done by a laboratory technician. That took time, but there was no way around it.

A couple of hours later, the laboratory called with the results of the blood smears. The husband had vivax malaria and the wife had falciparum. Who would have guessed that?

She called Bud, and he agreed with her treatment and management plans. He said he'd be happy to see the patient and review the chart. Victoria thanked him and encouraged him to just tell the ward team what should be done if he had any suggestions. He didn't need to run it through her.

Victoria met once again with her team to bring them up to date and make certain that they were all on the same page. She reminded them that they should call her at any time, day or night, if there were any issues they needed help with. Then Victoria was off to her lab. She finished up there just in time to go pick up Tess and Jasmine at school.

The girls were very excited.

"Jasmine did the best in reading today," Tess said, "so she got to go for a ride on Walter."

Jasmine was beaming. "I love Walter."

"You're not too big to ride on Walter?"

The girls giggled. That was silly.

They dropped Jasmine off at her house, then Victoria planned a quick stop at the grocery store. That should get them home in time to hear her dad speak. She wasn't certain about live TV coverage, but the entire rally was to be streamed on the internet.

In the store, Victoria told Tess that she could pick out a treat for after dinner. Big mistake. Tess couldn't make up her mind. They had been in the cookie aisle for several minutes, and Tess finally picked up a small package of Oreos. She looked like she might be just about to put the package back when it was snatched from her hand.

It was Miguel, the man who had grabbed Victoria's purse the day of her father's arrest. He stared menacingly at Victoria, clearly recognizing her. Tess seemed stunned and confused, not understanding what was going on.

A security guard moved up behind Miguel. Presumably, the guard had been following him around the store. Miguel had a bag nearly filled with groceries. He added the Oreos to his bag, then glanced back at the guard and started walking toward the door. Victoria watched him leave the store.

With rising inflation, families all over America were

struggling to put food on the table. Not Miguel. His groceries were free—at least for Miguel. But someone had to pay for that food. A portion would probably be absorbed by the store, but much would be passed on to already strapped consumers. What percentage of inflation in America was the result of rioting, looting, and shoplifting? How many businesses would finally give up and simply close their doors forever?

"Are you folks okay?" the security guard asked.

"We're fine," Victoria said. "Just about done."

The security guard shook his head. "There's not much we can do, as long as they're just stealing. Even assaults have to be pretty serious for the police to do anything. And even if the police come, there are almost never prosecutions. It just gets worse and worse. I don't understand why the people in charge are letting this happen. Don't they understand what it's doing to the country?"

"It's clearly some kind of plan they have," Victoria said. "It's obviously deliberate. For whatever reason, they want to put the public through this. They want all this turmoil, this chaos. Otherwise, they would put a stop to it. These politicians really don't seem to care what happens to people. They have something more important on their minds."

"I'd be happy to walk you to your car, ma'am, if you like."

"Thank you. I think we're okay. And thank you for chasing that man away. I'm not sure what he might have done."

Victoria grabbed a package of Oreos and smiled at Tess. Her daughter seemed mystified by what had happened, but not upset. Sometimes, not understanding what was going on was a blessing.

She paid for their handful of groceries and walked through the sliding doors to the parking lot, a small bag of groceries in one hand and her daughter's hand held tightly in the other.

She saw Miguel standing with a group of men maybe 100 feet away. It was as if he had been waiting for her. He reached into his bag, pulled out the Oreos, and began waving them in his hand, laughing at her, taunting her.

Victoria moved quickly to the car. The passenger-side door was unlocked. She was certain she had locked it. Had Miguel broken into her car?

With new urgency, she buckled Tess into the front passenger seat and, walking around the back of the car, took one last glance at Miguel. He was still laughing and waving the Oreos.

She pulled out of the parking lot, faster than she should have, her only thought, to quickly put as much distance as possible between them and Miguel.

Suddenly, a large form loomed from the backseat. He had a gun.

"Jennifer!" Tess screamed delightedly.

"Hi, Tess. How would you like to go for a ride in the country and see some horsies?"

19

The crowd was enormous. Many thousands had come to hear Dr. Alex Walker, suddenly famous after his false imprisonment and dramatic release. The movement believed that it had found its leader.

Alex Walker gazed out over the crowd in astonishment. It was a moment that they had hoped for, planned for even, but perhaps, Alex thought, he could never truly be ready for. He was a seasoned speaker with decades of experience, but, never before, outdoors in front of a cheering crowd that stretched nearly as far as he could see. And he had never previously given a political speech. Before the emergence of this current, existential threat to the country he loved, he would not have been able to imagine himself in such a position.

There were signs of all shapes, sizes, and sentiments. One, near the front, pictured a fentanyl capsule.

MADE IN CHINA – HAND DELIVERED BY THE SINALOA CARTEL

There were hundreds more.

U.S. BORDER – A CRIME SCENE STRETCHING THOUSANDS OF MILES

AMERICA – GREAT WHILE IT LASTED

IMPEACH THE TELEPROMPTER

INFLATION IS THE WAY DEMOCRACIES DIE

WELCOME TO POST-CONSTITUTIONAL AMERICA

Ham Hobart and his friends had very deep pockets and had spent extravagantly on a sound system that included remote speakers spaced throughout the crowd. Professional videographers had been hired to livestream and record the event. The so-called mainstream press was, naturally, nowhere to be seen.

After Ham delivered a brief introduction, Alex had to wait several minutes for the crowd to calm down. Then, he decided, he was as ready as he would ever be. He spoke without notes.

"Friends, we are at a treacherous moment in American history. One political party looses its minions to riot, loot, and commit arson, assault, and even murder—with impunity. Leaders of that party openly support this mayhem, and, in the same moment, demand defunding of the police. Arrests are few, and there is little interest in prosecuting even those few. This permissive attitude toward those early riots now extends to the vicious lawlessness that grips so many of our cities. Crimes against persons and property are rampant, and the perpetrators have little fear of consequences. The occasional arrest for a crime of violence frequently results in immediate release without bail. Felony charges, when brought, are often quickly downgraded to misdemeanors.

"At the same time, persons of a different political persuasion, people who oppose the regime currently in power, face a very different legal system." Cheering and applause broke out in the crowd.

"The FBI may not be able to bring to justice those who torch public buildings and assault police officers, but they are extremely proficient at investigating citizens who speak out at school board meetings to protest racist indoctrination of their children. The attorney general has set up a special task force dedicated to this cause. Their message is straightforward—the regime wants this racist message to be taught, and, if you speak against us, there will be consequences.

"In the aftermath of the January 6 hysteria, some individuals accused of the dastardly crime of walking inside the Capitol building have been able to show, at trial, that they were waved into the building by the Capitol police. They have been acquitted. Others have not been so fortunate. There is a warning in this for all of us. Given the current state of persecution of those who disagree with the regime, perhaps we should all take care to keep a video record of our activities, lest we fall victim to false arrest and ginned-up criminal charges. Otherwise, we may find ourselves in jail awaiting trial for an alleged crime as inconsequential as stepping on the grass."

The crowd erupted. There was no stopping them. Several minutes passed before Alex could continue.

"My friends, there is an open assault on our fundamental freedoms. Equal application of the law is basic to our democracy. And, of course, our society cannot function without the freedoms of speech and assembly.

"This next may seem like an obvious point, but it is an important one—our freedoms are under attack because people are attacking them. These people, these attackers, must be stopped. This is still America. If you attempt to deprive me of my freedom of speech, you are committing a crime. Those who strive to take away our basic rights must be held to account.

"You may be surprised to hear that I do not blame the president for any of this. How do you blame a man for the words on a teleprompter that he cannot even read correctly? No, I hold responsible those who dragged into position a man they knew was incapacitated and unable to perform the duties of the presidency. During the campaign, they hid him in a basement—at a time when any other candidate would have been out campaigning in order to prove his ability to the voters. The reason for this odd campaign tactic is obvious. Those close to the president were fully aware of his declining mental capacity. Where were his friends and family? Was there no one who loved him enough to say, respectfully, your time has passed? Was there no one who loved this country enough to say, we cannot do this?

"This is not the first time in recent memory that the denizens of the Washington swamp have pulled this trick. To investigate the Trump Russia collusion hoax, Robert Mueller was appointed special counsel. Acquaintances of Mr. Mueller knew of his mental decline prior to that appointment. Anyone who witnessed the special counsel's testimony before Congress saw a man who was frequently befuddled and clearly lacked knowledge of many basic aspects of the investigation. The chairman of the Intelligence Committee, a highly partisan Democrat, wrote that he found Mr. Mueller's cognitive decline 'heartbreaking,' and that he instructed committee members to keep their questions simple so as not to confuse the special counsel.

"It was clear to all who had knowledge of these events that Mr. Mueller could not have been, in any meaningful way, in charge of the investigation of the Russia hoax, a fraudulent investigation that harassed the previous president for nearly two years. Mr. Mueller merely served as a figurehead to provide the thinnest veneer of respectability to what was, in reality, a political witch hunt based on a preposterously false narrative and controlled by a person or persons whose role was unknown to the public. And, importantly, those actually running the investigation were essentially unaccountable. They were not being supervised in any substantial way by the mentally incapacitated man serving as special counsel during the course of the so-called investigation. And they were shielded from Congressional oversight by the interposition of Mr. Mueller, with his limited mental capacity, to testify before Congress.

"I bear no malice toward Mr. Mueller for this. He was, like the president, merely a man who had reached a point in his life when he no longer had any business driving the car. It was the responsibility of those who loved him—and those who understood the harm he could cause—to tell him that he could no longer drive. If he was unable to understand his limitations, the car keys should have been pried from his hand.

"Mr. Mueller's activities are, fortunately, behind us. Unfortunately, the president still has nominal control of the country. The American people are entitled to know who is writing the words into the teleprompter that the president struggles to make sense of. We are entitled to know who is making the decisions that are determining the course of our country.

"When the president is asked, as he was recently in Japan, 'Are you willing to get involved militarily to defend Taiwan?' and the president answers, 'Yes,' do we accept that answer, or do we rely on the statement issued by persons at the White House who tell us to disregard the president's statement? On what authority do persons in the White House contradict the president? In short, who is in charge? Who is actually making the decisions that decide the future of America?

"If the president is not competent to perform the duties of his office, surely the laws he has signed, and the executive orders that he has issued, are not valid. And he certainly cannot be permitted to act as commander-in-chief, with the perilous responsibilities inherent in that office.

"The American people are entitled to know—and must

demand to know—whether or not this man is competent to serve as their president. If he is, he must prove himself by submitting to prolonged questioning from a press prepared to ask tough questions. I do not mean the submission of a handful of puffball questions from a few pet reporters. A president cannot demonstrate his competence merely by correctly identifying the flavor of ice cream in the cone he holds in his hand. If the president is able to demonstrate that he possesses the mental acuity to perform his duties, so be it.

"If the president cannot demonstrate his competence, he must be removed from office. I know that this is a discomforting statement for those of you who lack confidence in the abilities of the current vice president. I assure you that I share your concern. However, replacing the president would return accountability. We would know who is making the important decisions—even if we don't agree with them—and we can hold that person responsible for her actions. Our Constitution requires a functioning presidency. It does not permit a president to act merely as a figurehead while unelected, unknown persons, hidden behind a curtain, operate the levers of power.

"So that is my first point. Our nation deserves—requires—a competent, accountable president. My second point is that the ever-increasing chaos that currently grips our country is not an accident. It is a deliberate policy. I have come to this position reluctantly. It was, at first, very difficult for me to accept the idea that powerful people wanted to destroy America. I wanted to believe that this was simply a wild, unfounded conspiracy theory. I knew, of course, that Marxist dogma calls for the destruction of a society in order to build the socialist state. This is analogous to the demolition phase in construction—the tearing down of an old building to make way for the construction of a new one. However, I simply could not imagine—did not want to believe—that leaders of the greatest country this world has ever known could be so benighted that they would pursue such a demonstrably evil policy and attempt to establish a system that has failed so miserably and caused so much despair everywhere it has been tried. But my eyes have been opened. I see incessant rioting and looting, ever-increasing crime, open borders, direct, open attacks on our basic freedoms, and efforts to erase our nation's history and inoculate our nation's school children with vicious, divisive racist hatred and gender confusion. I have come to understand that the Democratic party, formerly the party of slavery, of the Ku Klux Klan, and of segregation and Jim Crow, has now morphed into the party of Marxism and socialism.

"Classically, Marxism depends on class warfare to gain control of a population. That model has not worked well in this country. The vast majority of Americans recognize the nearly unlimited potential for upward mobility that this nation provides. So, American Marxists have turned to other means to divide and conquer the population. Their use of racism is particularly repugnant, and more than slightly ironic, given the history of the Democratic party. In addition to the history I have already mentioned, it is worth noting that when it came time for Congress to pass the Civil Rights Act of 1964, a higher percentage of Republicans than Democrats—in both the House and the Senate—voted for passage. Indeed, 74% of the no votes in the House and 78% of the no votes in the Senate were cast by Democrats. Democratic Senator Robert Byrd, the former leader of the West Virginia Ku Klux Klan, led the filibuster against the Civil Rights Act. Lest anyone think that Senator Byrd was some peripheral figure, it should be recalled that he served as majority leader of the Senate for the Democrats when they were in power and as minority leader when they were not. In classic Democratic doublespeak, he was anointed the 'conscience of the Senate.' Hillary Clinton called Byrd her 'friend and mentor.' Joe Biden delivered a eulogy at Byrd's funeral in 2010. Can you imagine what the Democrats would do to a Republican who referred to an openly racist Ku Klux Klan member as a 'friend and mentor?'

"The Democrats' use of the charge of racism is clever, if disgusting. It is such a vile charge that it frequently accomplishes its clear goal, to silence opposing views. No one wants to be called a racist or a white supremacist, especially by a person of color. The Democrats level charges of sexism in the same way. To be clear, these labels are used purely for raw political purposes, not to benefit aggrieved minorities. Anyone paying even the slightest attention to the American political scene is aware that black lives matter only in the extraordinarily rare event that a white policeman shoots a black person. These occasional occurrences spark political outrage and riots in the streets with all their attendant criminal activity. Yet the commonplace, almost daily, murders of black children in our nation's once great cities cause nary a ripple on the waters of American politics. You see, black lives don't really matter to the Left, but they *are* politically useful. Both types of black deaths, whether at the hands of police or perpetrated by other blacks in our nation's cities, foment the civil unrest and chaos that Marxist and socialist political elements strive so assiduously to promote.

"Another obvious and deliberate epicenter of chaos, actively promoted by the current administration, is found at our southern border. The flow of millions of migrants into our country can only be accomplished because the administration is so willing to openly and flagrantly violate federal law and blithely disregard the civil rights and welfare of both U.S. citizens and migrants. To accomplish its goals, the government must tacitly work hand-in-glove with the Mexican drug cartels, without whose consent—and compensation—migrants cannot cross the border. U.S. border agents are deflected from their normal duties to care for the new arrivals, which opens the door—literally—for the smuggling of drugs into our country. This is a double win for the cartels. They make billions of dollars selling the illicit drugs after having already collected billions of dollars from the migrants they traffic into the United States.

"The human tragedy is well known. Migrant deaths are reported almost daily on the U.S. side of the border. The unknowable death toll on the Mexican side would undoubtedly stagger the mind. The number of women and children who are sexually abused as they migrate has been reported to be as high as 80%. Young children, toddlers even, are found abandoned in the desert, left to live or die on their own. And, of course, the lethal consequences of the administration's policy are not limited to migrants. Deaths from illegal drugs in this country now exceed 100,000 per year. The amount of crime associated with the sale and consumption of these illegal drugs—from the lunatic actions of drug-crazed individuals to the myriad crimes they commit to fund their addiction—is incalculable.

"What does the administration think of this human catastrophe? It is difficult to come to any other conclusion than that, in line with their attitude toward black crime victims in U.S. cities, they simply do not care. Let me repeat that. It's important. The actions of the administration clearly show that they don't care about the human tragedy their policies are creating. In the vernacular, they simply don't give a damn. Like the revolutionists they emulate, they have their goal, and nothing must be allowed to get in its way. You have to break a few eggs to make an omelet. These little people are merely fodder for their revolution.

"We have to recognize that those illegally crossing our borders are not really migrating, they are being imported. Like barrels of oil, they are being imported for consumption. They are flooded into our country because the Democratic party believes that this human wave will give them a political advantage. It is widely believed that the aim is simply to augment the supply of voters dependent on the failing Democratic party for their survival. This may be true, at least in part, but I fear a more sinister motive. How are these new immigrants to survive? The two most obvious support systems for them are the largess of the already strapped American taxpayer and the tender mercies of the drug cartels to whom most of these people are indentured for the cost of their importation into the United States. Those seeking employment will be competing directly with U.S. citizens. The arrival of this vast new underclass is a prescription for social unrest similar to the ongoing immigration catastrophe in Europe. It is likely this European disaster that the administration is attempting to copy, in the hope of creating similar chaos here.

"Before I begin to speak about solutions and resistance, I want to say a few words about the role that so-called 'climate change' plays in this scheme. You will recall that this purportedly incipient catastrophe used to be called 'global warming.' When that became a tough sell, they came up with the new name so that *any* change in the weather could be used to promote their goals. As a man of science myself, I find their 'science' very difficult to follow. But what *I* believe is irrelevant. What matters is that these political leaders, those who are shoving 'climate change' down your throats, don't believe what they are telling you. We have, for example, the specter of the recently retired President Obama purchasing not one, but two, multimillion-dollar, oceanside mansions. Does it sound like he's concerned about the oceans rising? The incumbent climate czar pollutes the world as he jaunts from continent to continent in his private jet. Do you think he's worried about his carbon footprint?

"And the current president, in his first actions on assuming office, shuts down a climate-friendly oil pipeline and takes aggressive steps to throttle American oil production. What does this do for the environment? It forces Americans to turn to "dirty" oil, produced thousands of miles away, that must be transported by gigantic, highly polluting ships. This tradeoff is an environmental nightmare. And, at a time when the invasion of Ukraine is so starkly demonstrating the catastrophic consequences of European nations' permitting themselves to become dependent on an unreliable external source—in their case Russia—to meet their energy needs, the administration has just committed this country to exactly the same course. America was energy independent prior to the actions of this administration, and, without government interference, would have remained so for the foreseeable future. But now, we are forced to go cap-in-hand to the likes of Russia, Iran, Saudi Arabia, and Venezuela and beg them to supply the oil required to meet our energy needs. Three of these countries are natural enemies of the United States, and the fourth, Saudi Arabia, won't even return the president's phone calls. What happens during a time of international crisis when these countries are either unable or unwilling to provide the oil our nation runs on? Under the previous administration, this would have been a catastrophic issue for much of the world, but not for the energy-independent United States. Now, however, this new administration has subjected the welfare of American citizens and the security of our country to the whims of our enemies. Shame on them.

"My point is, of course, that the draconian measures that the Left proposes to address 'climate change' have no more to do with climate change than their opposition to voter identification has to do with civil rights. In reality, their climate change proposals are, like everything else they do, efforts at increasing their political power and their control of the population. Imagine when you can no longer drive to the gas station to fill your car or truck whenever you want, but, instead, are dependent on a government-controlled—and likely highly unreliable—electrical grid. Do not doubt that Washington will tell you exactly when and how many miles you are allowed to drive. Meanwhile, the cost of energy is soaring, a major contributor to the economic uncertainty and inflationary chaos currently gripping the country.

"So, friends, we have all seen, and been touched by, this rising chaos that threatens our nation. Most of us understand that this is intentional. When crime goes unpunished, crime increases. When a prosecutor announces, as occurred in the city of New York, that the crime of resisting arrest will no longer be prosecuted, what message does that send to criminals? What message does that send to law enforcement officers who daily risk their lives to protect us? Civil society cannot survive in this environment. Those who are driving this chaos understand that as well as we do. So, why are they doing it?

"I hate what they are doing, and I am terrified of where they are planning to take us. This is the answer that I have long resisted, but can no longer ignore. These people are about power and control, and they will never have enough of either. My belief is that they intend to use the chaos they are deliberately creating as their excuse to crack down and further deprive the American people of their personal and economic liberty. As Shakespeare might have said, their plan is *to cry chaos and let slip the dogs of tyranny.*

"This is the classic route that socialists take to power. One need look no further than Nazi Germany to see how it is done—the Reichstag fire; Brown Shirts in the streets, committing their crimes with impunity. The destruction of the family, the erasure of a nation's history, the indoctrination of children in their schools—these are all tried-and-true pathways to socialist takeover. Where will it end? My guess is, even they do not know. They probably cannot even imagine. At some point, today's plotters will fall by the wayside. They will be disfavored—on the outside looking in. That is the way revolutions work. Power becomes concentrated in fewer and fewer hands.

"I have to confess, I do not understand the allure of Marxism. Clare Boothe Luce said, 'Communism is the opiate of the intellectuals.' I believe that there's truth in that, but I also think that most of the plotters see themselves as part of a wealthy, ruling overclass and the rest of us as their half-witted subjects. That's the way socialism typically works—Marxism for thee, but not for me.

"So, what are we to do? To put it simply, we must fight back!"

Once again the crowd erupted. The most boisterous cheering yet. Alex held up his hands to quiet them.

"For those of us desperately clinging to the belief that we are still living in a democracy, however tenuous, it is voting that must be our primary focus. The vote is the cornerstone of this democracy. Without it, we have nothing. If you cannot say that all persons voting are legally entitled to do so, that all legal ballots are being counted, and that all illegal ballots are being denied, you cannot say that the vote is honest. You cannot have confidence in the integrity of the process. If it is not racist to require identification to enter the White House, it is not racist to require identification to vote!

"If only one party is counting the ballots, and the other party is prevented from even observing the counting, you are not even pretending to have an honest election. If thousands of ballots are being counted that have no documented chain of custody—so you can have no idea whether or not they are legal votes—you are not even pretending to have an honest election. If you deliberately and repeatedly ignore election laws—even if a corrupt judge winks his approval—you are not even pretending to have an honest election.

"I believe, then, that our first order of business is to make certain that our nation's elections not only are conducted fairly, but have the appearance of being run fairly. We need to restore the public's confidence in the electoral process. Screaming loudly in Washington will not accomplish this goal. This work must be done locally. The other side has long recognized this fact and has, in many critical locales, taken over complete control. The only way to reverse their stranglehold is for us to roll up our sleeves and do the work. There is no one to do it for us. We must volunteer and run for office. We must get involved in the election process at the local level and demand its integrity.

"We live in a representative democracy. Power is supposed to be held in the hands of the people. The Constitution strictly limits the powers of the federal government. Over time, the national government has usurped much of the power that was reserved for the states. We must begin to reverse that process. It won't be easy. It won't be quick. We must however commit to restraining a federal government that can no longer restrain itself. We cannot allow our daily lives to be controlled by some anonymous, unelected bureaucrat in the Department of Commerce who is accountable to no one.

"The importance of local and state government, of course, extends far beyond the conduct of elections. The other side discovered this while we were sleeping. Billionaires like Adam Michaelson understood what their money could accomplish locally and contributed enormous sums to offices that the public was not paying sufficient attention to. That's why local school boards, city councils, and prosecutor's offices have become a Leftist catastrophe. The sober population far outnumbers the radicals now in control of these offices in many cities. All we need to do is assert ourselves and commit to the hard work required for us to regain control. We must run for office or find strong candidates who will. We must support them with our money and our vote. And we must educate our fellow citizens so that they understand what is at risk.

"Finally, and perhaps at the most basic level, we need to begin to vigorously, vociferously resist the Leftist lies. We must call out their attempts to shame into submission those with alternative points of view. I am not a racist just because I happen to disagree with you!"

Again, loud cheers of agreement.

"This behavior is obnoxious, puerile, and dishonest. Its purpose is to prevent the expression of opposing points of view. They are not making an intellectual argument that we can respond to, and we should not pretend that it is. They are spouting fatuous nonsense. I believe that we should utilize our understanding of bovine scatology in response, and express ourselves loudly and forcefully."

There were a few snickers in the crowd.

"So, when they say that the way to end inflation is to print even more money and spend ever more trillions on public programs, we simply reply, BS! When they say that white people were born racist and can never eradicate the stain, we say…"

"BS!" The crowd was joining the game.

"When they say that gender is a matter of choice, not genetics, we say…"

"BS!"

"When they say that people who disagree with them on

COVID or climate change are anti-science, we say…"

"BS!"

"When they say that our southern border is under control, we say…"

"BS!"

"When they say that requiring voter identification is racist, we say…"

"BS!"

"Thank you, my friends. Now we begin." Alex raised a clenched fist and began to lead the crowd, "Fight back! Fight back!" The chant continued as he left the stage.

Hamilton Hobart returned to the stage, and the crowd finally quieted.

"Ladies and gentlemen," he said, "we have a special treat to close our event today. I am proud to call to the stage Harley Bask…" And that was as far as he got. The crowd went crazy.

Harley Bask, the famous country singer and songwriter had taken the 100-year-old song, 'Lovesick Blues'—later turned into a hit by Hank Williams—and changed the lyrics. It was now known as the 'Woke-Scam Blues,' and it had become an anthem of the movement.

Harley walked onto the stage wearing his signature cowboy hat, jeans, and boots. He always wore a crisp blazer over a button-down dress shirt. He was clean-shaven. His smile was contagious.

He waved and began playing an introduction on his guitar. The crowd quieted as Harley began to sing. For this song only, he deliberately tried to sound like Hank.

…I got a feelin' called the blues, oh Lord
Ever since this woke scam broke
I'm about to get canceled
Doesn't matter what I do, oh Lord

You can kiss your freedoms good-bye
Your vote don't count so why try
They'll tax more, they'll spend more
They'll trigger more inflation
Lord, I hate to hear them say they want to go glo-o-obal

That's their socialist dream
I hate to think it's all over
My country's lost it seems
We've got to beat this scam somehow
Lord, let's impeach that teleprompter now
I say, Let's go Brandon
I've got the woke-scam blues

Well, I'm in love, I'm in love with America's Dream
They want to take it from me
Well, I'm in love, I'm in love with America's Dream
Won't let them steal it from me
Lord, I tried and I tried to deal with all their lies
But what a price to pay
So now that I am canceled
This is all I can say

…I got a feelin' called the blues, oh Lord
Ever since this woke scam broke
I'm about to get canceled
Doesn't matter what I do, oh Lord

You can kiss your freedoms good-bye
Your vote don't count so why try
They'll tax more, they'll spend more
They'll trigger more inflation
Lord, I hate to hear them say they want to go glo-o-obal

That's their socialist dream
I hate to think it's all over
My country's lost it seems
We've got to beat this scam somehow
Lord, let's impeach that teleprompter now
I say, Let's go Brandon
I've got the woke-scam blues

When Bask finished, the crowd erupted once again. After a few minutes, he got them to quiet down so that he could be heard.

"I've got a new one for you this afternoon," Bask said to more applause. "It's based on another century-old tune called 'Cocaine Blues.' Johnny Cash had a big hit on that. It's one of those tunes, once you get it in your head, it's hard to get it out. Anyway, I've kept the tune and written new lyrics. I call it the 'Mean Old Teleprompter Blues.'

The crowd cheered, and the music began.

Thinkin' about what was bummin' this town
That woke teleprompter tryin' to take our country down
When a bold plan popped into my head
Steal that teleprompter, hide it under my bed

Got up next mornin' thought this would be fun
Grabbed that teleprompter and away I run
Had a good plan but I was too slow
They caught up with me just outside of El Paso

Shut in my jail cell with time to kill
In walks the po-lice from Capitol Hill
They sent word back the prompter had been found
Said you dirty thief you shut the White House down

You left Joe Biden with nothin' to read
Without that old prompter there's no way he can lead
He shuffles and scowls and looks quite ill
He's under medication from his doctor Jill

They slapped me in leg irons and they took me back
They said by the way don't expect any slack
Said a guy like you won't get no bail
You'll just get solitary in the DC jail

Lyin' around locked in solitary
When I get bad news from my attorney
You can forget all the plans we made
You just drew a judge known as Honest Abe

Couldn't believe how bad was my luck
A DC jury and a hangin' judge
Thought one cute juror would save my day
But then she shot me the finger and turned away

The jury went out, and they came back late
They were all smiles, so I thought I would skate
But, oh no, they found I was guilty
Said, Judge, please lock him up and throw away the key

The judge he smiled as he looked up at me
Not a man known for his mercy
Twenty-five years – no parole
That's an awful long time in a federal hole

Come on you folks don't feel sorry for me
2024 I'll be pardoned and free

20

"Tess, why don't I lift you up and put you in the backseat next to me?" Jennifer asked.

"No," Victoria said. Her voice was even, but firm. She looked in the rearview mirror and locked eyes with the man. There was something different about him. He'd shaved his beard.

"You're not in any position to be giving orders. I can do whatever I want with Tess."

It was a chilling thing to say. Victoria was suddenly overcome by nausea. She thought she might actually vomit.

"If you try to move Tess into the backseat," she said, "I will crash this car right here and now. I have no idea what the consequences will be, but that is what I will do."

There was no response from Jennifer. Good. It was a small victory but an important one. Victoria had wrested a tiny bit of control from their captor.

"Later, then," Jennifer said.

The man was a sadist. Add that to what she knew about him. He was a pedophile, probably some kind of sexual omnivore. He was vicious. He was huge. She knew of only one weakness that offered her a potential advantage. Jerome Robert Brown, also known as Jennifer Beaulieu, was dumber than cheese dip.

All the clutter and complexity in Victoria's life had been instantly swept away the moment she saw him in the backseat of her car. Her future came immediately into crisp, clean focus. Her existence now had only one purpose—to save Tess. Nothing else mattered. The realization was liberating and empowering. It was her second advantage.

"Turn left here!"

"Don't yell at me!" Victoria said, deliberately missing the turn. The turn would have taken them quickly to the freeway, the fastest route out of the city. Victoria felt instinctively that surface streets offered more, and safer, options for escape. She was on the lookout for a police car, someone she knew, any chance opportunity she could exploit.

"If you disobey another order, I'll shoot the kid."

Victoria reached over and touched her daughter's leg. "It's just a game, Tess. Don't worry." Tess appeared anxious, but not panicked. Not yet.

"Turn right at the next corner."

They were headed away from the freeway now. Had Jennifer changed his plan, or was he just testing her, making certain she would follow his instructions?

"Turn left at the next corner."

"Mommy, we're going to the park!" Her daughter's spirits instantly picked up.

Victoria had no doubt that Tess was right. Jennifer had changed his plan. The park was huge with plenty of secluded areas. Before rioting and crime overtook the city, the park was a favorite for family picnics and teenagers' romantic getaways. As a child, Victoria had loved swimming and sunbathing at the park's large lake. She and Brian had taken Tess to the park. Tess especially loved the baby ducks in the spring. Occasionally, there were migrating swans. However, even then, the park could be dangerous, especially after dark. There had been robberies and murders. Bodies had occasionally been dumped in remote areas. Now, many considered the park too dangerous even in broad daylight. It was a site of drug sales, prostitution, and gang violence.

Victoria knew that they had little time left. She searched desperately for her least-worse option. No police in sight. Very few people around. Then they were at the park, and she made her decision.

She knew the entrance that Jennifer likely had in mind. She would act before they got there.

The spot she was looking for was just as she had remembered. A small group of people huddled nearby. They had lawn chairs and were probably planning a picnic. They were far enough away that she would not be putting them in danger.

Victoria hit the button to roll down her window, cranked the steering wheel hard to the left, and gunned the engine.

"Hey!" Was all Jennifer said.

Ten seconds later, the car was plowing into the lake. Tess screamed with delight.

"I can't swim!" Jennifer was in full panic. "I can't swim!"

Victoria almost smiled. Jennifer's terror gave Victoria an unexpected edge. She had to act quickly before Jennifer discovered what Victoria already knew from her happier days at the lake—the water here was quite shallow.

And then Victoria's plan fell apart.

She pushed on the door, but she couldn't force it open. It was the weight of the water pressing from outside. Water was already seeping through the floorboards, but it would take a long time for the interior of the car to fill with water and equalize the pressure so that the door could be opened more easily. Victoria knew that she could push herself through the window, but she couldn't take Tess at the same time, and she couldn't leave Tess alone in the car. She could easily put Tess through the window, but it was too dangerous for her daughter to be in the water by herself.

She looked behind at Jennifer. He was regaining his composure but was still in survival mode. He was trying to force one of the backdoors open with his feet. His shoulders were pressed against the opposite door. He was making headway. A little water was seeping in around his door.

Then Victoria sensed movement to her left. A woman was wading toward the car. Others were watching from the bank. Victoria unfastened her daughter's seatbelt.

"Are you okay?" She was Hispanic, approximately fifty years old.

"We're about to be," Victoria said. "Please, let me hand you my daughter." Then, to Tess, "I'm going to hand you through the window to this nice lady." Tess was confused, and therefore compliant.

"Please go on ahead to the shore with Tess and call the police. I'll be right behind."

"My sister already called. What about the other lady?"

"*He* will be fine."

"He?"

"Please hurry. I'm right behind you." Victoria was already pulling herself through the window.

Escaping through a car window was not an option for a man of Jennifer's size. He was fully occupied with his struggle with the door—which he was slowly winning. Sirens could be heard, growing louder by the second.

Victoria waded ashore and took Tess in her arms. Tess seemed unfazed by the excitement.

Jennifer was now free of the car and wading toward the shore, but away from them. Victoria warned her rescuer that the man, dressed as a lady, had tried to kidnap them, and that he had a gun. They needed to be very careful, but it looked like, for now, Jennifer was more interested in escaping the police than harming them.

Two police cars arrived first, with a fire truck close behind. When she told the officers that she'd driven into the lake to foil a kidnap attempt, and that the man had a gun, they immediately got on their radios. Within minutes at least a dozen police cars swarmed into the park. They quickly found where Jennifer was hiding and had him in handcuffs.

Victoria told the officers what had happened and everything she knew about Jerome Robert Brown, AKA Jennifer Beaulieu—including his arrest record. A couple of medical technicians arrived with the fire department contingent. They recognized Victoria from encounters in the ER. She told them that she and Tess were fine. They just needed to get home to some peace and quiet. Tess wondered if she could ride in the fire truck.

A police sergeant named Thompson appeared to have taken charge of the scene. Victoria repeated her story to him. He said that there would need to be a more detailed, formal interview in the near future, but they had enough for now.

Thompson said that the car would be taken to a police holding facility for evidence gathering. It would likely be released in a few days. Frankly, he said, with the car's engine having been submerged, it will probably not be worth trying to fix. She should talk to her insurance company.

Victoria hadn't even thought about the car. It occurred to her for the first time that her purse with her cash, credit cards, and identification was still out there in the lake. And a new question entered her mind, "How am I going to get home?"

Thompson smiled. "My officers will be happy to give you a lift." He looked thoughtful for a moment, then added, "You did good, Dr. Townsend. This thing could have gone sideways a hundred different times. You kept your head, and you saved your daughter and yourself. You should feel proud."

"Thank you," Victoria said, but the only emotion she felt was relief.

The ride in the police car brought Tess to a new level of excitement. "I bet Jasmine has never ridden in a police car!"

Victoria got Tess into a warm bath and called Brian. He wanted to drop everything and come to them.

"We're fine, Brian. It's over. Just drop by after you wrap things up at work."

21

Dennis had recommended that they make their getaway while Harley Bask was singing. Otherwise, they would get caught up in the massive, departing crowd, which had the potential to cause all sorts of problems. Best to just avoid it.

Hamilton Hobart and Alex Walker were in the backseat of the SUV. Ralph, Ham's driver, and Dennis, who had planned security for the event, were in the front. The plan had worked. They were free and clear.

"I have to go over to the law school tonight," Hobart said. "It's my alma mater, and every year I give a speech to the students. I talk about the early days of the civil rights struggle and how far we've come. I tell them about some of my first cases—important cases that these young folks have probably never even heard of. The idea is to inspire them to make a contribution, to show them there is a legal world outside of big corporations and Wall Street.

"I just give a short talk, then there's a question-and-answer session. After that, they always treat me to a nice dinner at some fancy restaurant. It's a small party at the dinner, just a handful of faculty and a couple of students who've distinguished themselves in some way. It's supposed to be a big honor for the students who are invited. Anyway, it's always a pleasant evening. You're more than welcome, Alex, to come along. I think you'd find it interesting."

"Thanks, Ham. I'm sure I'd enjoy it, but right now I just want to get home. I need to see my daughter and granddaughter and savor a bit of normalcy before we move on to what's next. I've got a flight scheduled for tomorrow, but I thought I'd see if I could find a red eye that would get me home sooner. I usually don't have any problem sleeping on a plane."

They dropped Alex off at his hotel, then headed for the law school. Ham's talk would be given in Hobart Hall, an honor bestowed more than three decades earlier in recognition of his contribution to the civil rights effort. Ham had made no financial contribution toward the construction of the building. In fact, Hobart Hall was named before Ham began to take on the wealthier clients that had eventually made possible his generous donations to the school.

A large crowd was gathered outside the Hobart building. It appeared to be a demonstration about something, but the protestors appeared unfocused at the moment. As the SUV brought them closer, Ham looked over at the protestors and saw that they weren't students. These were protestors of the rented variety. Some carried signs, but they were too far away for him to read.

"I wasn't expecting this," Dennis said.

Ham shook his head. "Fortunately, it has nothing to do with us."

As they slowly made their way toward the front door of Hobart Hall, some of the signs became legible.

INSURRECTIONISTS ARE WHITE SUPREMACISTS

GO HOME UNCLE TOM

NO SPEAKING PLATFORM FOR RACISTS

UNCLE HAM

Dennis quickly had his phone out and made a couple of calls. "Let's get you inside, Mr. Hobart. Mobs like this are pretty unpredictable."

Dennis ushered him up the steps and into the building without incident. Inside, they were met by a tall, thin man in his late forties.

"I'm Dean Stafford," he said. He offered his hand in a manner that appeared somewhat reluctant. "I'm sorry for the commotion."

"This is nothing," Hobart said, taking his hand. "In the old days, it was the police dogs you had to watch out for." So this was the new dean. Ham had not previously met the man.

"There's been a bit of a change in plan," the dean said. "I won't be introducing you. This is George Long, one of our first-year students. He will be doing the honors this evening."

"How do you do," Hobart said, offering his hand. The hand was ignored.

Hobart turned back to the dean. He had vanished.

"This way," Long said.

Hobart followed, with Dennis close behind.

Long stopped. "Who's he?" indicating Dennis.

"He's my plus one for dinner," Hobart said.

"Oh, I'm supposed to tell you that there won't be a dinner this evening."

They were led into what was essentially a large classroom with tiered seating. Its capacity was probably somewhere on the order of 300 people. There were maybe 100 here tonight, much smaller than Hobart's usual crowd. Typically, when Hobart appeared for his annual speech, he was given a standing ovation as soon as he entered the room. Tonight, he was greeted by silence.

George Long went to the podium. Instead of introducing Hobart, he said, "Susan Gardener has a statement to read."

A young woman in the third row stood and began reading. "Mr. Hobart, your presence here is unwanted. Your open support for the white supremacist insurrection is antithetical to everything this law school represents. This law school will not provide a platform for the proliferation of your racist dogma. Your very presence is a threat to the safety of every member of this community and is offensive to our values.

"We support the recent statements by former President Barack Obama and former Secretary of State Hillary Clinton that the deliberate spread of lies and disinformation must be stopped. If we do not stand against racism and treason, what can we stand against?

"Mr. Hobart, you cannot hide behind the color of your skin. There is a name for what you are. No one wants to see any violence here. Please, just do the decent thing and leave."

She sat down. The room was silent.

Hobart was thinking that he would have no trouble answering her arguments. They were puerile and intellectually silly—not to mention, counterfactual. They lacked even the most basic understanding of both freedom of speech and the practice of law. An attorney defends his client. He doesn't adopt his client's views. And, of course, Alex Walker was not a racist, and the fraudulent charges against him had been dismissed with prejudice. Hobart stepped to the podium to respond.

"Shame! Shame!" The students began chanting.

Hobart waited. He was a patient man. They would tire and he would be heard.

When the chanting at last subsided, he began to speak.

This time, they began screaming profanity and crude epithets. Many stamped their feet. Others pounded the walls. It was impossible to be heard above the din. There was little reason, with this group, to try.

Hobart glanced at Dennis. Dennis nodded and took out his phone. They left to the sound of applause at their backs.

When they reached the front door, he saw that Dennis had summoned additional security backup. They were as prepared as they could be for whatever awaited outside.

The security detail went through the doors first and cleared a path for Hobart. When Hobart emerged, someone with a bucket tried to throw some kind of liquid on him. Hobart remained dry, and the assailant ended up with the bucket on his head and immediately began screaming, farcically, "Police brutality!"

In less than a minute, they were securely in their SUV and on their way. A second SUV was close behind.

Hobart's eyes were welling with tears.

"We have come so far," Hobart said. "We're not perfect. Of course not. But we have achieved much. Now, all of a sudden, we are slipping back into darkness. How can this happen? How can future attorneys not understand the importance of freedom of speech, of civil discussion? I weep for our nation's future.

"John Adams warned, two centuries ago, 'Remember, democracy never lasts long. It soon wastes, exhausts, and murders itself. There never was a democracy yet that did not commit suicide.'

"I fear that what we are witnessing now is his prophecy coming true."

22

The phone rang. At first, she didn't recognize the sound. A police siren? She didn't know where she was. She didn't know what day it was, let alone what time of day.

"They've released him," the voice said.

"What?"

"Jennifer. They've let him go."

"Brian?"

"Wake up, Victoria. Sorry to wake you, but this is urgent. I'll wait while you clear the cobwebs."

She sat on the edge of the bed. It was light outside. She looked at her phone. She had only been asleep for an hour or so.

"Sorry, Brian. I was sound asleep. I didn't understand what you were saying."

"I called my sources in the prosecutor's office. Mostly I wanted to know if they were planning to turn the case over to the Feds, because of the kidnapping. They said that, for now, there wasn't a case. They cut the guy loose."

"I don't understand. You mean he made bail? Or did they let him out on one of those no-bail deals I keep hearing about?"

"No, Victoria. I mean he wasn't charged."

"He kidnapped us—not to mention what he planned to do. And he had a gun."

"They didn't find the gun. He probably threw it out into the lake somewhere. The problem with that is, even if they eventually do find a gun in the lake, it may be impossible to trace it back to Jennifer. The water, over time, erodes evidence like fingerprints and DNA. We might get lucky, but most likely the gun, as any part of a case against Jennifer, is gone."

"I still don't understand why he wasn't charged. It's obvious I didn't just make all this up."

"His story," Brian said, "is that he was in a supermarket parking lot, and he asked you if you could give him a ride to the park. You said sure, but then you panicked and drove into the lake when you discovered that he was transgender. His lawyer says that you have previously demonstrated that you are transphobic."

"That's nonsense."

"Of course it's nonsense, but the prosecutor's office serves nonsense for breakfast. Their entire theory of the law is nonsense."

"I *knew* who he was, Brian, from that episode at the school. That's pretty well documented. So, I didn't just 'discover,' today, that he claims to be transgender2."

"The problem is, he has a witness."

"A witness?"

"One Miguel Santiago."

"The purse snatcher?"

"I presume so. He claims he saw the whole thing at the store, and he completely corroborates Jennifer's story."

It dawned on Victoria, for the first time, what had actually happened at the store. It seemed so obvious now.

"Miguel was harassing Tess and me at the grocery store. He grabbed a package of Oreos out of Tess's hand, then, when we went into the parking lot, he taunted us. At the time, it just seemed like that, childish taunting, bullying. Now I realize that he was trying to distract me. He knew that Jennifer was in the car. Miguel wanted me to pay attention to him so I wouldn't see Jennifer. He essentially participated in the crime."

"An accessory," Brian said. "Hard to believe that Miguel and Jennifer had coordinated this thing in advance. Miguel probably just happened to be at the store, saw a chance to be a creep, and took it. How do you suppose Jennifer happened to be there?"

"No idea. It's our neighborhood grocery. When we filed that lawsuit against the school board, I got doxed. My name and address were all over the internet. So, it would have been easy to find out where I live. I don't know how long Jennifer might have been hanging around the neighborhood, waiting for an opportunity. The thing I worry about most is that he may have become obsessed with Tess. He appears to be a pretty determined pervert."

"The most important thing right now is to protect you and Tess, which I will do. I could stay at your house, but it's probably safer for you to stay at my place, at least for tonight, then we can plan for the future."

"Thanks, Brian."

"I'm on my way. Just double-check all the doors and windows to make certain they're locked. Probably best to close the drapes and shutters. Don't answer the door. I'll be there in half an hour or so to get you."

You saw every day, in the newspapers and on TV, stories about violent offenders being released back onto the streets, and the crimes they committed at a time when they should have been in jail—women terrorized by men who had previously attacked them, sometimes repeatedly; the mentally ill who viciously assaulted random citizens on the streets, released again and again to commit ever more violence. You knew it was happening, and you knew it was wrong, but it seemed distant. It was happening to other people. People you didn't know. Now it's happening to us, Brian thought, and he felt ashamed that that made such a difference. He was no longer just concerned. He was angry.

High-level crimes were prosecuted reluctantly. Lower-level crimes were completely ignored. Combine that with the "defund the police" movement and you had a prescription for the rampant lawlessness that gripped America's cities. It wasn't as though people like "Let 'Em Go" Larry didn't understand this. On the contrary, breakdown of civil society was a big part of their plan. They had to be stopped.

The situation, long untenable, had become catastrophic. Seattle, for example, a city that had been, for many decades, controlled by Democrats—the champions of the women's movement—had recently announced that it no longer possessed the resources to investigate adult rape cases. Think of that. A woman reports that she has been raped, and not only is there no arrest, there is not even an investigation. There is no possibility of an arrest. No possibility of justice. The newly elected mayor says that he wants, instead, to emphasize the investigation of "visible" crimes. In another part of the city's crime promotion campaign, Seattle has long since banned most car pursuits by police, so car thieves and carjackers can just wave good-bye at those pesky flashing red lights in their rearview mirrors.

And, of course, at a time when overwhelmed police forces are unable to respond in a timely manner to 911 calls, leftists want to make certain that citizens are completely defenseless—by banning firearms. They make statements like, you don't need an AR-15 rifle for hunting. Someone needs to remind them that the Second Amendment has nothing to do with hunting.

Brian drove by a long line of recreational vehicles parked end-to-end in what had recently been a very nice middle-class neighborhood. Otherwise "homeless" individuals lived in these vehicles, many of which were unable to move under their own power. For liberal planners, these conditions fulfilled two goals. On the one hand, down-on-their-luck folks, many of whom were drug-addicted or mentally ill or both, could live in unhealthful, unsafe conditions, while, on the other, a once-thriving neighborhood was blighted. And, of course, everyone got to enjoy the wave of crime against persons and property that the "homeless" brought to the community. Liberal politicians said they recognized the problem, but the new condominiums that their financial supporters in the construction business were building to resolve the issue were quite expensive. Taxpayers were going to have to come up with a lot more money. This cozy relationship between politicians and those who funded their campaigns had come to be known as the homeless-industrial complex.

A similar quid pro quo existed between the liberal politicians and assorted leftist "non-profit" groups that were hired to provide the various services that encouraged the homeless to continue their current lifestyle. Some of the taxpayer money doled out to these groups was simply kicked back in the form of campaign donations. Some of it was paid back by "in-kind" donations—employees of these groups were a ready and eager, prepaid, source of staffing for political rallies and protests.

Brian's route took him by the park, and he shuddered to think what might have happened but for Victoria's quick thinking. The lake came into view, and he pulled over near the spot where Victoria had driven into the lake. Her car was gone, but you could still see tracks where it had plowed across the shore and into the water.

It was chilly in the early evening and the park was mostly empty. Someone was walking along the shore about 100 yards from where Victoria's car had entered the water. The person bent over at the waist, repeatedly, as though looking for something in the weedy overgrowth at the edge of the lake. Brian got quietly out of his car, thinking to himself, no one could be that stupid.

Brian moved cautiously from cover to cover so as not to be seen. When he was as close as he dared get, he snapped a couple of photos with his phone. Then he watched and waited until, a few minutes later, Jennifer found his gun. Brian took some more photos, then some video of Jennifer examining and wiping the dirt off the gun. Then he dialed the police department and asked for Sergeant Thompson.

"Charlie, this is Brian Townsend. I'm in the park near the spot where Victoria drove into the lake this afternoon. I have pictures and video of a very large man, dressed as a woman, searching for and finding a pistol in the weeds about 100 yards north of where the car went into the water."

"We're on our way," was all Thompson said.

Brian remained where he was while he waited for the cavalry. Jennifer had decided he needed a rest after his strenuous search and was sitting in the grass near where he had found his gun, clearly feeling both proud of himself and bulletproof.

The first squad car arrived with flashers on but no siren. As soon as he saw the flashers approaching, Brian started to take video again. Jennifer saw the flashers moments after Brian, and immediately hid the gun in the weeds then broke into a run toward a wooded area not far from the shore.

Once the police officers were out of their car, it took them about five seconds to notice the large form hightailing it for the woods. It didn't take them long to run him down and get him in handcuffs. Jennifer wasn't built for distance running. The officers hadn't seen Brian.

Minutes later, Thompson arrived, and Brian flagged him over. They knew each other from the old days.

"Your guys aren't going to find the gun on him," Brian said. "He's hid it again, but I've got the whole thing on video."

Brian showed Thompson the video. "No matter what," Brian said, "You've at least got a convicted felon in possession of a firearm. That should give you enough to hold him until you sort out the kidnapping."

"You'd think, wouldn't you?" Thompson said. "I bet we got close to a hundred cons on bail right now with weapons charges. No one cares."

More police arrived and Brian showed them the video to help them find the gun. It didn't take long. It was high and dry. They didn't think there would be any problem getting fingerprints, and, of course, they had the video.

"If you can part with your phone," Thompson said, "that's the cleanest way to do this from the evidence point of view."

"I've got an older phone for backup. It would be a big help to me, though, if I could take the SIM out of this phone, so I could use the number."

"I don't see a problem with that. By the way, how did you happen to be here?"

"I was driving to pick up Tess and Victoria, thinking they'd be safer with me. My route took me by the park, and I realized this was the spot where Victoria had driven into the lake. I stopped to take a look, and there he was."

"She really did a good job. I didn't put it together that she was your ex until you called. I'm sorry we had to put this guy back on the street. The prosecutors want to put everybody back on the street. It's a mess."

"The whole county's a mess," Brian said.

Thompson had a few more questions, then Brian was on his way. He reached for his phone to let Victoria know what had happened, then remembered that he didn't have a phone, just a SIM card.

It had been quite a day. He had never been prouder of Victoria. She had come through under incredible pressure. But luck was involved, especially in his happening to see Jennifer. Why had he come back for his gun? Maybe he was afraid that his fingerprints were on it, and that someone else would find it. Or maybe just because the gun was valuable and would be difficult to replace. Or maybe experience had taught Jennifer that he could pretty much get away with anything these days. He had a pretty successful scam going. Only time would tell if he was right.

23

"This man is a problem," Adam Michaelson said. "We've seen this before, in Eastern Europe. Some guy comes out of nowhere sparking nationalist and populist fervor and destroys everything we've worked so long to achieve. He's got to be stopped, one way or another."

Michaelson and Thomas Fielding were in the library at his estate. They had just finished watching Alex Walker's Washington speech on the internet. Despite their efforts, Walker's speech had gained national attention. Almost overnight, he had become a major political force.

TV and news media had generally handled the rally well. Most simply ignored it, giving it no coverage at all. Media that did not ignore the rally portrayed it as a white supremacist gathering and wildly understated the number of persons attending. The rally was described as "disturbing" and "a threat to our democracy." Readers and viewers were reminded of the rising tide of white supremacy in the country, the greatest terrorist threat that America faced, and the need to be vigilant lest the nation face a repeat of the horrors of the insurrection of January 6 when armed white supremacists nearly succeeded in toppling the government.

Social media also performed well. Invoking white supremacy, racism, and insurrection, social media attacked, deleted, and banished anyone mentioning the rally or Alex Walker in a positive or even neutral way. Most social media permanently banned Hobart's accounts.

Compliant members of the House and Senate demanded hearings. How could the rally have been permitted so soon after the insurrection? The threat was palpable. They clamored for permanent, more substantial barriers around the Capitol. The Capitol police force must be augmented—at least doubled in strength. Strong consideration needed to be given to a permanent National Guard presence around the Capitol and, more broadly, throughout Washington, D.C.

"We made a big mistake," Michaelson said, "in focusing solely on Hobart. That part went well, though. He's not broken yet, but he will be. Hobart will quickly recognize that he has a stark choice. He can either abandon this movement he's trying to energize and end his association with Alex Walker or face permanent ostracism from everything he holds dear. Various bar associations are already planning to remove him from his committee roles.

"By the way, Thomas, I want you to look into how much it will cost me to change the name of Hobart Hall. We'll throw a few million at the law school if they rename it, say, Martin Luther King Hall. See what the law school wants and offer it to them. Also, check to see if there are any scholarships that have Hobart's name on them or that he has a strong association with—not just at the law school, anywhere. Same thing with charities, advisory committees, and so forth. Be sure they understand the risks of their being linked to Hobart and this white supremacist movement. Assure them that we'll fill any financial shortfall that might occur as a result of their separation from Hobart. And back this up with a media campaign. What's happened to Hamilton Hobart? No longer the man you think he is. Civil rights figure turned racist. That sort of thing. We need both editorials and headlines."

As usual, Fielding said nothing and took no notes. His expression never changed. He did nod occasionally.

"But we need to go after Walker more aggressively, as well," Michaelson said. "This snake has two heads. We don't know enough about Walker. We need to know everything. When we do, we'll turn his world upside down and separate him from everything that's important to him, including his good name. He'll come to look back fondly on his time in jail."

George appeared, dressed as always in an immaculate dark suit.

"Dennis has arrived," he said.

Dennis was shown in, his size, age, and casual dress striking an incongruous note.

"So, Dennis," Michaelson said, "What have you got for us?"

"Lutz has cobbled together a group of people, mostly young, mostly with inherited wealth, and they're planning to buy real estate in areas that have been depressed by rioting. It looks like they're concentrating on locales that were prosperous before the riots. They're counting on a quick turnaround—and a quick profit—as soon as things get back to normal."

Dennis handed over his written report. Michaelson and Fielding exchanged furtive, knowing glances.

"They haven't pulled the trigger on many properties, yet," Dennis said. "They've mostly been trying to line up financing. Lutz wants to leverage this thing to the hilt, in part because he doesn't have much capital. Right now, they're not buying much. My read is that they think that more riots are on the way, and that will depress real estate prices even further. Meanwhile, they're all throwing cash into their partnership. Lutz is already strapped. He had to borrow money to finance his share of the principal. He's always been the kind of guy who spent every dime he had and borrowed to spend more. He has a fancy condo he can't really afford, and he missed last month's payment on his Porsche. It's all in my report."

Michaelson smiled. "Thank you, Dennis. We had suspected that Leonard might be overextended financially. That can make him susceptible to all manner of temptations that could affect our organization adversely. We have to keep an eye on things like that."

Michaelson handed the report to Fielding, then returned his attention to Dennis. "How well do you know this Alex Walker?"

"Hardly at all. I've been around him a couple of times. I set up the security for Hobart at the rally the other day. I don't remember any direct interaction with Walker. If you saw his speech, you know as much about him as I do."

"We need to know more," Michaelson said. "We'd like a full background report, everything that's known about him, and then some. As soon you can."

"Yes, sir."

"Thank you, Dennis."

That was his cue that he was dismissed. Dennis left the library and took the backstairs down to the area on the lower floor that was the technical nerve center for the security operation he had set up at the Michaelson estate. Dennis would spend the rest of the morning talking to his men and reviewing, once again, the entire operation.

"So, what do you think?" Michaelson asked.

Fielding put the report on Michaelson's desk and shook his head. "I think that Leonard sniffed out our plan and figured he'd make a little money on his own."

"There's plenty of money for everybody, of course. The problem is, he's likely to screw up and let the cat out of the bag. That runs the risk that the public will come to view our philanthropy—our generous expenditure of billions of dollars to rebuild America's blighted cities—as mere profiteering. We can't have that."

"I can have someone talk to him," Fielding said, "and explain the unpleasant things that will happen to him if he doesn't abandon his real estate dreams—or, for that matter, if he ever again tries to front-run one of our projects."

Michaelson considered this. "Leonard is a slimy bastard, but, in the end, he's *our* slimy bastard. We own him. He's pretty much capable of anything, which makes him useful to us, but also dangerous. For now, though, I think we can handle this with a little more subtlety. We can teach Leonard a lesson, for now and for the future, without his ever knowing that we discovered what he was up to.

"Dennis has provided a typically thorough report. We know where all Leonard's financing is coming from— everything from his real estate dreams to his mortgage and his car loan. He is dealing with institutions and individuals with which, to say the least, we have considerable influence over. They need to hear—not from us, but from mutual friends—that Leonard and his little band are erratic and unreliable. Their lenders will respond with higher interest rates and greater capital requirements. New funding will evaporate.

"Meanwhile, the few properties they've bought are eating up their capital reserves. Leonard and his group are not developers. I'm sure their plan is to buy properties and flip them to new owners when order is restored and the financial outlook for cities and businesses improves, but that's not going to happen any time soon. Leonard has made a classic rookie mistake. He has invested too early. By the time market conditions improve enough for him to turn a profit, he and his friends will have run out of money. Most likely, Leonard will come begging us to save him.

"One other thing, Thomas, for now, let's see that

Leonard's Porsche gets repossessed. That will be a humbling experience and provide a first taste of just where his greed is taking him."

24

At least for now, Jennifer was in jail. Brian had checked. Sergeant Thompson said that, these days, "convicted felon in possession of a firearm" was a weak charge. Bail, if even required, would be modest. Jennifer would soon be free to commit more mayhem. If the case ever did go to trial, it wouldn't be for a couple of years or so. So, they had to make the kidnapping charge stick. Finding the gun helped with that. A lot. In the old days, say two years ago, Jennifer would have been convicted on Victoria's testimony alone. Slam dunk. The gun corroborated Victoria's statement and showed that Jennifer had lied. Thompson didn't see how the prosecutors could walk away from that, but, in the current political climate, you never knew.

Brian asked Thompson if he thought they would charge Miguel. In a word, Thompson said, no. He explained that Miguel, being in the country illegally, was in a protected class. Even if Jennifer was successfully prosecuted for kidnapping, the only charge they would likely have against Miguel was making a false statement. There was only one circumstance under which Thompson could imagine that Miguel would face a false statement charge. If Miguel turned out to be a high-ranking Republican, Thompson was confident that the prosecutors would lock him up and throw away the key.

It was a chilly evening, just turning dark. The street was not lighted the way it used to be. Most of the shops that, two or three years ago, would have been doing a thriving business at this time of the evening, were now boarded up, and the street was deserted.

Brian was huddled in the doorway of an abandoned drugstore. It had been run by a national chain that had tired of operating the business as a charity for shoplifters and looters. They had, regretfully, closed several of their stores in the area. That was a blow to the many locals who had depended on those stores to fill prescriptions, but the chain's management said that it wasn't purely a profit and loss decision. Lax law enforcement had instilled in criminals a sense of entitlement, and they had become increasingly violent in asserting their right to steal. Management had come to recognize that these stores were no longer safe for either customers or employees.

Brian was staked out across the street from one of the city's struggling hotels. Tourists, formerly a financial mainstay for downtown hotels, no longer came. Hotels tried to survive on the increasingly meager flow of business travelers and by hosting local events. The bar association was having its quarterly dinner at the hotel tonight. Brian was waiting for "Let 'Em Go" Larry to come out.

Larry typically showed up for the cocktail hour, wolfed down his dinner, then bolted before the speeches began. Brian's plan had been to intercept Larry as he headed down the street to retrieve his car from the lot they all used, but, as time dragged on, he was beginning to worry that Larry was going to be a no-show. Then, there he was, scurrying out of the front door like a rat with a cat on his tail. He was pudgy and balding and had squinty eyes and prominent upper front teeth. Larry the Rat. His scraggly Van Dyke beard did nothing to improve the look.

Brian had performed a thorough reconnaissance of the area and carefully planned how this would go down. He crossed the street and fell in about twenty feet behind Larry. After a few seconds, Larry, aware that there was someone behind him, quickened his pace. Brian began to move faster so that Larry would be in no doubt that someone was trying to catch up to him. He let Larry wonder who that might be for a few more seconds before saying anything.

"Larry, it's Brian Townsend. We need to talk."

"Make an appointment!" Larry threw the words over his shoulder. He didn't even bother to slow down.

Brian broke into a trot. Larry tried to get away, but his weight and sedentary lifestyle worked against him. Brian got ahead of him, and, at the calculated moment, turned in front of Larry, forcing him to stop. When Larry tried to maneuver around him, Brian grabbed him by the lapels of his suit and backed him into one of the many darkened doorways that lined the street.

"Assault!" Larry yelled. "I'll charge you with assault. And kidnapping! You're kidnapping me. You won't get away with this, Townsend!"

"Kidnapping, Larry? Really? You don't have a very well-developed sense of irony, do you?"

"You're going to jail, Townsend."

"Actually, Larry, I have personal knowledge that your policy on kidnappers is not to file charges. You're not suggesting, are you, that it's different now just because the alleged victim happens to be you? That's not going to look very good on TV."

Larry wasn't dissuaded. "I'm not kidding. You're going to prison for a long time."

"You have a problem, Larry. No witnesses. You know, there was a time, before you slithered into office, when this street would have been filled with people at this hour. Not anymore. Thanks to you, it's not safe. Back then, all these stores had security cameras. Not now. I checked. What would be the point? They video someone committing a crime, and nothing happens. And I'm pretty sure that even you are not stupid enough to think that a police car is going to roll by on routine patrol. You've defunded the hell out of them. And if a cop should happen to spot a crime in progress, what's he going to do? He's gotta be thinking that you're as likely to charge him with a crime as the guy he arrests. You've taught the cops that they're better off if they just don't get involved. So, Larry, it's just you and me. For once, you're lying in the bed you made. Not much fun, is it?"

"Help! Help!" Larry started screaming and wouldn't stop.

Brian punched him in the stomach—not too hard, just enough to take his breath away and make him stop screaming.

"If you're going to vomit that fancy dinner, Larry, please don't do it on my suit."

Larry managed not to vomit. His breathing became less labored. He looked like he might cry.

"Pay attention now, Larry, this is important. I'm here to tell you, straight to your face, that I'm ashamed of myself. I think a lot of people in this city should be ashamed of themselves. We watched you destroy what was once a great city, and we did nothing. And you know what? That's not the worst thing you've done, not even close. People have died because of you. We all knew that, and we did nothing. You released people who should have been in jail, and they murdered, raped, and robbed the citizens of this city. And we did nothing. People were nearly beaten to death on the streets, and we did nothing. Those crimes are on you, Larry. Without you or some other lawless Leftist freak in the prosecutor's office, many of those murder victims would be alive today. They would be with their families. Do you ever think about a woman or a child who was raped by someone that you should already have put in prison for decades—

someone whose last rape you pled down to misdemeanor assault? Do you, Larry?"

Larry was silent.

"I think that the reason most of us didn't do anything was that those crimes seemed so distant. We didn't actually know any of the victims. That's what I'm ashamed of. We told ourselves, well, it's not our responsibility. And, in a very narrow sense, that was true. You know whose responsibility it was? It was your responsibility, Larry. So many of those people were underprivileged and poorly educated. They were a pretty defenseless group, and it was your job to protect them, and you just didn't care.

"My daughter and my former wife were kidnapped by an armed sexual predator, and you let him go. He wasn't even charged. There is every reason to believe that he specifically targeted my daughter and her mother. What was the first thing he did after you let him go? He went back to the crime scene to retrieve the gun he hid there—the gun that your understaffed police force wasn't able to find. What do you suppose he was going to do next? Was he going to come after my family again, or would he just attack some other woman or little girl whose terrible misfortune it was to happen into his field of view? It's certainly nothing more than a stroke of luck that he's back in jail now. He needs to stay there. You're paid to protect the citizens from people like him. It's time for you to start doing your job.

"When all this happened, my first thought was, there's nothing I can do about it. Your particular brand of corruption is difficult to prove in court, especially in a city packed with judges up to their necks in the same corrupt ideology. Then I thought about the various political options. The best, and quickest, would be for you to just resign in disgrace, but, of course, you're not about to do that. Then I thought about a recall, but you'll be up for reelection well before a recall vote could get on the ballot. So, politically, the only recourse is to find someone to run against you and vote you out of office. I'm committed to that. I have money. I have friends with lots of money. We're going to make certain that you're not reelected. Even Adam Michaelson doesn't have enough money to keep you in office. So, that's a given. Come November, you're done. But, November's a long way off, and something has to be done now. That's why we're having this little talk."

Looking at Larry, Brian could see that he wasn't convinced that his political career was over. You had to say one thing for the guy, he knew enough about the law to exercise his right to remain silent.

"Larry, when you let somebody go who ought to be in jail, and that guy goes out and kills somebody, you're responsible. The first time you do it, it's a mistake. The second time, it's because you're stupid. The third time, it's intentional. You have become an active participant in the crimes that are committed—crime after crime, time after time. When someone who should have been in prison is not there because you chose not to enforce the law, you're a partner in the crimes that he commits. When he murders somebody, you're just as guilty as he is. You might as well be holding the gun yourself.

"And I'll tell you something else, when you and your buddies in this city and across the country act in concert to deliberately not enforce the law in order to achieve your personal political goals, that's a criminal conspiracy. That's clear as day to me. And the people of this country are suffering severe harm as a direct result of the wave of crime that your little criminal enterprise has inflicted on them. I'm not sure, yet, what view the legal community is going to take of this, but I can tell you one thing for certain, the public will understand the concept immediately. It makes crystal clear exactly what you're up to. Still, Larry, even that will take a while, and, while we're waiting, your gang's reign of terror will continue. Meanwhile, you and I have urgent business.

"Tonight, Larry, is the beginning of real accountability for you and people of your ilk. My daughter and her mother, and many other innocent citizens, will be in grave danger if this man who calls himself Jennifer Beaulieu is released from jail. My sources have told me that your office is already in the process of trying to plead his case down to some trivial charge. What I want you to understand, Larry, is that, if he is released, I will hold you personally responsible. I don't mean legally or politically. I mean physically, like tonight, only much more severe. Gone is the day when you can inflict terror on the citizens of this city, then go home to a nice dinner and a quiet evening by the fire. The people of this country must begin to hold people like you accountable in a meaningful way. You can't be permitted to deliberately unleash a torrent of crime and suffer no consequences for your actions.

"So, Larry, if this Jennifer character is released, I'm coming after you. At the same time, I will do everything I can to protect my family, but, if they're harmed in any way, you will pay an extreme penalty. Do you understand that?"

Larry managed a smirk, and it was too much for Brian. He hit him once again in the stomach and put a lot more into it this time. Larry doubled over and fought for breath.

"What's going on here? Do you need any help?" The voice was that of a tall, well-dressed black man of about fifty. He was the only one of the three of them who had had the sense to wear a topcoat against the cold night.

Brian had been so focused on Larry that he'd failed to keep an eye on his surroundings. He understood that he would now have to pay a steep price for his session with Larry, but, in that instant, thought it was probably worth it.

Larry was regaining his composure enough to speak.

"This man assaulted me and held me against my will. He threatened to murder me."

"I wasn't talking to you," the man said. "I saw the whole thing from across the street. You attacked this fellow here for no apparent reason, and he defended himself." He turned to Brian. "I only came over to give you my card, so you could contact me if you decide to press charges and need a witness. I'd be happy to testify."

Brian turned his attention away from Larry to take the man's card, and in that brief moment, Larry produced a gun. Larry was a leader of the anti-gun crowd, but, of course, their intention was that only the hoi polloi would be disarmed. Important people like Larry were above all of that.

"You're dead, Townsend," Larry said.

"I'm not so certain of that," the stranger said. From somewhere he had produced the biggest handgun Brian had ever seen. Mice could live in the barrel. He leveled the gun about six inches from Larry's head.

"Put down the gun, Mr. Prosecutor. You're too stupid to be playing with guns."

"If you shoot, I'll kill Townsend."

"Is that the man's name? It means nothing to me. Two things I'm sure of. The first is, if you don't hand over that gun right now, I'm going to kill you. The second is, you're not going to kill me. Now hand the gun over so I don't get blood all over my clothes."

Larry handed the gun over, his resistance gone. His back against the wall, literally, he slid down into a sitting position.

"You have a nice day, now," the stranger said as he put Larry's gun into the pocket of his topcoat, then turned and walked into the darkness.

Brian studied Larry's pathetic form huddled in the doorway. He realized that he was still holding the stranger's business card in his hand.

"Larry," he said, and waited for the prosecutor to look up. "Don't make the mistake of doubting anything I said tonight."

Brian turned and crossed the street, headed in the direction opposite the one the stranger had taken.

25

The homeless camps were spreading. Where Brian lived, the camps had been a constant presence for many years, but he didn't like that they were now sprawling out to within blocks of Victoria's house. No matter what you thought was the best way to deal with the homeless problem, everyone agreed that the camps brought crime and unsanitary, unhealthful conditions everywhere they went.

Some said that the homeless in the city's core were being displaced by the new immigrant arrivals. The federal government was flying migrants, by the hundreds, into the city. They arrived in the middle of the night, without notice, and typically without the ability to support themselves and their families. The strain on the city's resources was severe, and the situation was growing increasingly desperate. Churches and other charities continued to provide what they could, but their resources were not unlimited. As the competition for assistance grew, people in need were forced to scavenge for sustenance farther and farther from the city's center. This was just one more of the increasingly large number of social problems that were fully anticipatable but completely ignored, and therefore manifestly deliberate— part of the deep-laid plot painstakingly designed to generate chaos and undermine social stability.

Brian arrived at Victoria's house, let himself in, and was surprised and pleased to find her father ensconced in his favorite chair in the living room. The two men were fond of each other, and the divorce had not changed that.

"Alex," Brian said, as they shook hands, "so good to have you back. I can see that we need to get some food into you." Alex had clearly lost a good deal of weight. He looked like he had aged ten years.

"I'm afraid that prison food is about as bad as you'd expect, and the environment is not especially conducive to the appetite. Overall, I'd say that jail was not a pleasant experience, but I survived. It's behind me. Others got much worse than I got."

"They put him in leg irons," Victoria said. "Can you believe that?"

"That was mostly when they were moving me around." Alex smiled. "It made me feel like a real desperado. I'll tell you though, when they have you in leg irons and your handcuffs are good and tight and attached to a big leather belt around your waist, you feel pretty helpless. It's all about control—and, of course, it's meant to be humiliating."

"We've been trying to bring each other up to date," Victoria said. "Dad, I haven't even asked you yet what's going on with you and the medical school."

"Ham says that the first thing to do is to file our malicious prosecution claim with the federal government. He's demanding 90 million dollars—says that leaves lots of bargaining room. At any rate, once the claim is filed, he'll send a letter to the school formally informing them that all of the charges against me were dismissed with prejudice. He says he'll attach a copy of the claim, so they'll have all the facts. The idea, Ham says, is to make clear that the school is holding a losing hand and wait to see what they come back with. If that's unsatisfactory, we can always sue. Meanwhile, with the clinic closed, I'm in no hurry. Besides, I seem to be acquiring some new responsibilities."

"I watched your speech on the internet," Brian said. "It

was terrific. What's the plan going forward?"

"Still in strategy meetings about all that. We have to be careful. There's nothing they'd like better than to lock me up again. They'll use any excuse."

Victoria shook her head. "Have you seen those signs, 'Where Is America?' What happened to free speech and the right of assembly? They throw you in jail, but the government and press can pretty much say whatever they want. We saw all that horrid stuff on the news calling you a racist and a white supremacist. How can they get away with that?"

"That's an old trick. Stick a terrible name on someone, and that justifies anything you want to do to them. You expect that kind of thing from the odd sleazy politician, but I never imagined it would become an administration's standard policy. It's what Putin did when he invaded Ukraine. He said he needed to denazify the country. That was his excuse for the invasion. After what happened to them in World War II, there's nothing a Russian can think of that's worse than being called a Nazi, so Putin used it to rally his people behind his war."

Alex turned to Brian. "Victoria said you left your old firm, over all that school board nonsense. Anything new with your lawsuit?"

"Ida says she's almost done with the depositions, just a couple more to go. Based on the information she's developed so far, she says that the board is in an untenable position. They just don't know it yet. Her plan is to finish the depositions, then go public with what we have. Ida expects parents and other concerned citizens to be outraged by what she's learned, and they'll put pressure on the board that it won't be able to withstand."

"Will that resolve things for you at the medical school, Victoria?" her father said.

"I assume so. For now, I'm just going about my business as though nothing has happened. I've made it clear to them that I will never submit to their Maoist reeducation agenda. It's kind of a standoff at this point."

There was still one more elephant in the room. "Did you tell your dad about the other thing?"

"Jennifer? Yes. Dad understands that Tess and I are safe now."

"Regarding Jennifer," Brian said, "I've been debating with myself whether or not to tell you what I did tonight. I think I should. I've been disgusted by the idea that has evolved in this country that district attorneys are allowed to ignore the law when it suits their personal political ends—and then face no consequences. They choose not to prosecute dangerous felons and just put them back on the street to commit more mayhem. That puts real people in grave danger. This is not some abstract philosophical point. Citizens are murdered, raped, robbed, and otherwise brutalized by people who should have been in jail. I know I'm not telling you anything you don't know, but why are prosecutors allowed to do this with impunity? They're not held to account in any measure consistent with the amount of harm they cause. A prosecutor fails to perform his duty, and what's the worst that can happen? He, eventually, gets kicked out of office, either by recall or failing to get reelected. Someone dies, and maybe, eventually, a prosecutor loses his job. Someone is raped, and, just maybe, the prosecutor doesn't get reelected. People who are victimized by these prosecutors deserve justice. So, tonight, I took it upon myself to explain to 'Let 'Em Go' Larry that what he had done to my family put him at risk for a whole lot more than just losing his job."

Then Brian told them what had happened. He tried not to leave anything out.

"I truly believe," Brian said, "that Larry would have killed me if the guy with the gun hadn't shown up."

"Any idea who your savior was?" Victoria said.

"Actually, I do." Brian pulled the man's card out of his pocket. "Lucius St. John, President and CEO, St. John Development. The name doesn't ring any bells with me."

"I think they build luxury homes," Victoria said. "I ran into the name when I thought Tess and I might move. Their stuff was way too pricey for me."

Brian had his phone out, seeing what he could find on the internet. "You're right, Victoria. They're privately held, build luxury home developments all over the country. Estimated to have annual revenue well into the billions. Let's see if I can find anything personal about the man."

Minutes later, Brian was shaking his head. "This is really awful. When I search on Lucius St. John, it brings up news stories about some guy named Lopez, an illegal immigrant, who was repeatedly arrested for drunken driving—at least three times. Absolutely nothing done until the third time when he was diverted into a recovery program which he didn't bother to attend. Meanwhile, he commits a bunch of felonies that were pled down to misdemeanors—lots of burglaries, one armed robbery. All this time, Immigration and Customs has a detainer on him, but, of course, ICE detainers aren't honored in our fine sanctuary city. So, instead of being deported, he remains here to commit his fourth documented DUI. This time, sadly, he kills someone—Mrs. Lucius St. John. So, we don't know how Lucius St. John came to be near that hotel tonight, but we do know why he's not a fan of our district attorney."

"Brian, you could get in real trouble over this," Victoria said. "What if Larry decides to prosecute you?"

"I'm guessing he won't. He would probably worry about Mr. St. John testifying. Larry doesn't know that I would never let Lucius St. John commit perjury on my behalf. That hasn't occurred to Larry because he wouldn't bat an eye at presenting perjured testimony. On the other hand, Larry knows that a trial would risk bringing a whole lot of his dirty laundry into public view. I'm also wondering, would a jury of my peers ever convict me? I think most people in this city feel they've had enough of Larry's crime wave, and it's way past time to do something about it. Are we supposed to just sit on our hands and passively accept whatever hell the people in charge decide to throw us into?"

"This worries me," Alex said, "this rise of vigilantism. We're hearing reports from all over the country of people taking the law into their own hands. I don't mean that it's not understandable, justified even, and I'm certainly not criticizing you, Brian, but you can see that this could get out of hand in a hurry. I see vigilantism as a predictable result of what government, at all levels, has done to us. When you take away all of the structures that a civil society depends on for the protection of its citizens, you force people to fend for themselves. If I see this as a very predictable result of what the leftists controlling the government are doing, they can certainly see that as well. They may even be counting on it. Could this rampant vigilantism be the force majeure they're counting on to finally rip up the Constitution once and for all?

"I don't know how far the Left is willing to go. What's their endgame? Is it troops in the street pointing guns at citizens? It certainly looks to me like the military is using woke ideology to purge the ranks, the same way totalitarian regimes purge their military of disloyal elements. They're also discharging troops who refuse the COVID vaccination. Troops who refuse vaccination are probably a pretty conservative, often religious, bunch. Pretty soon, the political ideology in the military will be no more diverse than it is in the Harvard faculty. Mao said, "Political power grows out of the barrel of a gun." Is that where we're headed?

"Brian, you acted tonight in an effort to force an official to do the job he is supposed to do. Others will look at the situation and say, the judicial system and law enforcement are not fulfilling their responsibilities, therefore, I have to do it for them. I have to act to defend my family. It falls upon me to punish wrongdoers.

"I think about the movies we've all watched set in the Old West. The bad guys are running the town, and the townspeople are helpless. Lawlessness abounds. Usually there's some rich rancher behind it all. He hires the corrupt sheriff and local judge. He controls the town council and sets the rules. He runs the local elections, so there's no voting the bad guys out of town. It's the rich rancher's hired hands who come into town and shoot up the saloon and terrorize the people. These favored rioters can do whatever they want, but the townspeople better not step out of line. Justice is swift and severe for the little people.

"The townspeople face three choices. They can leave town. They can resign themselves to living in the chaos and tyranny that is being rained down upon them. Or, they can rise up using the only means left to them, physical force. We watch the movie and ask ourselves, why don't they fight back? There are more townspeople than bad guys. The townspeople are well-armed. Why don't they do something? And, finally, they do. And we cheer.

"I can't help but worry that we're approaching such a moment in this country. Polls show that, right now, only about 20% of the people believe that the country is headed in the right direction. That's an astoundingly low number. What recourse do the people have when they feel that way? In the end, just one—they can vote the bums out. Our democracy, the very existence of our nation, depends on the ability to do just that. And, not only must we *have* free and fair elections, but, equally importantly, the American people must *believe* that the election process is free and fair.

"The 2020 presidential election process has been so muddied and politicized that it's almost impossible to sort out what actually happened. However, there certainly have been enough irregularities exposed that a fair-minded person could rationally question the results. The government needs to put all of these concerns to rest. If people believe that ballot signatures were not properly certified, you adjust the verification process to eliminate that question. If people say, look at this video, there's evidence that some individuals are dumping hundreds or even thousands of ballots into collection boxes, you make certain that, in future elections, that can't happen. If one political party says that they weren't allowed to participate meaningfully in the ballot counting process, you establish a system that prevents them from being excluded in subsequent elections. This is not rocket surgery. It's simple. And, one other thing I would add, if you want the public to believe that the process is fair and above board, you conduct the vote under the laws that the legislature has passed. You don't ignore those laws, and you don't make up new laws in the middle of an election.

"This is all very straightforward. It's common sense. So, what does the Democratic party do? They double down. They demand that all the practices that have caused uncertainty become a permanent part of the election process. Under their scheme, you can't ask people to prove that they're who they say they are, and that they are qualified to vote. That's racist! This is the equivalent of saying that you want to denazify the election. The Democrats want universal mail-in ballots. The 2005 Commission on Federal Election Reform, headed by none other than the sainted Jimmy Carter, cautioned that mail-in ballots were the largest source of potential voter fraud. Congressional Democrats even attempted to pass a law making it a crime to spread "falsehoods" about elections, making such crimes punishable by a $100,000 fine and up to five years in jail. Recent experience in politics and on social media has demonstrated that there is likely to be disagreement, split sharply along political lines, about what is fact and what is fiction.

"If Americans cannot have confidence in the election process, they're going to feel that their country is being stolen out from under them. Then, what recourse remains for them? Maybe that's why the Left is so intent on disarming the population. Maybe that's why they cracked down so hard on the so-called January 6 insurrection. The January 6 crackdown was merely practice for the greater challenge to come. They wanted to see how much suppression of individual rights the population would obediently tolerate.

"I try to understand what the Left's goal is in all this. It's certainly not the pablum they espouse about protecting the underprivileged and safeguarding democracy. All you have to do to dispel that notion is look at the way their leaders conduct their private lives. As near as I can tell, all they care about is money and power—the very thing they accuse the Right of.

"I recently ran into something Gore Vidal wrote. He wasn't one of my favorite people, but he certainly understood the liberal mind."

Alex searched his phone. "Here it is. 'It is difficult to find a reputable American historian who will acknowledge the crude fact that a Franklin Roosevelt, say, wanted to be president merely to wield power, to be famed and to be feared. To learn this simple fact, one must wade through a sea of evasions: history as sociology, leaders as teachers, bland benevolence as a motive force, when, finally, power *is* an end in itself, and the instinctive urge to prevail the most important single human force without which no city was built, no city destroyed.'

    "I ask myself, could it really be that simple? I fear that the answer is yes."

26

Leonard Lutz was lost. It was well after midnight, and he was driving through an area of the city that wasn't safe in broad daylight. It had been one of the first parts of town to be destroyed by rioting and would certainly be the last to be restored—if that ever happened at all. Leonard was here because he was desperate. And he needed a gun.

He had an address, but the streetlights were mostly out, and the darkness made it nearly impossible to read any of the few remaining street signs, the ones that hadn't been torn down and sold for scrap. Leonard had been so focused on the cash he had to scrounge—to buy the gun he couldn't afford—that he had left his condo without his phone. In happier times, he would merely have turned to the GPS in his Porsche, but, of course, the Porsche had long since been repossessed. On hearing of that calamity, Michaelson said that, naturally, Leonard needed a car, and that he would be happy to provide one.

This had given Leonard hope that he would soon be once again riding in style, but then the replacement was delivered. He was handed the keys to a 2013 Mitsubishi Mirage. The car had fading red paint and a badly dented rear bumper, but there was worse news under the hood—a three-cylinder engine that delivered something like 75 horsepower. Needless to say, there was no GPS. He would make Michaelson pay for his little joke, but, for now, Leonard needed the car. These were desperate times.

Leonard's investors were growing increasingly restless. He had promised quick profits. They wanted instant profits. He had promised major, widespread rioting far exceeding all they had seen so far. It hadn't happened—yet. There had been nothing more than the typical background level of looting, murders, and generalized mayhem that big city governments had been encouraging over the last couple of years. This furthered the Left's goals of perpetual chaos and disruption of normal, civil society, but there had been no discernible move toward the ultimate socialist dream of a total collapse of law and order that would lead the public to demand that the government step in and take whatever draconian measures were necessary to restore order. Leonard told his investors to be patient, it's coming. Why did they think all those politicians were working so hard, 24/7, to stir up racial animosity? Why did they think politicians were declaring that white supremacy was the greatest threat that America faced? They were doing the hard labor of laying the groundwork for the upcoming riots. They were creating the tinder. All that was needed now was the spark.

Their investment model was quite simple—buy property during the height of the upcoming riots and sell when the government stepped in and calm returned. He knew from his political connections that the riots were scheduled for this summer and that the government was locked and loaded, ready to commit whatever force was required to stamp out the unrest. It was the intractable delay that was killing them. More than one of his investors had commented that they were waiting for Godot.

There had been progress on other fronts. Trillions of dollars of profligate government spending had, at long last, generated the desired rampant inflation, and the Federal Reserve had been admirably slow in responding. Inflation was by itself a horrific force fully capable of singlehandedly shredding a democracy. What you got at first was just some annoying price hikes and a little chipping away at savings, but over time, with continued government support, inflation would explode. Average people would no longer be able to afford food and housing. They would see their lives' savings dwindle to nothing. Then would come shortages of everything. Food riots. Corporate earnings would dissolve and the stock markets would crash, but that wouldn't stop the government from blaming the economic devastation on corporate greed. Finally, the moment would arrive for the socialist cavalry to ride in and remedy the disaster they had fomented. Runaway inflation and the despair it caused were a perfect excuse to institute wage and price controls and take over the entire economy—a major step on the road to achievement of the socialist paradise.

Tired of waiting, Leonard's collection of trust-fund investors had threatened to bolt. They saw the investment they had made in Leonard's scheme being shrunk by inflation while there was easy money to be made shorting the stock market. They wanted out, and Leonard felt the walls closing in. Every penny he had was in the scheme. He had even taken a second mortgage on his condo. If he lost his investors, he lost everything. Desperation time.

There was a streetlight up ahead—actually providing some illumination for a change. He could make out a figure standing in the glow. Instinctively, Leonard guided his car away from the curb. Getting closer, he could make out a dapperly dressed man of about forty within the arc of light. He looked like someone waiting for a bus. Leonard pulled to the curb and rolled the passenger-side window down. Before Leonard could ask for directions, the man had half his body through the window and his face next to Leonard's.

"Nice ride," he said. "Tell me you're not with the po-lice."

Leonard had no idea what the man wanted. He assumed

his request was mere sarcasm.

The man became more insistent. "*Tell* me that you're not with the po-lice. Say it."

Leonard shrugged. "I'm not with the police."

"That's better. Now, what can I do you for? You lookin' for white, black, Asian? I got 'em all. Or maybe, you lookin' for a handsome young man. I got that, too. Or, if you just want something to suck up your nose, I got you covered." He pulled back a little, his forearms resting on the window sill.

"How much?"

"How much for what?"

"For a girl."

"Now, you talkin'. You just want car service, it'll cost you a hundred."

"Where would we go," Leonard said, "to be inside?"

The man pulled his head out of the car and pointed to a nearby building. Not a light to be seen in any of the windows.

Leonard stomped the accelerator. The little car's response was not exactly neck-snapping, but the man didn't appear to have any interest in chasing him.

"You be back," the man yelled, "just as soon as you get your courage up."

When Leonard finally took his eyes off the rearview mirror, he couldn't believe what was right there in front of him. Underneath a few layers of graffiti, he was pretty certain the sign said Bowker Market. The market was burned out, but the metal sign was still there. Leonard made the turn, and, a few blocks down, found the Bowker Street address he was looking for.

His instructions were to park his car and wait, so that's what he did. He kept the engine running and the windows rolled up. The neighborhood looked derelict and hopeless, like most of this part of town. Waiting did not help his anxiety level, but he worried that waiting might be a whole lot better than whatever came next. He didn't have long to worry.

Half a dozen figures emerged from the darkness and began milling around the car. They all wore hoodies that partially covered their faces. Leonard imagined that they were teenagers, part of a gang. He had never felt so defenseless in his entire life—or so stupid. Desperation, the mother of stupidity.

A larger figure loomed out of the darkness and approached the car. He rapped on the window with a knuckle and motioned for Leonard to roll the window down.

"You the man wants to buy something?"

Leonard nodded.

"Name?"

"Lawrence," Leonard said. It was the name they were expecting.

"You got the five hundred?"

Leonard nodded again.

"Give it over."

"I have to have the gun first."

The man snickered. "Don't work that way. You give me the money, then I give you the gun."

"Let me see it."

The man shrugged and pulled a handgun out of his belt. It looked okay. What did Leonard know? He reached under the seat and pulled out the sack with the money and handed it to the man. He counted it carefully.

Satisfied, he tucked the money away. "You have a nice day now," he said.

All of the teenagers were now showing guns.

Leonard started to say something, then stopped himself. He didn't need to make himself look like any more of an idiot. He put the car in gear, and the gang moved so he could pull away.

"You have any more money you want to give me," the man said, "you know where I am."

27

It took some maneuvering for Brian to arrange a meeting with Lucius St. John. The first hurdle was that St. John had no reason to recognize Brian's name, and Brian could hardly introduce himself to St. John's secretary as the guy who beat up the district attorney. And he couldn't say, I'm Brian Townsend, the guy who Mr. St. John offered to commit perjury for. So, Brian told the secretary that he was an attorney, and that this was a personal matter, a type of message he had actually used many times before to maintain privacy in matters related to divorces, lawsuits, and so forth. The following day, the secretary called back to say that she would need more specific information about why he wanted to speak to their CEO. Her tone suggested that this was not the first time that someone had attempted to set up a meeting under false pretenses. Undaunted, Brian provided a nuanced version of his message. He told her the date that he and St. John had met, and that St. John had offered his views on a case that Brian and the district attorney had been fighting over. That worked. The secretary called back quickly to say that Mr. St. John would be happy to meet with him at his earliest convenience.

With their complicated schedules, setting up a meeting was a lot more difficult than it sounded, but they managed to arrange a time a couple of days later. Brian said that he'd be happy to drive out to St. John's office in the suburbs, and that was that.

The headquarters of St. John Development comprised several buildings spread over dozens of acres of what could have passed for well-tended pastureland. You fully expected to see horses. Brian was to come to the main building—easy to find, he was told, because it's the tallest. Inside, he was taken through the usual corporate security rigmarole. At the main desk, he presented identification and stated his business. The security man called upstairs to confirm his appointment, then told Brian to go right on up. He was expected.

Brian was quickly ushered into St. John's office, and the man rose to meet him.

"Mr. Townsend," he said as they shook hands, "I'm glad to have a name to attach to the face."

"Please, call me Brian."

"And I'm Lucius. I used to be Luke, but now my son is Luke, so, I'm Lucius. It's easier that way."

St. John appeared to be about fifty. He was very tall, perhaps six-and-a-half feet. He had a close-cropped military haircut. He wasn't wearing a suitcoat, just a white dress shirt and blue tie in the office.

He leaned over conspiratorially and said, "Have you heard from our friend?"

"No, you'll be relieved to hear that that's not why I'm here."

"You must have put the fear of God into him," St. John said.

"One of us did. I'm not sure it was me. I'm assuming that Larry had no idea who you were."

"That's what I'd assume."

"So, I doubt that he believed that you just happened to drop by. My guess is that he thinks I brought you as backup. I bet it's your gun that worries him, not your potential testimony."

"I'm fine with that."

"Since I knew your name," Brian said more solemnly, "I looked you up on the internet. I read about your tragic loss. I'm so sorry."

"Thank you. Unfortunately, it's not a unique story. District attorneys like ours are merchants of tragedy. It's deliberate, and it has to be stopped."

The office was enormous, befitting a corporate titan. One area had a long table made of some beautiful, exotic wood. It could probably seat twenty or so people for larger meetings. There was an alcove where St. John had his desk. They settled themselves in an area of soft seating near a large window that had clearly been designed for more intimate, less formal conversation.

"I'm sorry that you had to call more than once," St. John said. "I, of course, understand why you wanted to be vague about who you are. Once I had your name, I looked *you* up on the internet. Remarkably, I know your, I guess, ex-father-in-law. He's a fine man."

"Yes, he is."

"I imagine that he has a fine daughter."

"Right again. Victoria and I have a daughter, and we're very close."

"I'm pleased to hear it. Nothing is more important than family."

"How do you know Alex?"

"I've been working with him and Ham Hobart and some others to try to keep the Left from drowning the country in this socialist cesspool that they're so committed to. I wasn't able to attend the Washington event where Alex spoke, but I supported it financially. I watched it later on the internet. Alex was terrific. He's quickly becoming the face, and the leader, of our resistance."

Brian smiled. "When you speak, I hear just a trace of an

accent. To my unsophisticated ears, it sounds vaguely Caribbean."

"I was born in Jamaica. My parents brought my sister and me to New York when we were very young. We spoke Jamaican Patois—linguists call it Jamaican Creole—at home. I can still slip into that with fellow Jamaicans, but my American education has, I think, pretty much erased most of my accent in everyday conversation."

"The main reason I'm here," Brian said, "is that I wanted to thank you, in person, for what you did. If you hadn't come forward, I firmly believe that Larry would have shot me. It never occurred to me that he would have a gun. In retrospect though, he's just the kind of antigun hypocrite that I should have expected to be armed to the teeth. I did what I did in an effort to protect my daughter and her mother. I keep thinking, if you hadn't been there, my daughter would have grown up without a father. Thank you for preventing that from happening."

"We're fighting the same fight," St. John said. "I'm not a violent man. It's only recently that I've come to believe that I need to carry a gun. I hate that that's necessary, but what is the public supposed to do? The ranks of law enforcement are now so thinned that you can't reasonably expect help in anything approaching an emergency situation. What used to be the best areas of downtown, the heartbeat of the city's retail industry, are simply no longer safe. City government has abandoned the streets to criminals. And if there does happen to be a policeman around, he's hesitant to act, afraid that he's the one that is going to end up in jail if he has the temerity to interfere with a criminal who is merely exercising his God-given right to attack and rob anyone he pleases.

"There's a case out of Texas that I read about. The cops stopped this guy twice, and each time he just drove away. Finally, the guy drives into a dead-end street and finds himself boxed in. One of the cops gets out of his patrol car and suddenly finds himself about to be run over by the guy they've been chasing as he attempts to escape once again. The officer shoots the suspect and is charged with murder. His superiors say that he didn't follow proper procedure. He should have gotten out of the way and let the suspect escape for the third time. You never know what the facts truly show in cases like this, but the signal to criminals couldn't be clearer—resist arrest! Don't follow lawful police orders. The average citizen may not be aware of these new rules, but the bad guys certainly are.

"There was a recent incident in Seattle where police were pursuing a kidnapping suspect. He had the purported victim in his car. The suspect actually called 911, in the middle of the car chase, to complain that he was being pursued illegally and demanded that the pursuit be called off. Apparently, they've got these laws in Washington state that severely restrict who police can pursue. You can't make this stuff up.

"In Chicago, they've developed new rules restricting when police can pursue a suspect *on foot!* And, in New York City, the DA has told the bad guys not to worry, in most cases you won't even be charged for resisting arrest. The clear message to criminals is that they should disregard the police. They can drive away; they can run away; and, if they need to physically resist, that's okay, too. When you look at the terrible riots we've seen in this country over the last few years, virtually all have one thing in common, in the event that triggered the riot, the so-called victim resisted arrest. If he hadn't resisted arrest, there would have been no riot, the victim would still be alive, and there would be no question of wrongdoing by the police. So, one person resists arrest, and, as a result, dozens die, hundreds are injured, and billions of dollars' worth of property is destroyed, and what is the government's response? Pass laws that encourage resisting arrest.

"The man who killed my wife resisted arrest, repeatedly. That was just one more reason he should have been in jail instead of being drunk behind the wheel of a car. To me, this is a big problem with a simple solution. We need to start by teaching school children what we were taught—the police are there to help you, and you should do what they tell you to do. If people just followed that simple rule, think how much simpler life would be for all of us. Of course, the bad guys aren't going to comply, so they need to know that they will pay a very heavy price for resisting arrest—especially if they assault a police officer. Unfortunately, in our current upside-down society, everything is just the opposite. Children are purposely taught not to trust the police, and laws are passed to encourage resisting arrest. This causes disrespect for the law—and for the people in law enforcement—and leads to a breakdown in law and order. Sadly, this result is not an accident. The Left clearly sees civil disorder and the collapse of society as a stepping stone on the way to the achievement of their socialist paradise."

St. John smiled. "I'm sorry. I'm talking your ear off. I get a little carried away. I'm angry about losing my wife. I'm angry that I've been forced to carry a gun. And, I'm angry about what they're doing to this country.

"I've followed your battle with the school board, and I support your position unreservedly. That critical race theory they're feeding our children is nothing but rat poison, especially for minority children. The Left's socialist dream requires a permanent underclass, and minorities are the handiest initial target, so they teach them that they are oppressed and there's nothing they can do about it. They can't get ahead on their own, so they need to depend on their government overlords, their socialist saviors. It's a terrible, terrible thing, stealing children's dreams that way and deliberately leaving them hopeless.

"There was a great deal online about your lawsuit against the school board, but I had trouble finding anything regarding your issue with the district attorney and what happened to your daughter and former wife. All I know is what I overheard on the street the other night."

Brian told the story, from the beginning. "So, this guy who calls himself Jennifer is in jail for now, but being held only on the 'felon in possession of a firearm' charge, and the cops have told me that the DA doesn't consider that a very compelling allegation these days. I couldn't believe my ears. Then I saw on TV that terrible case in Los Angeles where a gangbanger, a convicted felon who should have been in jail for possession of a firearm, was released and took the opportunity to shoot and kill two police officers. Of course, the DA takes no responsibility for the officers' deaths."

"This is, for obvious reasons, another matter close to my heart," St. John said. "I'm no lawyer, but it feels like there's a crime there. There should be a way to hold these DAs accountable. To me, this is criminal negligence.

"I was looking through the legal statutes and came upon involuntary manslaughter. As I understand it, that is causing the death of a person through criminal negligence. There is no intent to cause death as would be required for a murder charge. The example that is frequently cited is an owner of a vicious dog who fails to properly restrain the dog, and the dog mauls and kills someone. Apparently, that's a classic example of involuntary manslaughter. There is no intent to kill, but the death results because of criminal negligence.

"Now, I understand that criminals aren't dogs that are owned by the DA, but the analogy seems pretty apt to me. Criminals tend to be recidivists. More often than not, they return to their life of crime. I'm not talking about someone who has served his time, paid his debt. I'm talking about people who have committed crimes, often serious felonies, that the DA chooses not to charge. And, I'm not talking about one guy they let go who then goes out and commits a crime. I'm talking about failing to charge people with such consistency that it creates a crime wave so severe that no one wants to live in the city anymore; a pattern so consistent and dependable that criminals do not expect to be charged. A prisoner in Los Angeles was recently recorded saying that he needed to hurry to make a deal with the prosecutor because he feared that the current soft-on-crime DA might soon be recalled, and the prisoner wanted to grab an easy deal while he could. Another LA convict was so enamored of the DA that he tattooed the DA's name on his forehead.

"How many people have to be murdered by people who should have been in jail before we can say that this negligence is criminal, that these DAs bear responsibility for these deaths? At some point, I think you can even make the case that this is not negligence, that these DAs know what they're doing. They would have to be profoundly stupid not to understand the crime they're causing, and no one is *that* stupid."

"And," Brian said, "when people understand that their government will not protect them, that criminals will not be punished, they feel they have no recourse but to take the law into their own hands. What a mess."

"We'll find a way out of this," St. John said. "We have to."

The two men agreed to stay in touch. There was much work to do.

"One last thing," Brian said, "if you don't mind. How did you happen to be there the other night, just when I needed you?"

"I've been keeping an eye on our friend Larry. Guys like him are dirty. They always are. I want to catch him. I have accountants researching his finances, and I have private detectives who watch him. Often, though, I feel the need to do the watching myself. There's a grim satisfaction in that. But I have to be careful. Sometimes, I feel a nearly overwhelming urge to give that evil little man the bullet he deserves."

28

It was a pleasant afternoon. The main terrace, shaded at this hour from the harsh summer sunlight, was a comfortable setting for the discussion of business affairs, the most pressing of which was the still unlaunched, unannounced American Revitalization Project. This selfless act of charity, Michaelson's heroic plan to rebuild the nation from its ashes, was destined to be the crowning glory of his philanthropic career. His name would surely be etched indelibly in the annals of the history of benevolence, and his altruism, his humanitarianism, celebrated around the globe as never before. But Michaelson's magnanimous project was on hold, awaiting that magical moment on which all of his philanthropic endeavors hinged, the moment of maximum profit.

The plan was simple. One final round of rioting would devastate the country and depress property values to an unprecedented nadir. Michaelson would then swoop in with his billions to rescue desperate owners who would scarcely believe their luck that someone was so foolish as to take their worthless properties off their hands. Next, the politicians would finally step in with oppressive measures to restore law and order—whatever it took. And then, at last, property values would begin to rise and Michaelson's investment would reap untold dividends.

The plan was simple, but so was the problem—no riots. Summer had fallen with unusual ferocity. The electrical grid had failed predictably. Brownouts abounded. The people were baking. Still, the scheduled rioting had not materialized. No inciting event had occurred. The firewood was dry, but the match was nowhere to be found. Politicians and the media were primed to loudly celebrate the highly anticipated event, but it had refused to appear.

"Why do you suppose," Michaelson asked, "that rioting has not erupted?"

It was a subject that Fielding had given considerable thought. "The people have been trained, and encouraged, to respond to anything that can be portrayed as unlawful police conduct. That's when they swing into action. I'm afraid that the handcuffing of the police has proved to be a bit of a double-edged sword. On the one hand, it has created lawlessness and civil disorder, just as was intended; on the other, it has alerted police to the increased risk they face. Those who have not quit the force have developed a more restrained attitude to the enforcement of the law. They have come to recognize that they face little hazard if they merely choose to observe criminal activity, whereas, if they attempt to arrest perpetrators and bring them to justice, they jeopardize their careers and risk severe legal consequences. And, for what? Unlike the police, criminals these days are unlikely to receive punishment that is in any way consonant with the crimes they commit. So why should the police make an arrest when the jeopardy is all on their side?

"Speaking for myself," Fielding said, "I now realize that I hadn't thought this thing quite through. I had expected that, as the crime 'wave accelerated, the police would continue to behave as they always have, protecting the public as best they could. But I've come to understand how unreasonable it was to expect them to act in a manner so obviously at odds with their own best interests."

George interrupted to announce that Dennis had arrived.

Michaelson examined his watch, then said that George might as well go ahead and bring Dennis on out to the terrace.

Dennis was wearing jeans, a black tee shirt, and heavy boots. Michaelson thought he looked like he had just got off a motorcycle—which he had.

"What have you found for us, Dennis?" Michaelson asked.

"First, I think I should tell you about an unusual request I had from Leonard Lutz," Dennis said. "He wanted me to provide him with a handgun."

Michaelson shook his head. "Well, that's easy. I'm sure you didn't give him one."

"Actually, I did."

"Good God! How could you be so stupid?"

"These days," Dennis said, "even a Leonard Lutz can get a gun, eventually, if he wants one badly enough. So, I assumed that, sooner or later, Leonard would be armed. Given that, I figured that it was best for me to provide the gun. That gives me an element of control—and, potentially, some insight. He trusts me. If he wants another gun, he comes to me. When he needs ammunition, he comes to me. That way, I may be able to get some idea of what he's up to. That could turn out to be useful to us."

"What does he want a gun for?"

"He claimed that he needed it for his own protection. That's plausible, given what's going on in the city. He said that it would be almost impossible, given current regulations, for him to legally acquire a handgun, and, even if he could, it would take forever."

"Fielding could have taken care of the red tape. We own lots of people at city hall. He could have gotten the gun legally—and quickly."

"He probably knew that, but that wasn't what he wanted. He asked me for a gun that was untraceable. An untraceable gun is, by definition, an illegal gun."

"Where," Michaelson asked, "do you find an untraceable gun?"

"You don't find one, you make one. You have to start with a clean gun, one that hasn't been used to commit a crime. That way you know that law enforcement hasn't recovered bullets fired from the gun and entered their unique markings into a database. The easiest way to be certain that the gun is clean is to buy one that is new and has never been fired. Then you drill out the serial numbers, and you're good to go."

"Which brings us back to the initial question," Michaelson said. "Why does he want the gun? Clearly, he has something nefarious in mind. We've been putting the screws to him financially, and he's probably smart enough to realize that we're the ones who are doing that to him, but surely he's not stupid enough to think he can get anywhere near us with a handgun."

Dennis became acutely aware of the small caliber pistol in his left boot and the sharply honed knife in his right boot.

"Maybe he's decided that it's time to end it all," Michaelson said.

"He wouldn't need an untraceable gun for that," Dennis said. "Probably wouldn't even bother with a gun if he was going to commit suicide. Whatever he's up to, my people are watching him closely. We'll find out."

"All that really matters," Michaelson said, "is that he doesn't do anything that comes back on us. That would be a disaster." Michaelson thought about that for a moment, then said, "Oh, well, I guess we'll just have to await events. What else have you got for us, Dennis?"

"I have the report you requested on Alexey Volkov."

"Alexey Volkov? Who the hell is that?"

"He now goes by the name Alexander Walker."

"Oh, my."

"He emigrated from the Soviet Union with his parents as a toddler. They adopted the family name Walker to better assimilate. The family went through the citizenship process, and all three became citizens while Alex Walker was still in grade school. There's not much consequential about the parents. He was a tailor. She a seamstress. They started with piecework and eventually owned their own small shop. Their main focus in life was their son. He was the pride of their life. Their goal was for him to become a successful, educated American. Both parents are now deceased.

"Alex Walker's brilliance was recognized at an early age. He attended the Bronx High School of Science and graduated at the top of his class. He received a full scholarship to Columbia University where he majored in biology with a focus on microbiology and genetics. He was the first author on several important papers while he was still an undergraduate. After Columbia he went to Harvard Medical School where he graduated first in his class. He trained in internal medicine at Massachusetts General and stayed at Harvard afterward to earn a PhD in genetics. The rest of his academic achievements, papers, faculty positions, and so forth are in my written report.

"While at Columbia, he met an exchange student named Irina Chernyak. She was a committed and active Marxist. They began a long-term relationship which culminated in marriage. They have one child, a daughter, the physician Victoria Townsend. Irina Chernyak went with Walker to Harvard. She was involved with every communist group in the Boston area. We could find no evidence of any employment. Alex Walker does not appear to have been politically active. Throughout his life, he has been a liberal Democrat, but never embraced socialism.

"While Walker was earning his PhD, Chernyak—who did

not change her name when they married—decided to return to Moscow. She abandoned her husband and daughter and never returned. Walker was devastated. Their marriage was never officially dissolved.

"Back in what is now Russia, Chernyak—ever the devout communist—seems never to have put a political foot wrong. She successfully climbed the ladder of Russian politics to her current position as a senior and very influential member of the State Duma. That's the…"

"We know what the Duma is," Michaelson said.

"Just one more thing," Dennis said, "that I think you'll find interesting. On January 4, 2021, two days before the events for which he was arrested, Alex Walker visited the Russian Embassy in Washington."

"Dennis," Michaelson said, "You're worth every penny we pay you." He thought for a moment. "Tell me, do you think that Alex Walker is up to some kind of hanky-panky with the Russians?"

"Absolutely not. My guess is, he misses his wife."

"Thank you, Dennis."

And, with that, Dennis understood that he had been dismissed.

"Well," Michaelson said, "I certainly think we have enough here to end any political aspirations that Alex Walker might be entertaining."

"You don't think," Fielding said, "that this might be a bridge just a bit too far. Do you think the American people are ready to swallow another Russia hoax this soon?"

"I didn't get where I am today by underestimating how gullible people are. They'll believe it because they *want* to believe it. They'll swallow it hook, line, and sinker and shout it from the rooftops. Politicians will campaign on the issue. They'll lure constituents to vote for their socialist paradise while they simultaneously scream warnings that the Republicans are controlled by the evil Russian communists— and voters, by the millions, will take the bait and not even blink at the contradiction.

"Let's feed the information to the reliable collaborating mainstream media and get hashtags going on social media. Really turn the bots loose on this one. We need a handful of influential congressmen and senators on board from the beginning. More will quickly follow. Be sure to feed it to those former CIA types that the lefty TV networks have hired. The left-wing ex-intelligence community will have a field day with this. Maybe they'll do another one of those letters that claim 'fifty former heads of U.S. intelligence agencies say Alex Walker's rise to prominence is a classic Russian disinformation operation.'

"This is going to be more fun than the last one!"

29

It was a bright, sunny day and Brian thought he probably had plenty of time to grab a sandwich before the press conference that Ida Silverstein had planned to let the world know what she had discovered in their lawsuit against the school board. It was good to get out of the office and stretch his legs. The transition to his own firm had gone well. He was busy, but still waiting for his previous firm to finally blow up so that Ted Bass would be free to join him and really get things under way.

Brian had taken all the necessary precautions for a stroll through the downtown area. He had his driver's license in one pocket—in case he needed to show identification for some reason—and, in another pocket, the small amount of cash required to buy lunch. His wallet, with all his credit cards and so forth, was safely tucked away in his desk back at the office. He followed the usual drill of walking purposefully, avoiding eye contact and verbal sparring with people who accosted him, and keeping a sharp lookout for hazardous waste that he didn't want to step on or in. He was making his way, lost in thought, when he happened to glance up and saw Hussein, the restaurant owner, sweeping up broken glass from the sidewalk in front of his cafe. Brian stopped and stared across the street at the destruction. Every window had been broken. The jaunty neon sign that proudly proclaimed Hussein's Café Americain had been badly battered and threatened to crash down at any moment. Brian crossed the street, waving at Hussein.

"Mr. Hussein, whatever happened?"

The café owner managed a little smile. "I had a party."

"That must have been some party."

"It was supposed to be nice, a community event. They called it 'Ice Cream with a Cop.' The idea was to get people to come downtown and show them that it was safe. Let the children meet some policemen and women so that they would see that they are nice people, to help them learn to trust the police. Parents brought their kids. There was ice cream, balloons.

"When they asked if they could use my place, I said, sure. I've got empty refrigerators, empty tables. I can take the plywood off my windows, open up again. Maybe this will be the start of something good.

"And at first it was fine. Everyone was having a good time. The children were laughing and playing, enjoying the ice cream. Suddenly, there was all this noise. Music blaring from loudspeakers. Then all these people showed up, probably a hundred or more. They looked like the rioters we see all the time. Some were dressed all in black and wearing the balaclava helmets. They were all screaming at us, profanity, saying terrible things about the police. They asked me, why am I helping these killers? I didn't know what they were talking about. They said I was a racist. How am I a racist? They even called me a white supremacist. Me, Hussein. They are screaming at me with a bullhorn in my face.

"They said I was spreading copaganda. Did you ever hear that word, copaganda? Apparently, if you say anything good about the police or help promote a positive image of them, you're guilty of spreading copaganda. That's why the protestors came. They don't want people to have a good impression of the police.

"So, the children are crying. The parents are terrified. These protestors are screaming at the police. They have their mouths next to the faces of the police and are spitting as they are yelling. Others have their phones out and are shooting video, hoping the police will react. The police are paralyzed, afraid to respond, but the rioters are already screaming about police brutality. Then they start throwing things. All my windows are broken. My sign is ruined. I guess it doesn't matter. I had a brief hope, but now I'm done. My restaurant is finished. At least no one was hurt. That's a good thing. The children got away safely."

"I'm so sorry, Mr. Hussein. You've worked so hard to build a life here. It's so unfair."

"I don't worry about me. I worry for my family. I worry for the country. If this continues, there will be no country. Where I came from, we had these people who could do whatever they wanted. They wandered around, terrorizing everyone. They could steal from you. They could beat you up. When people are allowed to do this, whether it's here or in my old country, it's because those in power want them to do it. The American government, the local government, could stop all of this crime and rioting in an instant, if they wanted to. They don't want to. They somehow believe that the chaos will benefit them, so they allow it. This is what I learned in my old country. When something bad happens— riots, looting, murders—and the government does nothing, it's because the government wants those things to happen. You may not understand why, but you know that the government is behind it. I thought I had left all of that behind me when I came here."

Hussein had been leaning on his push broom for support. He raised himself up and managed another small smile.

"I'm tired," he said. "Come in, if you have time. We'll have some ice cream. I still have lots of ice cream. I haven't figured out yet who to donate it to."

They went inside and Hussein produced large bowls of pistachio ice cream. It *was* really good ice cream. Except for shattered glass that had fallen into the restaurant, the inside was largely spared.

"What will you do, now?" Brian asked.

"I guess I'll put the plywood back up."

Brian started to say that he meant, what would Hussein do with his life. Then he realized that the man could still find humor in his situation.

"My brother says that I'm welcome on his farm. He'll find something for me to do. My wife and daughters are already there. But, I'm not a farmer, and I can't live off my brother. I have to find another way to support my family.

"How is *your* family?" Hussein asked, "Mrs. and the little princess?"

"They're fine," Brian said. In a way, that was the truth. No reason to burden Hussein with all that was going on in their lives. Brian worried about this man who had been forced to endure so much. Hussein managed to keep a brave face on, but what was going on behind the façade? It would be so easy for the man to slip into depression and despair.

"Are you finding things to keep your mind off all this, at least some of the time?" Brian asked.

"I still have my economics. No hope, anymore, of a university appointment, but I still allow myself to believe that something may turn up. So, I constantly update and revise my models. I now focus on the United States economy, which, in the past, was only in the background of my work."

"What areas interest you?"

"Oil and gas consumption has always been the heart of my work, but I model everything from industrial production to housing. It's all very intriguing right now because of the issue of inflation and the uncertainty of the Federal Reserve's response. It's interesting to look at the models and see how potential Fed decisions might affect various industries. Right now, for example, my housing model predicts only a slight dip in home prices unless interest rates increase very dramatically—much more than we've seen so far. On the other hand, if the administration gets its way, and the government prints even more trillions of new dollars, housing prices will soar."

"You know," Brian said, "I just can't believe there aren't companies out there who would be eager to employ someone like you. I know some corporate people. With your permission, I'd be happy to ask around, and see if I can find something."

"I would be grateful," Hussein said.

"It would be helpful if I had some information about your education, previous academic appointments, all that sort of thing, if you don't mind."

"It's all in my *curriculum vitae*. The *CV* also has all my contact information. Let me go in the back and get a copy for you."

Hussein returned with a printout that ran 75 pages. Brian glanced at the first page and saw that Hussein had a PhD from the London School of Economics.

"I can't promise anything," Brian said as they shook hands good-bye, "but I have a couple of ideas that I'm happy to look into."

"Thank you so much."

Brian left their impromptu meeting with a good feeling. He would be amazed if Lucius St. John didn't have a place in his corporation for a hard-working, immigrant, family man with Hussein's evident drive and ability, a man with the intellectual curiosity to maintain multiple economic models in his spare time while managing his faltering restaurant enterprise. Brian was already drafting the cover letter in his head as he walked away.

30

Ida Silverstein had insisted that a press conference was necessary to further their lawsuit. Brian was less certain, but he respected her expertise and had resolved from the beginning not to try to substitute his legal judgment for hers.

They had found a room of suitable size in a nearby hotel. Ida had arrived early to test the audio and video equipment and to talk to the security people she had hired. They were to be visible but not interactive unless things got out of hand. Ida's staff had contacted the press on rather short notice in an effort to prevent word of the press conference from spreading widely. It was not intended to be open to the public. The last thing they wanted was for protestors to show up and turn the whole thing into a circus. In the end, they had an audience of about thirty, a good mix of TV, radio, and print journalists. Several of the TV reporters had brought along camera crews. If the journalists reported fully and accurately what they were about to hear, the public would learn what Ida wanted them to know.

Ida was tall, slender, and, nearing sixty, still a beauty. She wore a dark blue dress that was serious without screaming "courtroom." She commanded everyone's attention the moment she walked to the front of the room. The audience fell immediately silent.

"Thank you for coming," she said. "My clients have filed this lawsuit, and we are here today, for one reason and one reason only. A first-grade teacher, Mrs. Judith Smith, denounced my clients' six-year-old daughter as a racist. The teacher did this without provocation and, of course, without any evidence to support such an outrageous accusation. There is no dispute about the facts of this case. In the first brief video clip that I will show you, you will see Mrs. Smith admitting that she called the child a racist. This video was recorded with Mrs. Smith's knowledge and consent. The other voice on the clip is that of Nina Bass, the world-renowned African-American artist, whose daughter is the lifelong best friend of my clients' daughter.

Ida played the clip with Nina speaking first.

"Jasmine said that you called out one girl in particular recently for being racist. Pointed right at her."

"The Townsend child, a classic case of white supremacy. Her parents are teaching her at home. How is that fair? A lot of families can't do that. We thought that doing away with homework would even things up, but some of these white families go ahead and teach at home anyway. These kids have math and reading skills way above grade level. They ought to make that against the law. I mean it."

Ida turned off the video. "So, Mrs. Smith admits that not only did she call the child a racist, she believes that she is, quoting her words exactly, 'a classic case of white supremacy.' She bases this on her suspicion that the child's parents have the audacity to help her with her studies at home. Now, I have no doubt that this kind of parental support greatly benefits a child. I wish all children were able to receive this type of assistance at home. While helping children with their homework may provide an advantage, it is certainly not racist. Ted and Nina Bass have said that they, like Brian and Victoria Townsend, are very involved in their daughter's schooling and work with her at home as much as they can. Does that make them racist? Should we label this African-American couple 'white supremacists?'

"Mrs. Smith's attitude is the expression of a hate-filled scam that has been given the name 'critical race theory' in order to make it sound harmless and intellectually sophisticated. But, make no mistake, critical race theory *is* racist to the bone. Fortunately, we have the assurance of school board president Edward Koontz that critical race theory is not taught in our school system.

"This next clip is from a recent school board meeting that was open to parents. It was a boisterous, contentious meeting because parents were irate about what was being done to their children. Not only were the children's heads being filled with racist nonsense, but also the school time eaten up by the teaching of critical race theory was stolen from the teaching of the basic subjects that the children were supposed to be studying. This short video has been edited so that you will see and hear a single question, asked by a student's mother, and the response of Mr. Koontz, the president of the school board."

Ida began the video.

"Mr. Koontz, we demand that the school system stop teaching critical race theory. Will you commit to that?"

"I cannot stop something, ma'am, that was never started. The school system does not teach critical race theory. It never has, and I can assure you that it never will."

Ida replayed the video to let it sink in.

"Now," Ida said, "I want to show you another portion of the recording of Nina Bass and Judith Smith. Again, this was recorded with the knowledge and consent of Mrs. Smith. The first voice you will hear is that of Mrs. Bass."

Ida began the video.

"So, why don't you just tell me, as best you can, how you're fighting the battle against racism."

"Well, it's not complicated. We want to turn these kids into anti-racist activists, but first they have to be decolonized.

You have to wash all that natural white supremacy and hatred right out of their brains. They don't even know it's there until you point it out to them."

"But they're so young. It must be very difficult."

"No. First grade, even kindergarten, is the best time. Their brains are really malleable. They're very subject to external influence. We just have to make sure that influence comes from us, not from their parents."

"Are you all alone in this, or are other teachers doing the same thing?"

"Everybody is *supposed* to be doing it. There are a few resisters, but they get a lot of pressure from the administration. There's a third-grade teacher who won't take part. I'm pretty confident that she won't be back next year."

"So, you are getting support from the administration."

"Oh yes. We've had formal training. They bring in outside people for lectures and special small-group sessions. One of the lecturers had a slide that really said it all. The slide said 'Burn Stuff Down.' Only it didn't say 'stuff' if you know what I mean.

"And that really gets to the meat of it. You have to burn all that crap out of these kids' minds and replace it with correct thinking. It's really similar to what they're doing downtown. You have to get rid of the old buildings, the statues, all of that false history and start over."

"In practice then, this is full-on critical race theory that you're teaching."

"Of course. We're not supposed to call it that, but absolutely it is."

"Do the children respond? How do you find the time?"

"They mostly respond. Once you get the hang of it, you can saturate almost everything you teach with anti-racist messages."

"And it doesn't get in the way of their other lessons?"

"Maybe, some, but you have to have priorities. This early age is the critical time to wash all that hatred out of their minds. They can pick up the reading and writing, the other basics, anytime. There's a new world order coming, and my job is to prepare these kids for it. It's not about being able to read and solve math problems, it's about social responsibility and racial equity. If a child can do the math but doesn't have the right answers when asked about social issues—which are much more important—then that child is not going to do well in my class or in the new world that's almost here. I'm not going to pass on to the next grade a white child who doesn't understand that he or she is a white supremacist."

Ida clicked off the video.

"We have gathered additional evidence from a number of other teachers and staff who confirm that critical race theory is not only taught throughout the school system, but that school administrators demand that it be taught and punish teachers who refuse. We have indisputable evidence that this is done with the full knowledge and support of the entire school board.

"Next, I'm going to show you a series of very brief video clips that are from the depositions of President Koontz and each of the other six members of the school board. In each case, you will hear me ask if critical race theory is being taught in the school, and you will hear full-throated denials by each and every one of the board members."

Ida played the tape.

"I want to remind you," Ida said, turning off the tape, "that these depositions were taken under oath. Each school board member, in turn, lied under oath. They were, of course, unaware of our evidence. Perhaps, they are so used to lying to the public and running the school system as though it were their own private fiefdom that they have lost any sense of obligation to parents and taxpayers. I wish that this was the most serious problem that was uncovered during the depositions. Unfortunately, it was not.

"I have one last series of video clips to show you. I promise that running the entire series will only take a couple of minutes. Each video shows a member of the school board being asked if he or she is a racist. In each and every case, the board member answers in the affirmative. Remember, all of the current school board members are white."

Ida played the last series of videos.

"I'm certain that these people will say that they are only asserting the primary tenet of critical race theory, that all white people are racist. They are white, therefore they are racist. I'm sorry. It doesn't work that way. If you search your heart and tell me, under oath, that you are racist, I believe you. I feel sorry for you. I am disgusted. But I have no choice but to believe you.

"If you call *me* a racist, I will call you a liar. I am not a racist. My clients are not racists. Their six-year-old daughter is not a racist. We are confronting, here, a sick political scam that has been carefully designed to advantage certain favored groups of people. It asks us to believe that all white people are racists from birth, a taint that they can never wash off. Everyone else gets a pass. This so-called theory is as silly as it is evil.

"We are demanding the immediate resignations of all current members of the school board. At this point in our investigation, we have two compelling reasons to require these resignations. One is that each board member has lied under oath. That cannot be tolerated. The second is that each board member is a self-acknowledged racist. We cannot allow such people to be in positions of responsibility in our community, especially with power over our children.

"It would not surprise me if these people attempt to squirm away from their admissions of racism. They may claim that they didn't mean it. They were only towing the critical race theory line to gain the approval of woke friends and colleagues. Inclusion in liberal circles requires obeisance to these woke theories.

"We have no intention of playing word games with these board members. If they now claim that they are not racist, then they have lied a second time under oath. Either way, they must resign.

"We have a printed handout for each of you. It reiterates the important points that have been made here today. In addition, there are DVDs that contain copies of all the video clips that I have shown you. I would be happy to take any questions."

The reporters seemed more intent on meeting their filing deadlines than asking questions, but one held up her hand.

"You're demanding resignations, but the evidence you've presented is from a single teacher who may be misinformed. You say that you have other evidence, but we haven't seen it. Do you really believe that the entire school board should resign based on what you've shown us today?"

"Let me make a couple of quick points," Ida said. "First of all, the school board members know the truth. *They* know that they have been caught lying. They know that it is only a matter of time until the truth is piled so high on top of them that they can barely breathe. I doubt that they'll want to hang around for that kind of total humiliation. My guess is that they will prefer to run and hide.

"Secondly, I would urge all of you reporters to get out there and investigate. The information that we've uncovered was not difficult to find. There are many teachers and administrators in the system who are eager to tell their stories. Search them out. Investigate."

The reporter appeared taken aback. Why on earth would it be her job to investigate? She tried another route of attack.

"What about unconscious bias? Critical race theorists argue that white people are so steeped in racism that they don't even recognize their bias."

"It's a very clever scam, isn't it?" Ida said. "The scam artists who promote it have been at this for a very long time. They've worked hard to cover all the bases so there's no way you can wiggle out of it. According to them, all that matters is the color of your skin. That's what makes critical race theory such an indisputably disgusting racist dogma. You don't have to have ever committed a racist act. You don't ever have to have had a racist thought. All that matters is that you are white. If you're white, you're racist. Case closed. It's original sin. And, if you are unable to see your own bias, that *proves* you're a racist.

"Unconscious bias is just something they thought up to strip you of any possible defense against the charge of racism. It's a way of controlling you. Once you accept that you have unconscious bias, people can accuse you of anything, and you have no way to defend yourself. You're a homophobe. You're a xenophobe. There's no limit to the number of unconscious crimes that you can be accused of. At the same time, your accuser claims to be bias-free. Do you suppose there's any chance that the people who peddle critical race theory might have a little bias of their own, unconscious or otherwise, or do you think they're just in it for the millions they make?"

The reporter didn't appear to have been convinced. She likely never would be. Perhaps she was one of those gullible Americans who had turned over access to their bank account to the wife of His Excellency Prince Abdullahi Abubakar, the imprisoned former finance minister of Nigeria. The wife just needed temporary access to the account so that she could deposit the billion dollars that her husband wanted her to immediately transfer out of Nigeria. For the use of the account, she would gladly pay a sum of $10 million to compensate for any inconvenience to the account holder. Meanwhile, could you please deposit $10,000 into the account of Mrs. Abdullahi Abubakar to cover the cost of transferring the money into your account?

Americans had lost many millions of dollars to various Nigerian email scams, but that was chicken feed compared to what the global critical race theory industry raked in.

31

Congressman Norman Sandstone was, Thomas Fielding believed, the most hated man in Washington. He certainly was the most obnoxious. Fielding had plenty of time to reflect on these thoughts while Sandstone kept him waiting, in the hallway outside the congressman's Capitol Hill office, while Sandstone hosted a parade of boy scouts, turkey farmers, and world-champion yodelers from his home district. Fielding had so far been kept waiting nearly two hours beyond the time of his scheduled appointment.

Sandstone's rudeness was, of course, not accidental, and it was particularly galling in light of the fact that the congressman had been bought and paid for, many times over. Michaelson had plucked him, a couple of decades ago, from a crowded field of equally unremarkable people who were running for Congress from an inconsequential, long-neglected district. It was Sandstone's personal qualities that set him apart and earned Michaelson's patronage. Sandstone was greedy, resolutely dishonest, and obscenely ambitious. He was in the race for money and glory. Politically, he was a blank slate. He spoke only in platitudes. Sandstone's first election was purchased for pocket change.

Over the years, Michaelson had funneled millions of dollars, directly and indirectly, into Sandstone's coffers. He had also provided numerous insider stock tips that had netted the congressman additional millions. When political winds began to blow unfavorably, Michaelson had designed and sponsored—behind the scenes, of course—several gerrymanders of Sandstone's district, rendering it one of the safest incumbencies in the nation. His position as congressman-for-life having been secured, Sandstone began to benefit from the magic of seniority. His route to power was characterized by two laudable achievements—staying alive and getting himself reelected.

Almost exactly two hours after Fielding's meeting with the congressman was supposed to have begun, one of his staffers emerged from his office.

"Mr. Fielding?" she asked.

Fielding nodded.

"The congressman asked me to check to see if you were still here. I'm sure he won't be much longer." And, with that, she disappeared.

With this latest insult, Fielding's slow burn threatened to flame out of control, but he managed to keep it in check. Sandstone wasn't the first politician he'd dealt with who had forgotten the true source of his power. A half-hour later, Fielding was still considering the proper retribution for Sandstone's insolence when his staffer reappeared.

"He can see you now, Mr. Fielding," she said, "but he asked me to warn you that it's a very busy day and he only has a couple of minutes. With all the demands being placed on him now, he's had to limit the amount of time that he can spend with lobbyists."

Sandstone's seniority and position had entitled him to one of the largest, most highly sought-after office suites that Congress had to offer. It was all leather and wood and thick carpeting. There was an unmistakable aura of power and rank. In the unlikely event that a visitor was not adequately impressed by all that, every inch of wall space was filled with citations, awards, and pictures of Sandstone grinning incessantly in the presence of all manner of important, readily recognizable world political figures, actors, sports stars, and assorted others.

"Thank you, Mr. Chairman," Fielding said, "for finding time to see me."

"It's a busy day, Tom. What's on your mind?"

The congressman had receding hair, dyed black. He wore an expensive charcoal suit, an expensive shirt and tie, and expensive shoes. He was tallish, fattish, and relentlessly obnoxious. No one—no one—called Thomas Fielding "Tom."

The staffer remained in the room. Sandstone knew better. Unbidden, Fielding took a seat in a comfortable leather chair, placed his briefcase on the floor, and waited. It was a standoff that Sandstone would not be allowed to win.

"Thank you, Beth," he said, finally, and the woman departed.

Having lost the battle, the congressman took refuge behind his desk and concentrated on the war.

"What?" he said.

"Do you know who Dr. Alex Walker is?" Fielding asked.

Sandstone considered the name. "Sounds familiar. One of the insurrectionists, I think. One of the January 6 traitors."

"He faced some charges, but they were dropped. Each and every one dismissed with prejudice. His arrest and trial made him a bit of a folk hero. When he was so unexpectedly freed, he immediately sprang into national prominence. It turns out, he's quite a natural speaker. The rabble love him. He's backed by a well-financed, well-organized group who are fomenting a new national political movement, which is, let's just say, unfriendly to our goals. Alex Walker is rapidly becoming the face of that movement."

"So?"

"So, Alex Walker is a Russian operative."

Sandstone instantly began shaking his head. "No, no, no!

We cannot go down that road again. Not while we're trying to somehow get through these January 6 hearings without ending up with egg all over our faces. Those damn hearings, we come up with someone who heard that somebody said that Donald Trump didn't eat his carrots, or, at the other extreme, that Trump tried to take over the controls of Air Force One and crash it into the Capitol to stop the counting of the electoral vote. The mainstream media are doing a remarkable job of making a silk purse out of that sow's ear, but it's really a tough sell, especially when we've now got a president who keeps falling down and has to be led off the stage by his wife. I don't see that we're making any headway on keeping Trump from getting elected in 2024. All we're doing is drawing ever more attention to the 2020 presidential election, and that's certainly the last thing we want to do. If we come up with another Russia hoax, with 80 percent of the voters saying the country is headed in the wrong direction, we're not going to get voted out of office, we're going to get laughed out of office."

Fielding waited patiently for Sandstone's anger to spend itself.

"This one's real," Fielding said. "We're not talking about alleged video—that no one has ever seen—of Trump cavorting with prostitutes. Alex Walker's real name is Alexey Volkov. He is married to a woman, Irina Chernyak, who is a senior member of the Russian Duma. We have documented that Walker visited the Russian Embassy just before January 6. This is serious, serious stuff."

Fielding opened his briefcase and pulled out an appropriately edited version of the report that Dennis had prepared for them. He stood and handed it to the congressman.

"This time," Fielding said, "there's a smoking gun."

Sandstone read through the report. "What do you expect

me to do with this?"

"We expect you to make it famous. We expect you to go before the cameras and denounce Alex Walker for the traitor that he is. We expect you to make certain that Walker is expelled from the national stage—permanently."

"Even if I accept everything it says here as true, and that's a big 'if,' there's still no 'there' there. Sure, it's awkward for Walker, but it's easy to see how there could be an innocent explanation for all of it. What if those innocent explanations are true?"

"We don't care about what's true," Fielding said. "You know that perfectly well. What we care about is what we can do with this while Walker and his group are protesting that they're innocent. Just look at what the Russia hoax accomplished. People still believe it even after they find out that Hillary Clinton's campaign paid for it, and that none of it ever happened. Half the country still thinks that Donald Trump is a Russian operative. That's a huge part of why he wasn't reelected."

Sandstone attempted to hand the report back to Fielding. "I won't do it. You can't expect the public to buy this crap. It could ruin me."

"We expect you to do this for us," Fielding said. "We believe that we have earned your cooperation."

"You mean you think you own me." Sandstone had turned bright red. He was yelling. "Well, you don't. I've served twelve terms in Congress and I'm the chairman of one of its most important and powerful committees. No one owns me. I work for the people of my district and the people of this country. It's time for you and Michaelson to get that through your fat heads."

The congressman picked up his phone. "Grace, what's next on my calendar?" He paused to consider whatever she said on the other end. "No, that's fine. I'm finished with Mr.

Fielding."

"We do hope that you'll reconsider," Fielding said as he left.

Sandstone sat behind his desk reveling in an intense sense of self-satisfaction. A major burden had been wrested from his shoulders. He was, at long last, free. He had been waiting for an opportunity to reorder his relationship with Michaelson and his crew, and, finally, he'd done it. No more tail wagging the dog. It was time they recognized who the big dog was now. He didn't mind working with them when it was convenient, but he was not going to be taking orders from Michaelson—not any longer.

The phone rang and broke his reverie.

"I have Leonard Lutz on the line," Beth said.

"What does that little twit want?"

"He didn't say—just that he needed to speak with you and that it's important."

"Oh, well, I might as well get it over with."

Lutz was not his usual, obsequious self.

"Good afternoon, Congressman. I'm calling to let you know that we're having to review our financial situation here at Toward a Fairer America. With the worst stock market in history and the economy being so rocky, our funding has reached a low ebb. We've concluded that we have no option other than to cut back on the financial support that we can provide to candidates, and I'm afraid that includes you."

This was not good news, but it wasn't the end of the world. Although elections could now cost many millions of dollars, these days prominent candidates were awash in donations from those who thought they could benefit from their election. Lutz's group had given Sandstone more than 2 million dollars in the last election cycle. That could be pared back a little without serious consequences.

"How much are you going to have to cut back?" Sandstone asked.

"All of it," Lutz said. "I'm afraid that, in the current election cycle, we're not going to be able to provide any funding whatsoever." There was a brief pause before Lutz said, "I'm sorry. I have an important call on another line. I have to go." And, with that, the phone went dead.

That was a blow. And the blows kept coming. Two more dark money groups called that afternoon to regret that they would not be able to provide the funding they had previously promised for the upcoming election. This was a disaster, but not one he couldn't survive. Times were tough. Opposition candidates would inevitably suffer similar constraints.

It had been a long day. There had been ups and downs, but there often were. Time to go home—not his home back in the district he represented, but his Washington home, in the rolling Virginia hills. The sky was cloudless. The sun was warm. And he had driven his pride and joy today, his 1967 Corvette Stingray convertible. He loved to get into that car, turn off his phone, put his cares in the rearview mirror, and just drive.

The Corvette was in mint condition. It had the rally red exterior and black leather interior. The V-8 cranked out 350 horsepower, and, with the four-speed manual transmission, could get from zero to sixty in 5.8 seconds. She was a beauty. He had always told people that there had only been one previous owner, and that had been a little old lady from Pasadena. Neither was true, and, as he aged, he began to think that the image of his taking over the wheel from that granny from Pasadena might not be quite what he was going for. Besides, in the song, granny had driven a super stock Dodge.

He could feel his worries evaporating as the elevator descended toward the parking garage. Most people would have considered his parking space one of the least desirable. It was a single slot, off in a corner, with concrete block walls on either side. It was inconvenient, but it protected his baby from dings, and that was all that mattered.

It used to matter. It didn't matter anymore.

Sandstone stared at his car in disbelief. It was sitting on its metal wheels. All the tires had been slashed. The windshield had been shattered. Every metal body panel had been bashed. The leather interior had been shredded. All the side windows had been broken. The soft top had been cut to pieces. The steering wheel was gone. The hood was up. Sandstone didn't know much about engines, but anyone could see that someone had cut a lot of the electrical wires.

He was startled by approaching footsteps. It was one of the security guards, waving at him.

"We just called your office, Congressman, as soon as we found this. One of the guys saw it on a routine drive-by. No one seems to have seen anything suspicious. Charlie has looked at all the video we have. He says it doesn't show anything. We just don't have any idea how this could have happened."

For the second time that day, Sandstone was red in the face and screaming.

"I demand an immediate investigation! It doesn't matter how much it costs or how much manpower is required. I demand to know who did this."

"Sure, we'll look into it," the guard said, "but there's only so much we can do. With all due respect, it's a vandalized car, not a murder. What do you expect us to do, call in the FBI?"

"That's exactly what I expect you to do. This happened on government property. The FBI has jurisdiction. If they can have hundreds of agents trying to figure out who put their feet on Nancy Pelosi's desk on January 6, they can sure as hell investigate this. I'm headed back to my office right now to call the FBI director himself, and he better jump on it."

Beth was still in the office when he got there. She was on the phone.

"It's your wife. She says she can't get you on your cell phone."

"I turned it off. Tell her you can't reach me."

"She says it's urgent."

"She always says it's urgent. Tell her I'm in a meeting with the president."

Sandstone went into his private office and slumped behind his desk. He hadn't been there thirty seconds before the phone rang.

"I really cannot talk to her now, Beth."

"It's not your wife. It's Thomas Fielding. He says it's important."

"*Him*, I'll talk to."

Fielding's tone was soft and respectful, almost contrite. "I'm just calling to offer my sincere best wishes," Fielding said. "We had kind of a tough meeting, and I feel especially bad about that in view of what happened later. I just wanted to offer our help if there's anything we can do."

"You destroy my car, and now you call to offer me, what, a ride home?" Sandstone was beside himself.

"Your car? What are you talking about?"

"My car was completely destroyed this afternoon in the parking garage. You're the only guys I know who could pull that off without anyone knowing, or at least willing to admit what they know."

"I don't know anything about your car. I was calling about your house in Virginia. I saw your wife on television. Haven't you heard?

"My house?" Sandstone's voice was a hoarse whisper.

"Totally consumed by fire. They suspect arson. Your wife and dog are fine. So, no damage that money can't solve."

"That house was filled with priceless antiques. They can't be replaced. And the house was a national historic landmark." Sandstone was devastated.

"I'm very sorry," Fielding said. "Let me know if there's anything at all that we can do to help. Oh, I was just thinking, I hope they didn't put anything in your gas tank. Guys who know what they're doing can put stuff in a gas tank that completely destroys an engine in just a few minutes. Wouldn't that be a shame."

32

The assault on Alexey Volkov, alias Alex Walker, was swift and brutal. Congressman Norman Sandstone led the charge. Sandstone was careful to make his attack in a speech from the floor of the House of Representatives so that his statements would be covered by the Constitution's convenient speech and debate clause. Under that protection, Sandstone had absolute immunity from any legal repercussions whatsoever, no matter how outrageously he lied or how slanderous his claims. He was free to say anything he wanted with no requirement that his words be tethered, even loosely, to reality. He found that gratifyingly liberating.

The leftwing cable channels played portions of the speech repeatedly throughout the day. The major networks excerpted Sandstone's words for the evening news. The small group gathered in Victoria's living room watched in silence.

"Intelligence sources tell me," Sandstone said, "that there can be no doubt that this man, Alexey Volkov, known to the world as Alex Walker, is an agent of Russia. Volkov has been skulking in America for decades, taking full advantage of our country's generosity, while patiently waiting for an opportunity to ambush the very nation that welcomed him so warmly. He is an American citizen, and this is treason.

"Volkov was a leader of the notorious January 6 Insurrection. Although charged for his crimes, he managed to escape conviction through a technicality. I am working with other members of the House and Senate to close the legal loophole that allowed him to escape justice and turned him loose once again on an unsuspecting nation.

"This man Volkov now heads a vile, white supremacist organization which seeks to overthrow our government. He spoke recently at a rally that this group held right here in Washington. He agitated the crowd to such a state that a massive police presence was necessary to prevent rioting and an attack on the Capitol and the White House many times more severe than the January 6 Insurrection. An outright coup was barely prevented. I personally called for the deployment of the National Guard and urged that regular troops be made ready. The survival of our nation hung in the balance.

"Today, I have spoken with both the attorney general and the director of the FBI and demanded a full investigation and consideration that Alexey Volkov be taken immediately into custody. I assure you that my committee will begin hearings on this threat as soon as possible. In the alternative, it might be advisable for the speaker of the house to institute a select committee in the nature of the January 6 Committee. I would be pleased to chair any such committee."

The news anchor said that her network had contacted both the Department of Justice and the FBI, but both had declined comment, citing ongoing investigations. An elderly former CIA director demonstrated no such reluctance.

"This is a classic Russian sleeper operation," he said. "Volkov's activities dovetail exactly with current Russian objectives. His goal is clearly to sow chaos and undermine the government of the United States.

"Given Volkov's role as the head of this very large, very active—and, I might add, unabashedly public—white supremacist organization, I am confident in declaring that this is the most significant and menacing Russian operation in American history. The fact that Volkov would enter the Russian Embassy openly and in broad daylight is particularly brazen and suggests that the Russians believe that this operation has progressed to a point at which America will be unable to prevent it from achieving its goals. The fact that this Volkov is a physician is particularly alarming. It raises the specter of a biological warfare aspect to the Russian scheme, especially in light of the world's ongoing struggle with COVID and the questions that has raised.

"I have spoken in the last 24 hours with numerous heads and former heads of intelligence agencies, both here and abroad, as well as with military leaders around the globe. I have never before heard such unanimity of opinion as to the serious nature of this threat and what it portends regarding Russia's intention to overthrow our democratic government. This is a pivotal moment in the life of our nation."

Victoria muted the TV. They had all seen enough. They'd been seeing pieces of this all day.

"I'm so sorry, Dad, that they're doing this to you, especially at such a difficult time."

"It's what they do," Alex said. "They have no souls."

"Clearly this is an all-hands-on-deck, all-out attack on you," Victoria said. "Are they going to arrest you again?"

Hamilton Hobart fielded the question. "I don't think they'll go down that road again. For now, their objective is to smear and harass Alex. They want to undermine his role as a leader. So far as we know, they only have a search warrant. If they had an arrest warrant, I would have been warned."

Hobart had contacts throughout the government, many adamantly opposed to the goals of the administration. Someone, either in the Department of Justice or FBI—Hobart was mum on his source—had tipped him that a search warrant would be served in a predawn raid at Alex Walker's home tomorrow morning. They had all assembled at

Victoria's for a final planning session, to make certain they'd thought of everything.

Hobart thought it best that Alex not be home at the time of the raid. They reviewed together very carefully just exactly what the FBI should be allowed to find. Hobart cautioned that removing too much from the home would alert the FBI that the raid was expected. So, Hobart suggested that the focus be on legal documents related to their claim against the government, and anything related to the budding protest organization that Alex had suddenly found himself leading. He also warned that there was a tendency for things to get broken or carted away and lost as a result of these raids. Whether this was deliberate abuse by design or merely sheer incompetence was difficult to know. At any rate, Alex should relocate anything of extreme sentimental value that he didn't want the government to "lose."

All told, there wasn't much that needed to be removed. Remarkably, Alex didn't have a computer in his home, but he made heavy use of his phone and there was much on it that the government had no business accessing. So, the phone was lost, meaning that the SIM card was removed and destroyed; the phone was wiped as one might do for resale; then it was hammered into pieces and the pieces broadcast over a wide area in a nearby lake. That was one lost phone.

Hobart had also taken precautions at his own office. The current administration was notorious for ignoring attorney-client privilege. It had no qualms about seizing privileged legal documents from the attorneys of its political opponents.

"Did you see that?" The crawl line running on the TV had caught Brian's eye. He grabbed the remote and clicked off the mute just in time to catch the end of the story.

"School board president Koontz cited only 'personal reasons' for his resignation. The two other board members made no statement. At this point, the resignation of the entire school board is widely expected."

"Finally," Brian said, "some good news. Maybe the tide is turning." His phone rang. It was Ida Silverstein. He went to the kitchen to take her call.

"This *is* good news," Hobart said. "The resignations will give Ida Silverstein enormous leverage. This should end the teaching of critical race theory nonsense in this city. Maybe other school boards will take notice." He thought for a second. "I've been meaning to ask, where is this Jennifer thing now? Is he still locked up?"

"I had a long interview with the prosecutors, going over everything that happened," Victoria said. "It was an unpleasant experience, but there was no way around it, I guess. And, of course, I'll have to testify when the time comes. The prosecutors said that the defense will undoubtedly want Tess to testify. They said that a favorite ploy of sexual predators is to act as their own attorney so that they can legally abuse and humiliate their victims in public on the witness stand. The prosecutors are pretty confident that no judge will force Tess to take the stand.

"They've added a charge of kidnapping, so, with any luck, Jennifer will go away for a long time. Meanwhile, he's demanding to be treated as female and be held in the women's jail. These guys really know how to game the system."

"Ida is pumped," Brian said, returning to the living room. "She thinks that the other dominos will fall pretty quickly, and then we'll be able to settle this thing. She views the resignations as just about as straightforward an admission of guilt as you're likely to find."

"Congratulations, Victoria and Brian," Hobart said rising to his feet. "Sometimes, the wheels of justice can move faster than we expect. Speaking of which, tomorrow's dawn is likely to come upon us faster than we expect. I think it's time for Alex and me to head for our 'undisclosed location.'"

Not even Victoria knew where her father would be hiding out for the next few days. Hobart thought that, if the authorities should ask, they should be able to honestly say that they had no idea.

As they were leaving, Hobart took both of Victoria's hands in his.

"I'm so sorry for your loss," he said.

"Thank you."

Hamilton Hobart arrived, deliberately, after the search was well under way. Several news crews had arrived well ahead of Hobart. He expected them to be there because his operatives had informed several outlets about what was to take place. Law enforcement usually told at least one TV station what was about to happen. The FBI liked to serve the warrant, then handcuff the homeowner for a few hours while they conducted their search. Putting the object of their search on TV in handcuffs insured maximum humiliation. Hobart wanted the news people there for his own purposes and didn't want to find out, after it was too late, that this was the first time in history that the authorities hadn't tipped them off. Since both local police and the FBI were involved in the search, either could have tipped off the media. If the FBI hadn't, they'd assume the locals had, and vice versa. This would never come back on Hobart.

There was one freelance camera crew in the crowd. They worked for Dennis. Hobart wanted his own record of what went on, so he didn't have to depend on the news outlets for footage.

Hobart identified himself to a policeman and demanded to see the search warrant. He was eventually led to the FBI agent in charge of the operation, who turned out to be a man Hobart knew.

"Well, well, John, this is a surprise," Hobart said. "What are you doing so far from Washington? Something you don't want the local guys to know about?"

"Just doing my job, Ham. Here's your warrant."

Hobart studied the document. "This is pretty comprehensive, John. I think your warrant covers nearly everything but the silverware. Must have been an oversight. Mind telling me what this is all about?"

"I'm not free to discuss anything. Where's your client?"

"He said he wanted a few days away. He's tired of all this harassment."

"We need his cell phone. It's covered by the warrant. Give him a call."

"That's the thing. He told me that I couldn't call him while he's away because he lost his phone. He said he kind of likes that it's not ringing all the time. He said that he wasn't going to bother to replace it until he got back."

The agent eyed him suspiciously, but didn't comment.

"You go ahead and do what you have to do, John. I'll be right over there talking to the press. I'll be telling them why you're really here and how much this is likely to cost the government."

The press was getting bored watching law enforcement agents walking out of the house with bags of "evidence" and welcomed Hobart's offer to explain what was going on.

"My name is Hamilton Hobart," he said. "I am Dr. Alex Walker's attorney. I came to be his attorney because of the government's harassment of my client, which clearly continues today.

"You are probably aware that the government maliciously prosecuted Dr. Walker because he happened to be on the grounds of the Capitol on January 6. They threw him in jail and denied bail. When Dr. Walker finally received his day in court, the government was unable to provide any evidence whatsoever that he had committed any crimes. Indeed, we have evidence that the government filed charges that they knew were false.

"Why would they do that? Because Dr. Walker has political views that are different from those of the current administration. This administration has demonstrated a clear pattern of using the FBI and the Department of Justice to attack its political enemies. This must stop.

"For its previous malicious prosecution of my client, Dr. Walker has filed a claim against the government seeking compensation in the amount of $90 million. Because the Department of Justice has failed to negotiate fairly to satisfy this claim, I am announcing that today I am filing a lawsuit for that malicious prosecution as well as other crimes against Dr. Walker. We will present incontrovertible evidence, including video taken on January 6, of government misconduct and false statements. Dr. Walker looks forward, once again, to his day in court, and another moment of complete vindication.

"Having failed so abjectly in its first attempt to ensnare my client with a pack of lies, the government has now embarked on a second effort to do so. They have taken a handful of well-known facts from Dr. Walker's life and attempted to weave them into something sinister. Let me set the record straight.

"Like many proud Americans, Dr. Walker began his life in another country. In my client's case, that country was the former Soviet Union. His family did not actually emigrate from the Soviet Union, they escaped. His parents brought Alex here for a singular purpose. They wanted their son to become an American. As evidence of that goal, the family changed its name from Volkov to Walker. This change did not serve some dark purpose. It was to make it easier for their son to be assimilated into American culture.

"Alex was a scholar. He attended Columbia University. It was there that he met the love of his life, Irina Chernyak, who was an exchange student from the Soviet Union. They were married and had a daughter, Victoria. Dr. Walker's politics, at that time, would best be described as liberal and very mainstream, in the mode of Franklin Roosevelt. Irina Chernyak had an entirely different world view. The fires of Marxism burned within her. In the end, that political philosophy became the driving force, the most important thing in her life—more important than her husband, more important than her daughter. She abandoned her family four decades ago, never to see them again. She has had a long political career in what is now Russia. Dr. Walker, of course, remained in the United States to pursue what was to become a storied career in academic medicine. His contributions to the fields of genetics and microbiology are well-documented and far too numerous for me to try to list. The clinic that he established in this city to provide medical care for the disadvantaged has served as a model for countless similar facilities all over the country. Alex and Irina's daughter, Victoria, also chose a career in academic medicine and has made her own contributions in the field of infectious disease.

"Although separated all these years, Alex and Irina were never divorced. Neither ever remarried. In late 2020, Alex learned that Irina was ill. She was in the midst of what was to be a long battle with cancer. Alex wanted to see her again. Perhaps, as a physician, he could even help her. Maybe she could be persuaded to come to the United States for medical care.

"He applied for a visa to enter Russia. On January 4, 2021, he was interviewed at the Russian embassy in Washington, D.C. in connection with that request. A few days later, Dr. Walker's visa application was denied.

"The final chapter of this story has just concluded. Irina

Chernyak has lost her battle. She passed away yesterday morning in Moscow.

"In this time of immense personal grief, Dr. Walker's enemies have once again launched a scurrilous attack for no other reason than that his political views are opposed to theirs. They have come in darkness to invade the humble home in which he has so quietly lived for more than thirty years, in vain hope that they might discover some new loose thread to weave into their tapestry of lies.

"Shame on them. Shame on them."

33

Two cops, bored as hell near the end of a long shift on a warm summer night. Things were quiet for once. That didn't happen much anymore, not with the chronic understaffing of the police department that the woke city government promoted.

They'd just stopped for coffee—again. No doughnuts this time. You had to watch the doughnuts. Greg Powell, the older of the two men, was coming up on 20 years on the job. Mitch Baker was ten years in. They'd been partners for a couple of years, but that was probably about to end. The department tried not to have two white guys working together if they could help it. In theory, that protected the officers and improved community relations. Maybe.

For now, the number of cops on the street was at an all-time low, and the latest recruiting class was only about half full—and some of those wouldn't make it through the rigors of the academy. Powell and Baker would be together until the new class graduated, then they'd probably be paired with rookies. That was always a crapshoot. You never knew how a rookie would react under pressure. The good ones understood that they had a lot to learn and carefully followed the lead of the senior officer. The bad ones thought they'd learned everything they needed to know at the academy. The worst situation, an aggressive rookie. Things could get ugly in a hurry.

"Jenny's dating a black kid," Greg said. Jenny was his

daughter from his first marriage. Baker and Powell had both been divorced. Powell had made the roundtrip twice.

"You good with that?"

"Sure. He's a great kid, a year ahead of Jenny in school. Serious. Good student. Headed to college. Good family. They study together, almost every night. I was suspicious. I know what happened when I was that age and 'studied' with a girl, but they really study. Jenny's grades are up. She's interested in school for the first time. Maybe *she'll* go to college.

"My big worry is that they're so young. I don't want them to get too serious, if you know what I mean, like what happened with Holly and me. I'm not sorry about Jenny. She's the most important thing in my life, the best thing that ever happened to me, but my marriage with Holly never had a chance. We were just too young. We didn't have a clue how to solve the kinds of problems that come up in any marriage—not that I did a whole lot better with Mary, but that was an entirely different situation."

A radio call came in of a 911 report of a bunch of gangbangers in an alley threatening residents. The caller told the dispatcher they were armed.

Baker hit the flashers. No siren. In the old days, multiple units would have responded to this kind of call—more units, less trouble. The theory was "overwhelming force." It worked. These days, though, in the era of "defund the police," citizens were lucky if the department even had one car available to send. Backup was out of the question.

Baker eased the squad car into the alley and saw six or seven figures, closely huddled together, about halfway down. This was where you had to be careful. You needed to take control of the situation without making anybody jumpy. They would be on drugs, that was a given. The most likely scenario, when the cops got out of the car, they would take off in half a dozen different directions. That would be the end of it.

The squad car rolled to a stop when they reached a point where the group was bathed in their headlights. They were crowded together in a way that hid most of them. The cops could only see the nearest two or three distinctly. The gangbangers were all looking down with their hoodies obscuring their faces. The way they slouched, you couldn't tell much about how big they were.

Powell and Baker got out slowly on either side and stood behind their doors. Baker got on the speaker for effect.

"Okay, we need to see everybody's hands. Get those hands up. Spread out so we can see all of you."

There was some movement. It looked like they were going to comply, then two shots rang out.

Powell felt the bullets whiz by his head and strike the wooden garage behind him. The bangers scattered, exposing the guy with the gun—which was pointed directly at Powell. Both officers fired. The gunman went down. The others started to run.

Baker yelled at them. "Stop or I'll shoot!" which, of course, he wouldn't have done. But they stopped.

"Everybody on the ground! Now! Keep your hands where we can see them!" Powell advanced deliberately as he gave the commands. He covered the group with his pistol while Baker searched them and handcuffed them with zip ties.

They were just kids. One had a pocket knife. No other weapons were found. The officers called for an ambulance and reported the shooting.

The kid they'd shot didn't look more than sixteen. Powell hoped he was at least sixteen. It went through his mind, same age as Jenny.

They'd hit him twice. One shot had struck him in the chest, the other in the upper abdomen. He was breathing. The bleeding didn't look too bad, but you never knew what was going on inside. It looked like he was moving his arms and legs a little, so, no paralysis at this point. Nothing to do but wait for the ambulance. Sirens could be heard, not too far off.

Powel picked up the gun, carefully. It was an old snub-nosed .38. He sniffed the barrel, then shook his head at Baker. The gun hadn't been fired.

Baker started yelling again. "Who's the guy who got away—the one with the other gun?"

Nothing from the bangers on the ground.

"It will go a whole lot easier for you guys," Baker said, "if you come clean and tell us who the shooter was."

Finally, one kid spoke up. He looked to be about eighteen, probably the oldest in the group. "Weren't nobody else," he said. "Weren't no other gun."

Probably, Baker thought, it was their leader who got away. He looked out for himself and left the others to fend for themselves. The kids he left behind were too afraid of him to give him up, knowing what would happen to them if they did. The gang squad will probably know who the boss was off the top of their heads. They pretty much knew all these guys, all the leaders, anyway.

The ambulance arrived and the medics went to work. They started IVs and compressed the wounds. They said it looked like it would be touch-and-go. They couldn't promise anything.

Bob McDaniel, the supervising sergeant arrived just behind the ambulance. Powell and Baker gave him a quick overview of what had happened.

"Sounds like a good shoot," McDaniel said. "Wish the shooter hadn't gotten away, but we'll figure out who he is. If we had the body cameras we've been asking for, there wouldn't be any question about what happened. The mayor says we can't afford them right now. I think it's more likely that, after screaming for so long that the cops had to wear the cameras so the administration could see what we were up to, they've now decided that they'd rather not have the facts—so they can blame us for anything that goes sideways. Your dashcam may have caught something. We might still get lucky.

"We'll throw a wide net around here, see if there's a gun in the bushes. One of these guys on the ground may yet turn out to be the shooter. The techs will check their hands for residue."

"Do you know who called 911?" Powell asked.

McDaniel shook his head. "Wouldn't give a name. We'll run down the phone number, see what we can find out.

"Meanwhile, your car stays here. Someone will give you a lift back to the precinct. You'll need to talk to the shooting team. You know the drill."

Time was running out for Leonard Lutz. The walls were closing in. If something didn't happen soon, he was finished.

Lutz made good money at the Toward a Fairer America Project. He maintained an expensive lifestyle, but, prior to organizing his real estate investment group, he was breaking even most months, tiding himself over with his credit cards if he came up short. But he'd had to borrow to come up with his share of the principal for the investment group, and that had sunk him. And that wasn't the worst of it.

His investors were about to bolt because the long-promised riot season had not materialized. Lutz was massaging them as best he could, while, at the same time, doing his best to prevent their discovering his altered financial circumstances. He used to meet them at fancy restaurants, showing up in his Porsche. That reassured them; made them feel like he was one of them. He couldn't very well now say, let's go to McDonald's, and arrive in a 2013 Mitsubishi Mirage.

So, Leonard was on the streets now, most nights, carrying his gun, searching. He had a pretty good idea what he was looking for, but, night after night, week after week, he hadn't found it. He had come close a couple of times, but had never quite been able to convince himself to pull the trigger.

He was learning how to survive on the streets, after midnight, on the wrong side of town. He was less afraid now. The gun gave him confidence. He had shown it a few times, when he was threatened, but hadn't been forced to use it. He had learned to walk purposefully, confidently, sending the message that *he* was the one to watch out for. *He* was the one to be feared. You think you're tough, bad guy, but you don't want any part of Leonard Lutz.

This new night wasn't the night of Leonard's previous experience, the old nights of upscale bars and high-toned restaurants and hookups with classy girls. This was the night of mostly empty streets and roving gangs and prostitutes and drug dealers. Leonard liked this new night. He was quickly becoming a part of it.

He walked in the shadows, almost exclusively in predominantly black neighborhoods, and around their edges, seeking just the right opportunity. Tonight, he finally found it.

Lutz heard voices, down the alley, as he walked past. He turned and made his way cautiously toward what turned out to be a group of stoned black kids completely oblivious to anything but themselves.

Lutz backed up to be certain he was out of earshot, then made the 911 call on his burner phone.

"There's a bunch of gangbangers, heavily armed, threatening anyone who comes near them. My neighbor says they pointed a gun at her and threatened to kill her. Right now, they're in the alley behind my house." He gave them the streets at either end of the alley and hung up. Now, all he had to do was wait.

Lutz had no problem positioning himself close to the stoned kids. They had absolutely no awareness or interest in their surroundings.

Lutz saw the squad car turn into the alley and slowly advance. He saw the car stop and the cops get out on either side. He heard the cop tell the kids to raise their hands.

That's when Leonard fired, careful not to hit anyone, positioned to be out of the way of any return fire. As soon as the cops fired their weapons, Leonard slipped away, back into the night.

Mack Smith saw the whole thing. He worked for Dennis, and it was his night to babysit Lutz. They had been doing this for weeks, trying to figure out what Lutz was up to. They watched him walk the streets, night after night, looking like he was going someplace but never getting there. Mack's bet was that Lutz had simply gone off the deep end. The best explanation for why someone was acting crazy was that they were crazy. In Mack's mind, Leonard's behavior tonight had pretty much confirmed the diagnosis.

Mack had lost direct sight of Lutz in the darkness. He had no idea that Lutz had pulled his gun until he fired it. Mack decided that Lutz was going for a thrill kill. His target must have been a cop, otherwise why would he wait to shoot until the cops arrived? Leonard had missed, and created a god-awful mess, but that wasn't Mack's problem.

Mack's assignment couldn't be more straightforward— follow Lutz and report back what he saw. He would let Dennis know in the morning.

34

Leonard Lutz waited until the first news reports were out to call Michaelson. Lutz had to be careful not to know more than had been publicly reported.

"I think this could be an important one," he told Michaelson. "Fifteen-year-old Deshawn Jackson gunned down by two white cops and now lying near death in an ICU. Good kid. No history of interaction with law enforcement. People around the district attorney are convinced that, when the kid dies, they'll be filing murder charges."

"Will he die today?" Michaelson, ever the pragmatist.

"All I know is what I saw on TV. He's on life support. He's a Catholic kid. They said he'd received last rites."

Michaelson said he'd look into it, then turned to Fielding who'd been listening on the speaker.

"See what you can find out. We can't risk backing the wrong horse. I don't want to get involved with some kid who's going to be hanging on in the hospital for months and months. We need imminent death, or, at the very least, irreversible coma. And the kid needs to have a reasonably clean police record. We can't rely on Leonard's assertions."

A few hours later, with Fielding's report in hand, Michaelson called Lutz back.

"Deshawn Jackson is a go. It's all hands on deck. Get your people on it. Let Reverend Small know that Toward a Fairer America will financially support his involvement."

"I understand," Lutz said, "that Lamont Jones is already

meeting with the family. He'll probably have a legal representation agreement signed by the family before the day is out."

"Lawyer Jones travels fast. Someone must have provided him some inside information."

Lutz didn't say anything.

"You've done good work here, Leonard. If it all turns out the way we expect, there will be a significant bonus for you."

You bet there'll be a big bonus, Leonard thought, but I'm taking care of that on my own. And there's going to be some big-time payback coming your way, as soon as I figure out the best way to screw you over.

But what Leonard said out loud was, "Thank you, Mr. Michaelson."

Michaelson disconnected the line, then turned to Fielding. "I believe that Leonard has learned his lesson. Maybe we should ease the pressure a little. We could see to it that he gets his Porsche back, for example."

"My advice would be to wait," Fielding said, "to see what happens with that spoiled group of investment brats he's assembled. They haven't completely folded yet. If it looks like they're starting to get active, we can always reveal Leonard's current financial straits. That should give them pause about following his investment advice."

Lamont Jones was a man of many appetites, the most obvious of which was food. Jones was a tall man, but not tall enough to support 300 pounds. His specialty was suing liberal city governments for the alleged racially motivated crimes of their employees, particularly their police officers. The magic of this kind of lawsuit, the inner beauty that attracted an attorney like Lamont Jones, was that the city's liberal administration could generally be depended on to share Jones' view that white police officers were racist bastards who deserved to be incarcerated. The facts didn't matter a great deal because the case would never see the inside of a courtroom. Both sides were eager to settle as soon as possible.

The general rule is that criminal trials have priority over civil trials. If you want to sue someone, you have to wait until any related criminal charges are resolved. That wait could easily be a matter of years. Importantly though, the rule applies to *trials*. A *settlement* can occur at any time and does not have to await the annoying and often cumbersome process of fact finding. Indeed, an important aim of this kind of settlement is to avoid the discovery of inconvenient facts that might disrupt the liberal narrative of the events in question.

From the point of view of the city fathers—and mothers— there is no better way to signal virtue than to agree to a quick and generous settlement of any claim of racist acts by white government employees. The higher the settlement, the greater the virtue. Cost is not an issue. After all, it isn't their money. Additionally—from the perspective of city administrators who immediately take it for granted that their racist employees must be guilty as charged—the big-dollar, rapid settlement has the added benefit of influencing public opinion, not to mention poisoning the jury pool. Thus poisoned, the subsequent criminal verdict can be expected to confirm their good judgment in agreeing to a quick and generous settlement.

This was the fertile ground on which Lamont Jones harvested many millions of dollars each year. However, since he was not the only astute legal scholar to have discovered this vein of gold, speed was essential. Jones employed individuals whose only responsibility was to scour TV, radio, internet, newspapers—any potential source—for evidence of a crime that needed righting. In additional furtherance of his pursuit of justice, Jones owned a private jet. He could arrive at the scene of injustice within hours, leaving his less nimble competitors frustrated and empty-handed.

There was, however, one tragic roadblock on the road to Lawyer Jones' next mammoth payday—the incumbent victim, Deshawn Jackson, was still alive. On the one hand, the attorney needed to act quickly while emotions were running high, on the other hand, for now, he was unable to scream, "Murder!" A deceased victim brought incalculable advantages, not only to the negotiating table but also in instigating public outrage. A gravely injured child, lingering in the hospital, did not stir the same emotions. Even dead children were forgotten quickly. Injured children were forgotten immediately.

Deshawn's mother, Desiree Jackson, turned out to be a hard sell. If it hadn't been for her fiancé, Marvin Snopes, Lamont Jones would not have even been able to pry her away from her son's beside in the ICU to speak with him.

"I don't care about money," Desiree said. "All I want is to take my baby home." She was inconsolable.

"Now, Desiree," Marvin said, "Deshawn is in God's hands now. If he does pass, there's going to be a lot of heavy expenses. You want him to have a nice funeral, I know. We can't afford that. And you got three other mouths to feed, still at home. It's not just about Deshawn. Let Mr. Jones help you out. Come on, baby."

It wasn't so much that Desiree was convinced, it was more that her disconsolate grief deprived her of any ability to resist. She signed the papers that Jones put in front of her and reluctantly agreed to attend the press conference that Jones was planning for that afternoon.

It was fine weather for an open-air press conference on the courthouse steps. Desiree came, barely able to stand in her anguish. Marvin was there. Jones talked Desiree into bringing her oldest daughter, but not even Marvin could convince her to bring her two youngest. "They're too young," Desiree had said. "They'd be afraid." No, the two youngest would stay with her sister.

Desiree didn't even know most of the folks assembled on the steps. Dignitaries, Jones had said. Many spoke to Desiree, expressing their condolences. More than once, Desiree had to say, no, DeShawn didn't pass. I'm hoping to take him home.

Jones assembled them on the steps, three-deep, in a semicircle. It looked like they were a church choir, and he was the choirmaster. At the last minute, a man came up behind Desiree and insinuated himself between her and Marvin, putting his arm around her waist. He was a short, heavy-set black man of about sixty. Desiree had no idea who he was. She assumed he was one of Lamont Jones' people. Whoever he was, he had a lot of nerve. She was later to discover that he was the Reverend Samson Small. She'd seen him on the TV. He looked different in person. Smaller.

Reverend Small flew first class, but he didn't have a private jet—which was why he barely made it to the press conference. He'd looked into it, but owning his own jet was a heavy lift, even for a man of Small's wealth. Buying a jet would also be certain to attract the attention of the IRS, depending, of course, on which political party was in power. They'd want to know where all that money came from. Small didn't want to open that can of worms. He had had some difficulties over the years—with both the IRS and some state revenue agencies—reconciling, to their satisfaction, his extravagant lifestyle and his declared income. And there were a couple of side hustles—the word *scam* had been used by certain racist media—that had drawn some negative attention. His investments in racehorses and a riverboat casino operation had received especially harsh criticism. But

when he got in trouble, he always had his ace in the hole—
racism. Call your detractors racists, scream it loud enough
and long enough, and sooner or later they back down.

Still, owning your own jet, that would be pretty sweet.

Small kept his assets distributed, so to speak—not too
much in one place and moving them around like he was
running a three-card monte. He made good money, just not
anything like Lamont Jones pulled in. Small had a number of
dependable sources of income. Patrons like Adam
Michaelson had bottomless pockets and didn't care how
much it cost to get what they wanted. Small was a contributor
on a bunch of the liberal TV networks, and that paid well. He
no longer had a church and congregation to hold him back.
He'd tried that for a while but soon realized that was a loser's
game. He did have a sort of virtual church, The Holy Rock of
Jesus, which was a website where the public could donate
funds to support his good work. Over the years, he'd
launched an array of racial justice groups and political action
committees, some of which had been quite profitable.

He'd tried the LGBTQ+ community a couple of times, but
that had turned out to be a bust. For one thing, the entry-level
requirement was that you had to agree that men could get
pregnant. Small had a lot of trouble saying that with a
straight face. For the longest time, he couldn't figure out how
that scam worked, then one day it hit him. If you call a
woman a man, then a man can get pregnant. He had thought
that there was some complicated biology involved, but, no, it
was just a word game. Old Abe Lincoln had a favorite riddle
that Small had been taught in grade school. How many legs
does a dog have if you call a tail a leg? Most of the kids said
five. No, the teacher said. The correct answer is four. Calling
a tail a leg doesn't make it one.

The Reverend Small took a sideways glance at the woman
he had his arm around, the soon-to-be-bereaved Desiree

Jackson. She was pretty cute. The reverend thought he might have to schedule her for some private counseling. He gave her waist a little squeeze.

Desiree was trying to decide just how hard to elbow this guy who had his arm around her when Lamont Jones began to speak.

"Friends, I am Lamont Jones. I represent the family of Deshawn Jackson, a fifteen-year-old black boy, gunned down by white police officers. Deshawn lies in his bed in the ICU in County Hospital, barely clinging to life, while those two white police officers still enjoy their freedom. They haven't even been charged!"

The crowd, mirroring Jones' outrage, began to chant, Justice for Deshawn! Justice for Deshawn!

Jones held up his hand, and the crowd immediately fell silent. "If there is one consoling note in this tragic, tragic event, it is that Deshawn, a devout Catholic, has been able to receive last rites before he passes."

Desiree looked around Reverend Small to catch Marvin's eye. The doctor had told her, not an hour ago, that Deshawn's condition had stabilized. He said her son's chances were improving. Did the lawyer know something that the doctor hadn't told her?

"Marvin," Desiree said in a voice that she hoped wasn't loud enough for Jones to hear, "What's going on? I thought Deshawn was better."

Marvin, a big man, stepped in front of Reverend Small and engaged him with what Marvin liked to call his baleful stare, looking down at the reverend with his face only a few inches from Small's. Marvin didn't move until Small relinquished his grasp on Desiree and moved over.

"It's okay, baby," Marvin said. "The man's just making a speech. There's bound to be some exaggerating, you know, the way they always do. He's doing it all for Deshawn."

Desiree did not appear convinced.

While Marvin was reassuring Desiree, Lamont Jones had gone on about the wave of police brutality that gripped America, describing previous incidents in great detail and with considerable indignation and outrage. A wave of brutality, Jones said, that this racist country did not care about and did nothing to stop.

As his moment approached, the Reverend Small searched the crowd for familiar faces. He recognized a few. They had done a pretty good job of turning out reliable protest groups on such short notice. More would flood in from around the country. This spot would become ground zero.

Jones introduced Deshawn's family, including Desiree's fiancé who was like a father to Deshawn. Then, Jones made his concluding remarks.

"I will have much more to say in the days to come. Of course, the family brought me in because of the obvious legal implications of the racist atrocity committed by these officers, but it is much too early to talk about legal consequences. For now, we must focus our thoughts and prayers on Deshawn, as he lies near death, cut down in his prime. Please, friends, pray for Deshawn's soul."

With that, Lamont Jones stepped solemnly back and began to console Desiree, and the Reverend Small barged to the fore.

The crowd had once again picked up the "Justice for Deshawn" chant, but Small wanted to move them in the direction of more general condemnation.

Small began the "No Justice, No Peace" chant, and the crowd quickly followed his lead. Then Small and Jones joined hands and began to lead the crowd down the street in the direction of the Third Precinct, the precinct to which Mitch Baker and Greg Powell were assigned. Desiree Jackson was left behind in grief and bewilderment.

The riots that followed were the worst that America had ever seen.

35

Some politicians on the extreme left openly supported the riots, many professing that the long hoped-for revolution had finally arrived. America, they said, was at long last done with the capitalist ruling class and its suppression of the people. Henceforth, Americans would live in harmony and experience true equity. This sentiment was shared by many in academia who called for the immediate destruction of all remnants of the nation's racist past. Any remaining statues built to honor old white men should be immediately pulled down. Buildings that reflected white supremacy and America's racist heritage should be razed, or, at the very least, renamed and repurposed. As equity became an economic reality, so should it become an academic reality. The traditional grading system, a long-recognized hallmark of racism and white supremacy, should be dismantled once and for all and replaced by an atmosphere of collegiality and social awareness. Traditional instruction in math and the sciences should be deemphasized and replaced with a curriculum that stressed social obligations. School, especially at the university level, should not be a place where students go expecting to learn a trade. Higher education must, instead, focus on preparing students for life in a new society free of racist, white supremacist dominance of employment and economic advancement.

The green new deal lobby, of course, had no intention of allowing this crisis to go to waste. Los Angeles, that great paragon of civic virtue, had, they pointed out, proposed a ban on the building of any new gas stations even before the latest riots. Now, with so many gas stations around the country having been set ablaze, was the perfect time to institute that ban nationwide. None of those burned-out filling stations should be allowed to rebuild. And, of course, very tight green regulations must be established before permitting any rebuilding of the many hundreds of businesses, homes, public buildings, and other structures that had already been destroyed in only the first few days of rioting. These regulations would, of course, make the cost of rebuilding prohibitive and leave large areas of urban America barren and desolate for generations, a situation reminiscent of the aftermath of the 1967 Detroit riots. Was this part of the plan or merely an unintended consequence? Whichever, proponents of the green new deal didn't seem to care.

Others on the left were less dogmatic, wanting to see which way the final wind would blow before crawling out so far on the Marxist limb that there was no hope of rescue if the branch should chance to break. There was, however, unanimous agreement on one point. The ultimate solution to this problem, as was true of so many others, was to throw money at it. Many trillions of dollars must immediately be appropriated to support the large, Democrat-controlled cities that had suffered so grievously. Additional unrestricted grants would be necessary at the state level, principally flowing, regardless of need, to traditionally Democratic strongholds like California, New York, and Illinois. Finally, a massive amount of funds needed to be made available at once to the president so that he, at his sole discretion, could make awards to various social activist groups, especially those focused on persons of color, to make certain that those groups could continue their important work supporting the country's most disadvantaged, regardless of citizenship.

It was by far the worst rioting Louis Robinson had seen in his 25 years on the force. The deliberately understaffed department had, for several years now, been unable to meet its routine obligations to enforce the law and ensure public safety. Fully staffed, the department could not have controlled the mobs that now flooded the city's streets. Louis thought of the rioting as similar to a forest fire. You couldn't put it out; you just tried to contain it. In firefighting lingo, it was the handcrews that had the responsibility to control the perimeter of the fire and limit its spread. The analogous law enforcement goal today was to limit the rioting to commercial areas and prevent it from spreading into residential parts of the city.

Louis saw his own job as more comparable to the role of the hotshots, the firefighters assigned to the most challenging and dangerous portions of a wildfire. A big difference, hotshots worked in crews, Louis was on his own.

He had stationed himself in a shopping area at a major intersection. The area was in the midst of what Louis called the looting phase. Early on, the looters predominated. Many of these were merely opportunists. They saw others grabbing stuff, so they joined in. There were also groups who were well-organized, often gang members. They were on the lookout for high-end merchandise that would be turned over to their leaders for resale. It was essentially the same organized crime activity that was already profiting so heavily from the decision not to prosecute shoplifting if the amount stolen was less than, say, a thousand dollars. That had become a big business. This looting, though, was potentially far more lucrative for the simple reason that there were no price limits. Help yourself to as much as you can carry, then come back for more.

Once the looters had had their fill, phase two would begin. That's when the professional rioters moved in, the leftists and anarchists who traveled the country sowing chaos as opportunities presented themselves. This was the militant, destructive face of the movement. These were the people, mostly male and white, who were largely responsible for inciting and perpetuating the riots. These were the arsonists and assaulters, the ones who threw the Molotov cocktails and attacked citizens and police officers. The looters were in it for the free stuff. The professional rioters were in it for the violence.

Louis stood beside his car, its flashers on, and awaited developments. He waded into the crowds to stop fights and settle arguments over which looter had rights over some piece of disputed merchandise. He offered first aid to those who had suffered injuries in the melee, the bulk of which were cuts related to the broken glass that was everywhere. Occasionally he had to go into the intersection to unsnarl traffic. There had already been a couple of fender benders. He told the drivers to notify their insurance companies. Overwhelmed and working alone, Louis had no ability to make arrests related to the blatant criminal activity he was witnessing. He certainly wasn't going to be filing reports on traffic accidents.

He didn't feel like he was in any particular danger. The looters didn't see Louis as a threat either to themselves personally or to their continued larceny. He was merely helping out where he could. Some even thanked him.

Louis was enjoying a brief lull in the mayhem and wondering if there was any way he could get a cup of coffee when he noticed a group of excited youngsters smiling and laughing and showing each other what they'd managed to abscond with. Most of them were kids that Louis knew personally from his volunteering at the Girls and Boys Clubs.

He saw Montel Brown, a great kid, probably about twelve or thirteen. Montel was grinning and proudly carrying a box under his arm that almost certainly contained a pair of brand-new basketball shoes. Montel's folks worked hard, but they would never be able to afford a pair of shoes like that for Montel. They also wouldn't approve of Montel's having stolen the shoes. The kid was probably already working on a way to hide his treasure from his parents.

As the group came closer, Louis and Montel's eyes locked, and Montel stopped dead in his tracks. Watching the kids, Louis had been careful to keep his facial expression neutral. He was observing, not judging. He was not projecting disapproval. Still, the grin vanished from Montel's face the instant he spotted Louis, and Louis understood exactly what was going on in Montel's head. He wasn't afraid; he was ashamed. Montel dropped the box and ran, much to the amusement of his partners in crime.

Louis wished he could go after Montel, talk to him, tell him it was okay. Everybody made mistakes. The important thing was to learn from them. But Louis couldn't leave his position. He and Montel would have their talk later. Montel's parents would never hear of his misstep.

A few minutes later, Louis was back in the street when he was hit by a car filled with looters and their loot. The driver didn't stop. Louis Robinson was killed instantly. He was the first of many black law enforcement officers who would lose their lives in the riots. He left behind a wife and two daughters.

Despite their best efforts, the thinned ranks of law enforcement were unable to contain the violence to commercial areas and prevent its spread into residential neighborhoods. In one area, gang members worked systematically from house to house, holding homeowners at gunpoint while they searched their houses, primarily for cash but also for jewelry or anything else that would bring a quick sale on the internet. The plan was working well until, halfway down the block, they were met with armed resistance.

Bob and Joan Covington were proud of the home, now paid off, that they had raised their family in. They had possessions in their house, also bought and paid for, that were of value, at least to Bob and Joan. Bob was a hunter. Over recent years, as it became increasingly obvious that politicians intended to make certain that law enforcement would be unable to perform its most basic duty, to protect citizens, Bob began to train Joan in the use of firearms for her own protection. She learned well.

They owned a variety of guns and were well-stocked with ammunition. Each had a nine-millimeter pistol holstered at the hip and carried an AR-15 rifle of the type much maligned by those who thought the Second Amendment was about hunting. Bob also had his favorite shotgun at the ready. You read about the hill someone was willing to die on. This was theirs. They stepped together out onto their front porch.

There were probably twenty or so gangbangers milling about on the sidewalk and street before they began their assault on the next house, which happened to be the Covingtons'. They were teenagers, but they were armed. One guy seemed to be in charge.

"Yo, grandpa, grandma, what's up with this? Too many of us for you to deal with. Don't be stupid."

"Gonna be a lot fewer of you if you try to enter our house. Don't *you* be stupid."

"What you gonna do if I just reach down, pull my gun out of my pants, and shoot you dead."

Bob leveled his gun. "I'll shoot before you ever get your gun out. My wife is already about to shoot that kid over there behind the tree who's fingering the butt of his gun."

They all looked over at the kid who quickly folded his

arms across his chest. I ain't doin' nothin'.

"One more thing," Bob said, "before you go to shootin'. Look behind you."

Behind them were Nick Jerome and Tony White, two guys in their forties who lived in the house across the street. Nick and Tony were real gun enthusiasts. They weren't hunters. Their area of expertise was personal defense. That's how they earned their living. When things began to go south earlier in the evening, the four friends had launched a sort of mutual defense pact. If trouble came, they'd defend each other.

Bob couldn't tell, in the darkness, exactly what weapons Nick and Tony had chosen. They were pointing long guns. They had taken a well-protected position at the curb behind a pickup truck.

"So," Bob said, "you boys should just move along before you end up with holes in your clothes. And don't come back. You've committed serious crimes on this street tonight. Next time, we'll shoot without warning."

The gangbangers struck some poses, but didn't say anything. Within a few minutes, they were gathering up their booty and heading down the street. The four armed neighbors followed them at a distance, making certain that they had left the area, then broke off to help their other neighbors who had earlier been robbed.

Let 'Em Go Larry was livid. "I will not have vigilantism in my city! I will not allow it! You can't have every Tom, Dick, and Harry thinking he's Wyatt Earp and going around shooting at people. Where will that end? That's why we have a highly-trained police force. It's their job to enforce the law, not some elderly couple spending their Social Security checks on guns and ammo. Get me the police commissioner!"

Long before the police arrived, the entire neighborhood had been mobilized to deal with the possible return of the gang or any other brand of felonious miscreants that might appear. Those experienced with firearms were armed, either with their own weapons or ones supplied by others. Those who were not armed served other useful purposes.

Two squad cars showed up—four police officers with vests and helmets, officers desperately needed elsewhere in the city. They pulled to a stop in front of the Covingtons' house. The heavily-armed neighbors grew closer. There were forty to fifty guns in plain view. They were as delighted as they were surprised that the city had heard of their plight and sent the officers to assist them in protecting their neighborhood. They literally cheered as the officers got out of their cars.

Bob Covington was less sanguine than his neighbors. He stood on his porch, the only person in sight not armed to the teeth. Joan was inside, covering him.

"Robert Covington?" one of the officers asked.

Covington nodded.

"We need you and your wife to come with us down to the precinct for questioning."

"What about?"

"We want to hear your version of the events that happened here tonight."

"Do you have a warrant for our arrest?"

The cop shook his head. "Not yet."

"Then I'll be staying here tonight, protecting my home and neighborhood. I'm not going anywhere. When things quiet down, I'll be right here. You'll know right where you can find me. If you do get a warrant, I'll be happy to speak with you in the presence of my attorney."

The cops looked at each other. They had no real idea why they were wasting time here in the first place. They were not about to get into a firefight with a group of folks defending their homes.

The cop smiled. "Have a nice day."

The neighbors cheered, louder now, as the cops departed, than they had when they arrived.

Hidden in the background, uncommented upon by the media, Deshawn Jackson was improving. The tube had been removed from his chest. He was eating a clear liquid diet. He had been moved out of the ICU. He was expected to recover, probably without significant health limitations.

His mother's gratitude to the doctors and nurses knew no bounds. Her prayers had been answered.

Lamont Jones' negotiations with the city were progressing well. There would be payments made directly to Desiree and additional millions to be held in trust for Deshawn. In an unusual agreement, Jones' fees would be paid directly by the city rather than subtracted from the amounts paid to Desiree and Deshawn. Jones would, of course, additionally receive one-third of the total amount of the settlement as the contingency fee agreed upon with Desiree. The exact number of millions of dollars to be paid was still being calculated. The city had, however, balked at paying an additional sum to Desiree's fiancé, Marvin Snopes, who was like a father to Deshawn.

The rioting, however, now progressed under its own momentum. It no longer needed Deshawn Jackson. There were always other martyrs to be found, myriad grievances needing to be assuaged.

Meanwhile, the nation was in flames.

36

The riots, this time, were different. There was a new atmosphere in the streets. In the past, you always had the feeling that the violence would be relatively localized and self-limited. You were confident it would burn itself out in a few days. The authorities would, however reluctantly, soon gain the upper hand. This time though, it seemed that the rioters were in it for the long haul. It was less of a riot and more of a brutal, committed revolution. Property destruction was wanton. Buildings were set ablaze throughout the country. New deaths were reported every day.

The stated purpose of the rioting depended on who you talked to. For some, it was all about past grievances. For others, it was about the future. The leaders on the streets were all of the far-left, Marxist/anarchist variety. They grew out of a variety of social activist organizations whose war chests had been filled over the last few years—to the tune of hundreds of millions of dollars—by the U.S. government, large American corporations, and wealthy leftist individuals. At long last, this was their moment.

In most jurisdictions, law enforcement officers were reduced to the role of spectator. They attempted to herd rioters toward areas where they might inflict the least damage, but these efforts were generally unsuccessful. There were simply too many rioters, and they were now, after so many years of largely unfettered practice runs, too experienced and sophisticated to be easily controlled. Their vastly superior numbers, and the strict limitations placed on the responsive actions that police were permitted to take, made one tactic especially effective. Rioters split their forces, with some groups specifically assigned to confront law enforcement. As a result, police were completely preoccupied with protecting themselves from attack, leaving the remaining rioters with free rein to pursue their destructive ambitions.

Police tried their best to protect the fire department and medical aid teams. Without aggressive law enforcement action, both came under vicious attack and were simply unable to perform their duties. Some governors in conservative states activated National Guard units which helped to bolster the numbers on the law enforcement side.

The most profound difference in this round of rioting was that citizens were armed—and they were resisting. They understood that the government was not coming to their rescue. Various levels of government—federal, state, and local—had demonstrated repeatedly during previous rioting and, more recently, in everyday law enforcement, that they did not prioritize public safety. Citizens were thus forewarned that they were on their own, and they were not going to give up without a fight. For the first time, deaths were not limited to the general civilian population. Rioters and their apolitical criminal fellow travelers had also lost their lives—at the hands of citizens.

So far, those deaths had clearly occurred as a result of citizens defending themselves. During previous rioting, these types of self-defense deaths had been vigorously prosecuted, but, this time, authorities were wise enough not to bring such preposterous legal actions lest the citizenry openly rebel. This was the great fear of the ruling class, that citizens, no longer content with self-defense, would go on the attack. Military minds understood that it was virtually impossible to win a war from a totally defensive position. You couldn't just sit there, day after day, covering your head and waiting for whatever the enemy decided to throw at you. This was a lesson that the American public was quickly learning, but had not yet acted upon.

Brian and Victoria had decided that he should move in with Victoria and Tess at their house. It was generally safer than downtown where Brian lived, and he wanted to be with them to provide whatever security he could. Commerce had generally ground to a halt in America, and Brian's legal work was accordingly minimal. What he needed to do, he could accomplish from home, which meant that he could watch over Tess who was no longer in school. Victoria still went to the hospital. Brian and Tess drove her there every morning and picked her up whenever she had finally finished her work for the day. Otherwise, the only time they ventured out was for groceries and other necessities. They quickly discovered that early morning was generally the safest time for shopping.

When Brian moved in, he brought along a shotgun. The gun had been a gift from a grateful client and had never been used. Brian was not a hunter and knew little about firearms, but, balancing the risks, he felt he needed to be armed. Friends instructed him on the use of the shotgun and how to handle it safely. Ammunition was becoming increasingly scarce, but Brian had managed to find shells. The shotgun was placed on the mantel over the fireplace in the living room where it could be quickly accessed but was safely out of his daughter's reach. Brian prayed that he would never have to use the gun.

When his phone rang, it was Ted. He and Nina were coming over with Jasmine for a hurriedly arranged potluck supper. Both couples said they had news to share and believed it would be relatively low-risk to get together so long as they were careful. They were especially eager to let their daughters share a little playtime. Their girls were chafing under the constraints of isolation and becoming a bit fractious.

Ted had made the prearranged call to let Brian know that they were a couple of minutes away. Brian took down the shotgun and went outside to meet them. He didn't see any unusual activity on the street. When they arrived, Ted got out first and reconnoitered the area himself before helping his wife and daughter out of the car with the dishes they had brought. Ted wore a 9-mm Glock pistol in a holster at his right hip. Unlike Brian, Ted had experience with firearms and had an open carry permit. He thought that it was important to warn the bad guys that he was not going to be an easy target. Lots of people agreed with Ted. It was no longer uncommon to see citizens walking about with holstered weapons. Some had permits; most did not.

Once the Bass family had made it into the relative safety of the house, everyone relaxed. The little girls were delighted to see each other and quickly ran upstairs to escape the old folks. The ladies did a little meal prep, then they opened one of the bottles of wine that Ted and Nina had brought.

"I'm just going to jump right in here and propose a toast," Brian said, "to the university's newest professor of medicine, Professor Victoria Townsend."

There was applause and congratulations. Victoria reddened.

"I think they felt like they had to toss me a bone," Victoria said. "The entire school board has resigned over this thing, and it looks like that sexual predator Jennifer will be going to prison for a very long time. The university administration didn't want to admit that they were wrong, so they did this to signal that it was all behind us. It's not a terrible way to end it."

"You would have been promoted months ago," Brian said, "if the woke administration hadn't made such asses of themselves."

"I'm just glad to get that aspect of this mess behind us. It seems so unimportant now compared to everything else that's going on," Victoria said.

"Regarding 'everything else that's going on,'" Ted said, "I have some disturbing news. Someone shot our friend Let 'Em Go Larry."

Victoria threw a searching look at Brian which Ted caught.

"What?" Ted asked.

"Oh," Brian said, "it's just the 'Jennifer' thing. Larry was so much in the middle of that, it's hard not to think about how anything that happens to him might affect the case. How's he doing? Will he be okay?"

"He's dead," Ted said. "I don't really have any details. It might have just been a random, senseless act. We may never know. You can imagine how it's almost impossible to investigate something like this these days. Anyway, that's not the worst of it. Remarkably, the mayor actually recognizes what a disaster the DA's office has become and is looking for an experienced prosecutor with a different point of view to come in and clean things up. He's looking for a real son of a bitch."

"Oh, no," Brian said.

"I'm afraid so."

Brian shook his head. "So much for Townsend and Bass."

"Bass and Townsend. This won't be forever."

"You've got rather an inflated impression of yourself, Ted, if you think I'm going to be sitting around waiting for you to finally get tired of putting away bad guys. Just think of all those bright young legal minds that are going to be looking for jobs after you throw them out of the prosecutor's office."

"There's one other thing," Ted said. "Nina's trying to make a decision. I think she needs a little encouragement."

"Finally going to try sculpture?" Victoria asked. "You know I've been supporting that for years."

"No, something entirely different. I've had it in my head for a while. I'm seriously considering running for a spot on the school board. At best, it's a thankless job. It's virtually anonymous—which is probably a positive thing from my point of view. Almost no one knows who's on the school board. Everyone assumes that decent, concerned people will run, but there's no real scrutiny by the voters. Look where that has gotten us—not just here, but around the entire country. School boards have been taken over by people whose primary concern is their woke, racist agenda. Their only interest in the children is to indoctrinate them with their leftist social views. Did you know that none of the recently departed school board members, not one, had a child in the system?"

"You know we will all support you," Victoria said, "but it's such an enormous commitment, especially on top of everything else you're doing."

"I think that's what goes through everybody's mind. We all know that we need good people on the school board, but we expect someone else to step up. *Everybody's* too busy. That's how we end up with these leftwing nutcases who have nothing else to do. It's the same problem we have with city councils. No one wants those positions either, except for these agenda-driven radicals."

All in all, it was a very pleasant evening. A moment of sunlight in the dark reality that had descended upon them. Jasmine and Tess begged to spend the night together, and the parents relented.

The lights went out just as Ted and Nina were about to leave. Blackouts were also a part of the new reality, courtesy of the administration's green rush to restrict the use of fossil and nuclear fuels. Under the current regulatory climate, it was beginning to look as though blackouts and brownouts were here to stay.

It was still uncertain what effect the blackouts would have on the rioting, but it was clear that the criminal elements immediately recognized that the blackouts had given them yet another advantage over their prey. The crime business was booming—yet another unintended consequence of the green agenda.

Ted and Brian went outside to have a look around before Nina left the house. Brian waited until Ted had the car running, then brought Nina out and shut the door behind her once she was safely in the passenger seat.

As he watched his friends drive off, Brian wondered once again, where is America? Was it gone forever?

37

Things were looking up for Leonard Lutz. Smoke filled the air and the horizon glowed a glorious shade of reddish orange—full-scale rioting, looting, and arson, a comfortable distance from his condo. He thought of the famous movie line, the army guy in Viet Nam who said that he loved the smell of napalm in the morning—it smelled like victory. Lutz took a deep breath, filling his lungs with the smoky air. The army guy was right. It smelled like victory.

Deshawn Jackson wasn't going to die, but Leonard was okay with that. Deshawn had served his purpose, and the nation had moved on. The prosecutor had hit the two cops with something like twenty charges each, but no one was paying much attention anymore. Leonard didn't care what happened to the cops. They probably deserved whatever they got—more even—for previous crimes they'd committed but hadn't been tagged with. They were, after all, cops.

The important thing was, there was no way this thing could come back on Leonard. Investigators had found two bullets in a garage wall right where one of the cops had said they would be. The prosecutor said, I wonder how the cop knew exactly where to look? He probably put the bullets there himself, or else knew they were there from some previous shooting. That alley was notorious. It was like a shooting gallery. You could probably find hundreds of bullets in the walls of garages and houses around there.

The prosecutor said, okay, you've got a couple of bullets,

where's the gun? The cops said, obviously, the shooter escaped in the confusion. The prosecutor said, right.

The only other thing they had was the 911 call. It gave Leonard the creeps when he heard it. He recognized his own voice, but there was no way the cops could link it to him. Sure, if Leonard was a suspect, they could match his voice to the call, but Leonard wasn't remotely on their radar. If you didn't have a gun, you couldn't match the bullets. If you didn't have a suspect, you couldn't match the voice. Case closed.

For several weeks, Leonard had been careful not to let anyone see him in his "new" car. A beat-up 2013 Mitsubishi Mirage was not exactly in keeping with the image he wanted to convey, either to his fellow investors or to the people who lived in his upscale condominium. But, after a while, he came up with a cover story. The Porsche had been burned out by rioters. Totaled. He was waiting for a check from the insurance company. Meanwhile, he'd decided he didn't want to go through that again with another expensive car, so he bought the Mitsubishi to drive until things cooled down. As soon as the rioting stopped, he'd buy another Porsche—or maybe a Ferrari this time.

Some smartass in his condo said he'd never heard of an insurance company paying off a riot claim. He said it was a standard exclusion. Leonard told him, yeah, the insurance company had tried to pull that on him, and his attorneys had had to get tough with them. My attorneys, Leonard said, I'm glad they're on my side, not against me. His fellow condo-dweller looked a little skeptical, like he wasn't buying what Leonard was selling. So, in subsequent telling, Leonard amended his story. Yeah, he'd say, I had to eat the cost of the Porsche, the whole 200 grand. Insurance companies won't pay for riot damage. It's standard.

His condo building had a communal garage. Leonard had

avoided it before he thought up his cover story. Now, he pulled right in. He got some glances. Everyone hadn't heard his car story.

He rode up on the elevator with a woman he'd seen around the building. He smiled at her. She nodded—slightly. She wasn't too bad looking, but didn't show any interest in Leonard. Probably a lesbian. Or maybe she'd seen the Mitsubishi.

He opened the door to his pitch-black condo, threw his keys on the mail table, and flipped on the light. He walked into his still dark living room to turn on the TV and there was someone sitting in his favorite chair, the one he'd paid nearly $4,000 for.

It scared the bejesus out of him.

"It's me," Dennis said.

"What the hell do you want? You can't just walk in here. This is a security building." The line sounded lame, even to Leonard.

"Where's the gun?"

"It's in a safe place." As soon as he said it, Leonard knew it was a bad answer. He should have said he'd gotten rid of it. But why would he get rid of the gun? That sounded like he was guilty of something.

"There's no 'safe place,'" Dennis said, "except at the bottom of the deep blue sea. Give me the gun. I'll take care of it."

"No," Leonard said. Finally, a right answer. He had worried about the gun, and what he should do with it. One thing he knew for certain, he couldn't just hand it over to somebody else, a piece of evidence that would link him to Deshawn Jackson.

"Leonard, the gun needs to disappear."

"I'll take care of it."

"See that you do." With that, Dennis rose from the chair

and headed for the door. He let himself out.

Well, that was easy. You needed to know how to deal with people like Dennis. They were hired help. You had to be firm with them. They were used to following orders.

Leonard went over to the bar and poured himself a drink, then he sat down in his favorite chair, still warm from Dennis. How long had the guy been in his apartment?

Dennis had rattled him. He hadn't been able to think clearly, wrap his mind around the problem—and Dennis. The drink helped.

First question, why did Dennis care about the gun? The obvious answer was that the gun was linked to Dennis. If Leonard asked himself, where'd you get the gun, his answer would be, from Dennis. But the link to Dennis was a little more tenuous than Leonard's answer suggested. Sure, he'd asked Dennis to get him a gun, but Dennis hadn't seemed too interested. In fact, at the time, he thought that Dennis had completely blown him off.

Then, a few days later, some guy stops him on the street, a guy whose name he never learned, a guy he'd never seen before—or since—and says, I hear you're looking for a gun. They did a cash deal. That's all there was to it. But where's the link to Dennis?

Suddenly, a tidal wave of understanding flowed through Leonard's brain. This wasn't about the gun, not directly. Dennis didn't care if Leonard had a gun. Dennis had provided the gun, no matter how hard he had tried to distance himself from the sale. What Dennis cared about was that the gun had been used. How could Dennis possibly know that? And how could Leonard not have realized that Dennis knew, while Dennis was still sitting right here in this chair saying that the gun needed to disappear? Because Dennis had flustered him, thrown him off balance. He wasn't thinking clearly.

And then an even more terrifying thought entered his brain. Dennis already had the gun. That's why he was such a pushover. Leonard said he'd take care of it, and Dennis had immediately accepted that Leonard would take care of the gun. "See that you do," is all Dennis had said, and then he left.

Leonard was already in a cold sweat before this last realization. Now he was nauseated. He was about to throw up. Leonard stood, took some deep breaths, and tried to get control of himself. Don't jump to conclusions. Just look. See if the gun is gone.

First, he studied the bookcase. Nothing appeared to have been moved. He took out his phone to compare the current position of everything in the bookcase with the picture he'd taken. He had deliberately placed his books, a couple of envelopes, a few odd sheets of paper, and a bunch of other things in the bookcase in a very haphazard manner. You couldn't move the bookcase without disturbing half the stuff in it. He always took a picture when he put things back, always checked the bookcase as soon as he entered the condo. Except for tonight. Tonight, he had been rattled. He forgot.

Leonard took the ruler from the bookcase and measured how far it was from the wall and from the corner of the room. It was exactly as he had left it.

Feeling a little easier, he began to remove some of the books from the case. It was a sturdy mahogany structure with a broad, heavy base. Leonard couldn't move it at all unless he removed some of the books.

He inched one end of the bookcase far enough away from the wall to allow him to access the cache. He removed the floorboard, and there it was, safe and sound.

He picked it up and held it lovingly. Holding the gun brought an almost sexual sensation. He'd never known anything like it. That's why he hadn't dumped it somewhere. He couldn't part with it. He often fantasized about using it again. The sense of power he felt holding the gun was titillating, almost overwhelming. He had fired two shots and torn the country apart—and stood to make himself millions into the bargain. That would be hard to top.

He returned the gun to its hiding place and began the laborious process of putting everything back in its place. Then, he took another picture. He needed to find a new place for the gun that would make it easier for him to visit it.

Leonard went back to his chair and began working on his drink again. There had been no need to panic. The gun was safe. No one could find it. He had no idea why Dennis had suddenly developed cold feet, but there was no way Dennis could know about Leonard's involvement in the Deshawn Jackson shooting. Dennis was in the dark, just like everyone else in the country.

Leonard began to relax. He looked about, soaking up the ambience of his pricey condo and feeling very satisfied with himself. He once again was able to focus on the very serious decision he had to make. Should he buy another Porsche, or, this time, move up to a Ferrari?

Dennis couldn't believe what a moron he was dealing with. How could the guy not have destroyed the gun, one of only two pieces of evidence that could possibly link him to the shooting? Not only that, he kept it in his condo! What a moron. Dennis knew that if he rattled Leonard's cage a little, Leonard wouldn't be able to resist the urge to check on the gun, so Dennis had set up surveillance outside, waiting for Leonard to appear and lead him to his hidey-hole. He figured he wouldn't have long to wait. He'd thought that setting up the digital camera surveillance inside the condo was probably a complete waste of time. No one could be that stupid.

Except for Leonard.

Dennis watched Leonard's entire performance on real-time video from the comfort of his SUV. He noticed how careless Leonard was, leaving his fingerprints all over the gun.

The next morning, Dennis waited outside for Leonard to leave his condo for the day. When he did, Dennis let himself in and, first, removed all the surveillance cameras he'd hidden about the condo the day before, then began to carefully follow the instruction video that Leonard had so thoughtfully let him record. He started by photographing the bookcase with his phone, then measured the distances to the wall and corner. He was able to easily slide the bookcase away from the wall without having to remove any of the books.

He removed the floorboard, then carefully lifted the gun with a cloth and placed it in the bag he'd brought for the purpose. He replaced Leonard's gun with a duplicate that was virtually indistinguishable from the gun he'd removed. Leonard would certainly never notice the difference. Then he returned everything to its previous position, measuring carefully and checking against the picture he'd taken initially.

Dennis stepped out into the sunshine, satisfied to have so easily accomplished his goal. Watching over morons tended to be an easy assignment, so he wasn't terribly surprised that his objective had been achieved so quickly. The problem with morons, though, was that they tended to be erratic. They could suddenly do something crazy and totally unexpected, like firing off a couple of shots in an alleyway and pushing the nation to the brink of civil war.

38

The onslaught of new, more ferocious rioting led to a near-total breakdown of civil order. The efforts of the police were completely consumed by the need to limit the damage caused by rioters, which left the more garden-variety criminals free to ride roughshod over the rest of the population. Looting was only restricted by the amount you could carry, or, among the increasingly audacious, the number of shopping carts you could commandeer and fill with plunder. Crimes against persons soared, and marauding gangs terrorized neighborhoods. Prosecutions were rare.

Citizens survived as best they could, mostly by hiding behind locked doors. When forced to venture out, they traveled in groups, protected by friends or acquaintances who were armed. Caravans of cars traveled about cities, transporting citizens to obtain groceries and other necessities. Shortages began to occur in everything from fuel to food products, causing prices—already sky-high due to government-caused inflation—to soar even higher. As always, it was the underprivileged and economically disadvantaged who suffered most.

The general population reluctantly recognized that they were on their own. They would have to provide for themselves whatever force was necessary to protect their homes, businesses, and families. Actual gun battles broke out between citizens and criminals, and it quickly became evident that the most highly armed neighborhoods were the safest. But citizens had to be careful. Liberal DAs who were loath to lock up violent criminals showed no such hesitancy when it came to what they liked to call vigilante homeowners. Prosecutors displayed their ingrained skepticism of claims of self-defense and often aggressively pursued charges against those who used firearms and said that they were only defending themselves. A favorite trick was to confiscate citizens' weapons pending charges that would never be brought.

With the populace virtually homebound, cabin fever was a problem. "Going out," in the usual sense of the term was completely out of the question, so people more and more tended to get together with friends and relatives in their homes. For Victoria and Brian, this usually meant arranging a meal with Ted and Nina, which provided an opportunity for Jasmine and Tess to see each other. Daylight hours were safer. They alternated between Victoria's house and the Bass's. Today, Ida and Sandy had joined them. The three couples had grown increasingly close as a result of both the shared ordeal of the ongoing civil disruptions and Brian and Victoria's legal battle with the school board.

They were just about to sit down to eat when someone knocked at the front door. Ted and Brian grabbed their guns off the mantel. Brian went to the door, but didn't open it.

"Who's there?"

"Special Agent Hilliard, FBI."

"Please show your ID through the window."

The agent complied, and Brian took a picture that included both the agent and his credentials. Hilliard appeared to be legitimate.

"Let me talk to him," Ida said.

Brian opened the door.

"I'm Ida Silverstein, Brian and Victoria Townsend's

attorney. How can I help you?" She didn't ask him to come in.

Hilliard took in what he could see of the house from the front door. "I'm a little uncomfortable," he said, "with everybody having guns in their hands."

"Welcome to the America that your administration has created," Ida said.

Brian and Ted glanced at each other, then put their firearms back on the mantel.

"I'm looking for Alex Walker," Hilliard said.

"He's not here."

"Then, I'd like to speak to Victoria Townsend."

"Regarding what?"

"Where her father is."

"She has no information for you."

"We can make this official," the agent said.

"You can," Ida said, "and I'm officially informing you that you—or anyone else from the Department of Justice—may not speak to my clients outside of my presence."

Hilliard looked at Ted. "Who are you?"

Ted considered telling him that it was none of his business, but said, "I'm Ted Bass, the city district attorney."

"You think you've got enough lawyers here?" the agent said to no one in particular.

He turned to leave just in time to watch a group of teenagers aimlessly sauntering down the street. One of them had something in his hand that looked like a tire iron. He casually struck Hilliard's car with it as he walked by, shattering the windshield.

Hilliard watched in silence, powerless to make any meaningful response. If he ordered the kids to halt, they'd simply ignore him—even if he drew his gun. They knew he wasn't going to shoot a kid for this kind of random vandalism. Not a chance he could run down the kid with the tire iron and put him in handcuffs. Even if he could, what was the point? People were assaulting police officers and burning down buildings, with no consequences, only a couple of miles away. The legal system had no time for a kid accused of breaking a windshield.

Special Agent Hilliard turned back toward the front door one last time.

"Big changes are coming," he said. "Soon."

"Soon" turned out to be six o'clock the next morning. The big change was martial law, declared throughout the country. Federal troops began patrolling the streets of major cities.

The response of most Americans—Finally! They saw the arrival of the troops as a chance, at long last, to restore order. Commerce could begin again. Jobs could begin again. *Life* could begin again. People might once again feel safe on the streets and in their homes.

This, of course, had been the plan all along. Why had government authorities for so long encouraged rioting, rising crime, open borders, homelessness, and so forth—all the chaos that was destroying the once great nation? Because the desire to end the chaos, the hope of returning to that happy life of distant memory, would make the citizenry amenable to the controls those in power were eager to impose. The purpose of the chaos was to soften the population, to render it compliant, submissive. The people were offered relief, a modicum of peace and personal safety, in exchange for the surrender of a large chunk of their freedom. Even greater power would flow to the already powerful who would happily reign over an increasingly obedient population.

The chaos was not an accident. It was the plan. Chaos was traded for tyranny.

For those with more mercenary hearts, the crackdown represented the financial opportunity of a lifetime. The civil unrest had driven down the value of financial assets, not just in real estate, but in the stock markets as well. Insiders who knew what was coming and had kept their powder dry suddenly unleashed their cash expecting a vast financial windfall as civil order was eventually reestablished. Not the least of these were members of Congress. There is a long, sordid tradition of senators and congressmen—and their families—achieving great wealth by trading on insider information. This was their finest hour.

For Adam Michaelson, the long-awaited moment had finally arrived. He began to furtively acquire depressed properties and propagated rumors that he was embarking on his most generous act of philanthropy ever, his commitment to rebuild America. This selfless project was scrupulously designed to generate many billions of dollars of profit for Michaelson.

Leonard Lutz and his small band of investors operated in what was, comparatively, the minor leagues, but they anticipated netting millions for themselves. Leonard had his eye set on a limited edition V12-powered Ferrari that could make 830 horsepower. Cost was not an issue.

For Alex Walker and Hamilton Hobart, there were far different considerations. They had expected a crackdown. They had not expected nationwide martial law. But, as they examined the way that martial law was being implemented, they saw how it could work to their advantage. Full-on martial law meant giving the military, and the executive branch, control of everything—police powers, the courts, everything. The manpower requirements of that kind of implementation were enormous, far more than what the administration could muster. Additionally, Democrat politicians were not about to cede power to the federal government. It was one thing to take over Republican-controlled cities and states, it was quite another to demand that Democrats surrender control over areas they governed. The problem, of course, was that it was the Democrat-controlled regions that were suffering most from rioting and crime. The patchwork solution that evolved generally kept local governments in charge, supported by federal troops.

Habeas corpus was never formally suspended, but the rules governing arrest and detention were, to say the least, relaxed. The wholesale arrests served the purpose of quieting the nation and restoring civil order, but the system was rife with abuse. Political arrests were frequent, especially of people objecting to the institution of martial law.

The Department of Homeland Security's Disinformation Governance Board, popularly known as the Ministry of Truth, was resurrected. The stated purpose of the board was to correct disinformation. Its real purpose was to control speech and shape public discourse to support the administration's policies and eliminate dissent. Most recognized that the board was merely a ham-handed attempt to abolish First Amendment rights.

Congress was eager that this crisis not be allowed to go to waste. Having caused record inflation through their profligate spending, leftist politicians now wanted to solve that problem with wage and price controls. Once that was accomplished, they believed, they could safely return to their old standby of extravagant spending balanced by onerous taxes.

And, while they still held very narrow control over both houses, the Left decided the time was ripe to consummate two very long-held desires—the elimination of the filibuster and the packing of the Supreme Court. There also began to be whispers that, in the face of the current social upheaval, elections should be suspended—indefinitely.

For Walker and Hobart, there could be no hesitation. The moment to act had arrived. It was urgent that they make their move while martial law was new and troops were still uncertain as to the limitations of their role. That uncertainty was their greatest ally.

There was much that could not be known until events began to unfold. The requirement of absolute secrecy during the planning stages had worked directly against their need for massive popular support on the ground. Their core group of leaders that they had been working with over the last several months believed they could guarantee a turnout of 25,000 supporters. They hoped for 50,000.

Walker and Hobart believed that the latter figure *might* be enough. If they could turn out 50,000 people, and if they could get them into position, then the movement would face its final hurdle. They had to convince their supporters to focus all their energy on a single, narrow objective.

39

They could not have ordered better weather. Highs in the mid-70s with overcast skies. It would be humid, but you couldn't have everything.

Small groups began to appear around 8:00 am. Families on holiday. Tourists. They were casually dressed for a day of sightseeing in the nation's capital. They wandered around the Mall, all the way from the Capitol to the Lincoln Memorial. That distance was over two miles. As the planners well knew, this was an area where you could easily hide many thousands of people—in plain sight.

Larger groups began to appear, tourist groups with guides herding them from site to site. Everyone happy and smiling. No shouting. No protesting. No signs. Just folks enjoying the day. There were police officers and occasional troops. Many of these visitors went out of their way to shake hands and thank them for their service.

By ten o'clock the counters estimated that they had their 50,000. As noon approached, the counters warned that they could no longer be confident of the number. It was certainly greater than 100,000, probably much greater.

At precisely noon, the code word was given.

"Stroll."

The "tourists" began to leave the Mall via broadly-spaced, predetermined routes. To an observer, there was no discernible pattern. Police scratched their heads at the number of people moving quietly along the streets, but there was no cause for alarm. It was great to see, despite all the recent turmoil in the country, large crowds of people returning to the nation's capital. They looked like a random cross section of America—men, women, racially mixed, and all ages, with one exception. A particularly perceptive onlooker might have noted that there were no children, no one under the age of 18.

Depending on their designated destination, some groups required more time than others to arrive at their assigned location. The organizers had allowed for this. Leaders, many posing as tour guides, shepherded their charges as inconspicuously as possible along their prescribed routes. When everyone was in position, a second code word was given.

"Gather."

From all points of the compass, they began to converge on the target. They were instructed to advance as far as possible, but not cross any barricades or police lines. This was to be the absolutely quintessential peaceful demonstration.

Law enforcement was befuddled. Walker and Hobart had counted on this. Individual police officers saw only a tiny portion of what was going on. At first, no one saw the complete picture. By the time they did, it was too late. When the White House was fully engulfed by a quarter of a million people—probably more—the third command was given.

"Picnic."

And that's what they did. Hampers were opened, and foodstuffs were sampled—sparingly. No one could know, at this point, just how far their supplies would need to be stretched.

Alex Walker and the other planners knew that their supply line was their Achilles' heel. As soon as the "picnic" command was given, they began to move in prepositioned supplies—food, water, portable toilets. The goal was to get as much in as possible before someone tried to stop them. Surprise, for the moment, was on their side. Authorities still had no idea what they were dealing with, and, for the time being, Walker's tourists were meeting no organized resistance. Supplies were positioned deep within the crowd and broadly spaced. They were also able to slip in the communications equipment for the speeches that were coming.

The authorities were in a quandary. Normal access to the White House and a large area surrounding it were completely obstructed. That was intolerable, but what could they do? Their estimators suggested that the crowd was now over 300,000. People kept coming and joining the periphery. The White House was completely surrounded by people quietly eating lunch. It was history's largest sit-in. They had no idea what these people wanted or who was responsible for this operation that had obviously been planned down to the minutest detail and accomplished with military precision. Importantly, government authorities could not identify anyone on the ground who was in charge. In short, they had no one they could talk to.

They sent uniformed policemen into the crowd. No one moved for them, but the cops were allowed to wade about freely through the mass of people. They met no resistance. Many were even offered food and drink. On the other hand, when authorities tried to move vehicles in, the dense crowd ignored them and refused to budge.

The FBI wanted to send in spies and agitators. Cooler heads thought that was a bad idea, but, of course, the FBI did it anyway. The agitators stuck out like sore thumbs in this mellow group, and were quickly outed. Almost immediately they were surrounded by people yelling, "Fed! Fed! Fed!" and forced out of the crowd. The spies were more difficult to detect. Presumably, they had a nice lunch. There was little else for them.

The media were now out in full force. Reporters from the few conservative news outlets in the country were the first on the scene—which provided a clue as to the general political persuasion of the group for anyone not smart enough to recognize that this quiet, well-mannered crowd was likely conservative. Liberal media were quick to label the picnic an Insurrection! and urged immediate action utilizing whatever force was necessary to disperse the threatening mob.

In the end, authorities decided to do nothing and await events. They didn't have to wait long.

It felt strange to Alex Walker, not having Ham Hobart at his side. Alex had always considered himself second in command, behind Hobart—and he still did—but Hobart wasn't here, in the crowd. He had other responsibilities. Hobart's role this day was behind the scenes. While Alex's role required him to play the front man, in full public view, Hobart's was necessarily private, secret even. Hamilton Hobart's decades-long struggles in the civil rights movement had won him the admiration, and often affection, of virtually every establishment liberal in the Democratic party since the 1960s. His recent defense of Alex Walker had tarnished his reputation in a few eyes, but not among the legendary party stalwarts whose cooperation he would be seeking today.

He and Alex would be working simultaneously toward the same goal, but from opposite ends. Their ultimate goal would only be achieved if each of them was successful in managing his portion of the operation. Their roles were synergistic.

Dennis and his associates had provided invaluable assistance and had been especially helpful when it came to the staging of supplies and planning the necessarily stealthy movement of the protestors through the streets of Washington. But the desire to avoid physical confrontation of any kind had led to the decision that it was probably better for Dennis to skip the actual event.

"Five minutes," Lucius said. Lucius St. John had been with them since the beginning and his role had grown to be one of the most pivotal in the movement. There seemed to be almost nothing he wasn't able, and willing, to do. He had recently brought on an associate named Hussein who was also extremely helpful. Both men had immigrated to America and had that deep understanding and affection for the country that, sadly, native-born Americans often lacked. Alex discovered that, remarkably, both men knew his former son-in-law, Brian.

As he climbed onto the makeshift platform from which he was to make his speech, Alex had two great concerns. How would the crowd react, and how would the administration react? If the speech was a dud, if the crowd did not enthusiastically embrace the plan, all was for naught. The movement would collapse on the spot. And, of lesser importance, he and his fellow conspirators would probably spend a considerable amount of time in jail. If the treatment of those accused of committing crimes on January 6 was any guide, it was not unthinkable that Alex would die in prison.

How the administration might respond was anybody's guess. So many members of the administration had supported the horrifically destructive riots of the summer of 2020, which had been declared "mostly peaceful," that it was difficult to imagine how they could characterize the current event as anything other than Americans exercising their right to peacefully protest—a right which the current administration had repeatedly claimed was enshrined in the Constitution. Still, it was hard not to think about the confrontation that occurred in Washington in 1932 when federal troops, supported by tanks, moved against World War I veterans who were protesting the failure of the government to provide the benefits that they were entitled to. Three people were killed. Hundreds were wounded.

Then, the moment arrived.

"Good afternoon."

Alex waited patiently for the crowd to recognize that he was about to speak and for them to begin to settle. Many would not be able to hear him directly. The organizers had arranged for livestreaming on several internet sites. It was also expected that, as the protest had attracted national attention, some television and radio networks would carry his speech live.

Cheering and applause broke out as people realized that Alex Walker was about to address them. Someone started a wave that circuited the White House several times before finally dying out. Then, Alex had their attention. He spoke, as always, without notes.

"In the wake of the Japanese sneak attack on Pearl Harbor in 1941," Alex began, "Japanese Admiral Isoroku Yamamoto reportedly said, 'I fear all we have done is to awaken a sleeping giant and fill him with a terrible resolve.' If the quote is accurate, Yamamoto was perceptive. Americans had been oblivious to the threat that loomed over them and thus were brutally surprised. But, once awakened, the American people answered the call, as they always have, and saved the country they loved.

"My friends, America has once again been caught sleeping and finds itself awakening in the throes of yet another brutal sneak attack perpetrated, this time, by our own countrymen. We see everywhere, in plain sight, the violence being done to our country, yet we have been slow to comprehend its meaning. The assault on our nation has been so diffuse and comprehensive that it has been difficult to recognize its source and goals. This was the intention of the attackers. This is how a sneak attack works.

"Those who *have* warned us often speak of creeping socialism or even Marxism. These terms are probably as useful as any for us to use, so long as we clearly understand their meaning. Do not confuse these philosophies in practice with the platitudes with which they are typically described. Socialism and Marxism are not about equality, the sharing of wealth, and equal opportunity. Their purpose is to concentrate power, wealth, and privilege among a small group of self-styled elites at the expense of the social and economic welfare—and freedom—of the general population.

"If you're like me, your mind probably resists the idea that there are people so selfish, so greedy, that they are willing to betray our country's ideals and ultimately destroy America in their pursuit of personal wealth and power. Of course, we see this type of self-serving behavior every day in the criminal class, but we naively expect better from those who are, so to speak, 'at the top.' I do not pretend to understand the psychological defect that creates this insatiable need for power and control. Why do men who are absolute dictators in their own countries, men like Hitler and Putin, lust to take their dictatorships—and armies—to new countries? They always gin up some fatuous explanation like Putin's claim that he is rescuing Ukraine from Nazism. This is the same approach that American politicians use when they cloak some of their most heinous actions under the veil of promoting civil rights.

"When liberal politicians support rioting and the destruction of cities in feigned outrage at the death of a single black man, yet ignore the deaths of thousands of African Americans in the cities that they control, it is clear that their concern is not the welfare of African Americans. They are not promoting civil rights. They are engaging in political theater in the pursuit of power. These riots occur, and persist endlessly with very little government response, because the politicians in power *want* them to happen. They *want* them to continue. Violent crime flourishes in our nation's cities, which are almost invariably under the control of liberals, because that violence suits those liberals' goals.

"When the administration flouts the law and opens the nation's borders to anyone who wants to enter, it is not acting out of compassion for those who illegally immigrate. What is compassionate about turning over control of the border to brutal drug cartels? What is compassionate about abandoning migrating men, women, and children to be murdered and raped by the thousands as they seek to cross the border? Is it compassionate to allow the cartels to charge thousands of dollars for the privilege of entering our country, ensuring that these new immigrants will be indentured to the cartels and forced to do their bidding for years to come? Because of this indentured servitude, women and children are forced into the sex trade after they arrive in the United States. Men and boys are compelled to participate in numerous other criminal activities including the cartel's multibillion dollar drug business which is now allowed to operate freely across the border and has cost hundreds of thousands of American lives.

"When was the last time you heard a senior administration official, much less the president, mention the human suffering that is being caused by the administration's project to illegally lure migrants across the border into America? When did you last hear them speak of the murders, rapes, and accidental drownings that are everyday occurrences? The most positive spin that you can put on the administration's actions is that it simply doesn't care about the human misery it is causing at the border and the consequent damage done to our nation. Unfortunately, it is likely that the Left, indeed, does care. It sees itself as gaining political power as a result of this massive influx of illegal immigrants, and judges the assaults, rapes, and deaths a small price to pay for the rewards they expect to reap.

"Orwell warned us about power. He wrote, 'We know that no one ever seizes power with the intention of relinquishing it. Power is not a means, it is an end. One does not establish a dictatorship in order to safeguard a revolution; one makes the revolution in order to establish the dictatorship...The object of power is power.'

"My friends, in the United States of America, power is vested in the people!"

The crowd, which had been listening spellbound, erupted and would not be quieted. The cheers and applause finally cascaded into a single chant, "Walker! Walker! Walker!"

It was several minutes before Alex could continue.

"Power was taken from us while we were sleeping. Those who stole it from us glimpsed an opportunity while our attention was focused elsewhere, and they seized it. But, now, once again, the sleeping giant that is the American people has been awakened. We must act now to take that power back."

Applause broke out once again.

"We find ourselves at a critical stage in the plot to wrest control of our nation from its people. At first blush, it is difficult to recognize that the myriad problems threatening our nation all arise from the same plan—the rioting, the violent crime besieging our cities, the unfettered human and drug trafficking at the border, and on and on. Looking closer, however, we find commonalities. First of all, these tragic conditions occur because they are allowed to occur; they thrive because they are encouraged. When rioters take over a city and the mayor describes their actions as a 'summer of love,' that encourages rioting. When a vice president supports a bail fund to get rioters back on the streets and says that the riots 'are not going to let up, and they should not,' she is encouraging rioting. When prosecutors release repeat, violent criminals immediately and without bail and seek to decriminalize the resisting of arrest and the assault of police officers, they are encouraging crime. When the brave men and women of the U.S. Border Patrol are reduced to providing concierge services for the customers of Mexican drug cartels, the degradation of their job encourages virtually unrestricted human and drug trafficking.

"The list of government-promoted disasters does not end here. There is the homeless industrial complex that` has rendered our cities unfit to live in, the substitution of political indoctrination for education in our schools, and the deliberate, anti-scientific effort to confuse gender identification to the point that a candidate for the United States Supreme Court is unwilling to even venture a guess as to what a woman might be.

"So, the first commonality is that all these disastrous conditions are permitted to exist because those in power want them to exist. The politicians want the problem, not a solution. The second commonality is that these conditions, individually and together, have caused the breakdown of civil society that each of us is experiencing every day. The chaos they perpetuate is not an accident. It is the lynchpin of their plan. Chaos is the gateway to tyranny.

"And here we arrive at the most treacherous aspect of their insidious plan. Many of you may still believe, as I once did, that the imposition of tyrannical rule in America would not be possible. The American people simply wouldn't stand for it. There would be open revolt. I fully understand why you would think that way. Now, let me ask you what happened when martial law was imposed—*martial law,* with all its curfews, interruptions of due process, and restrictions on our precious freedoms? The American people welcomed it!

"And that was their terrible plan from the beginning—sow

chaos and let it fester and grow until the people begged for a crackdown. Suddenly, the opaque becomes clear. We wondered why the gates of justice had become turnstiles. They claimed it was about justice for African Americans accused of crimes. Anyone could see the benefit for black criminals of a get-out-of-jail-free card, but, for ordinary, law-abiding black citizens, it was a disaster. Crime, especially violent crime, has reached epic proportions. Why did the politicians not see this? You'd have to be blind not to see the terrible harm these policies were causing. Now you have the answer. Crime in the streets was not a side effect of these policies, it was the goal!

"In this light, the government's laissez-faire approach to so many of our nation's problems becomes understandable—evil, unacceptable, but understandable. So, this is where we are and how we got here. Can we recover? Is the noose of tyranny already so tight that there can be no escape? I don't believe so, but we must act quickly. We must act now.

"In the long run, we must reverse the flow of power away from our top-heavy federal government and reestablish the federal republic that the founders gave us. That means returning power to states and local government. We must vote, to be sure, but voting alone is simply not enough. We have to campaign, but that is not enough. My friends, we have to run for office. We cannot continue to leave control of our school boards and city councils to a bunch of nutcases who simply have nothing else to do. The same goes for election boards and the state offices of secretary of state that are so essential to a fair and credible election process. This won't be easy. It requires a degree of personal sacrifice that we have not been making. Those who wish us ill have seen the power of these positions and have gradually taken them over. This has permitted a very small group of people to undermine the will of the vast majority. We can reclaim these grassroots roles by rolling up our sleeves and doing the hard work. It won't be easy, and it can't happen quickly. It won't happen today.

"So, what *can* we do today, and why are we here at this place?

"Under normal circumstances, in times of crisis, Americans of both parties turn to their president. He is the rock. He is the ultimate decision maker. The president addresses the nation in a way that clearly articulates the problem and explains the path to its resolution. He then answers very difficult questions from a fiercely independent and adversarial press. He continues the press conference until the press has spent itself.

"We do not have, today, a president who can do that. He ran for office hiding in his basement. When he did venture out, he sometimes thought he was running for the Senate. On the day he was elected president—the very day he was elected—he put his arm around his granddaughter and said, 'This is my son, Beau Biden, who a lot of you helped elect to the senate in Delaware.' His son, of course, had passed away and had never been elected senator anywhere.

"To my eyes, the president's mental condition has deteriorated even further in office. He has sometimes referred to himself as the vice president and to his vice president as the president. He has been unable to come up with the names of cabinet members who are standing beside him. He frequently appears lost at speaking appearances and has wandered off the stage inexplicably. He often makes statements that are simply gibberish. He appears confused by the words he's attempting to read on his teleprompter. We have no idea who wrote those words. It is not unreasonable to believe that the person or persons who caused those words to be written are the *de facto* presidency.

"It is simply not believable that this man is making the

decisions that are determining the course of our nation. Someone recently declared martial law. Was it the president? I believe that it is not credible that the president was, in any real sense, the person who made that decision. It is therefore reasonable to ask, is the martial law declaration legal? Are any of the president's executive orders legally in force? What about all the bills he has signed into law? Are those laws enforceable? When a president who we have all seen shake hands with someone who isn't there signs a law, is that binding?

"There is also the problem of accountability. Who can we hold accountable for the decisions that the president allegedly makes? It is widely understood that the president is merely a figurehead. Faceless persons in the government are making all the decisions that the president attempts to read. Who are these people?

"My friends, this is not the way our country works. This is not constitutional. This is not legal. We must have a president who is competent and able to say no to his subordinates when that is necessary. In this time of enormous crises, both domestic and international, we must have a president, a single decision-making individual, who is making the necessary determinations. That is what the Constitution requires. Without such a person in place, without public confidence that there is such a person in place, this nation is in grave peril.

"If the president is unable to meet the demands of his high office, he must resign. There is no other path. We must support him in this, regardless of what we think of his constitutional successor. This is the law. This is the Constitution we live by.

"In 1635, Oliver Cromwell famously said to Parliament, 'You have sat here too long for any good you have been doing. Depart, I say, and let us have done with you. In the name of God, go.'

"Mr. President, because the evidence before us shows that you are not competent to hold office, we demand that you resign."

The crowd took to their feet as one and roared. A chant grew and gained force, "Go! Go! Go! Go!" and continued for more than ten minutes.

When the crowd had finally quieted enough, Alex said, "Mr. President, we will not leave this place until you do."

This statement was greeted more enthusiastically than the last. Alex had a few more words to say, but decided against it. He quietly stepped down from his makeshift podium.

40

The walls were once again closing in on Leonard Lutz. Michaelson had fired him from the Toward a Fairer America Project, the dark money pool that he had been in charge of. The handsome salary that Leonard used to earn there had been his last source of cash.

Officially, Michaelson had nothing to do with the management of TFAP. In reality, he controlled it. Michaelson was the fund's principal donor. Without his patronage, TFAP would not survive.

Michaelson had sent Thomas Fielding, his consigliere, to do the dirty work. Fielding was a sadistic bastard who had always had it in for Leonard, and Leonard could tell that Fielding especially enjoyed this particular assignment.

"You've been caught poaching," Fielding had said. "We can't allow that."

Leonard feigned ignorance. He didn't have a clue what Fielding was talking about.

Fielding sighed and produced his evidence. They knew everything—everyone who was in Leonard's investment group, how much money each had invested, how much they had borrowed, the names of their lenders, everything.

"We trusted you," Fielding said. "We let you into our confidence. You betrayed our trust and put at risk a very important project."

So, Leonard did what he always did when he felt the walls closing in. He started drinking. He'd been drinking pretty much straight for the last 48 hours. Drinking, and trying to figure some way to get even with Michaelson. That wasn't going to be easy. The man was an impregnable fortress. Two or three European governments—and some in Asia—had tried, unsuccessfully, to bring him down. He just got richer, and those countries got poorer.

Leonard took a bleary-eyed glance around his condo. He loved that condo, but he was about to lose it. He was hesitant to leave it, even briefly, for fear that he would return to find that the locks had been changed, and he had been thrown out on the street. But, necessity is the mother of something— Leonard couldn't remember quite what—and Leonard was out of booze. Time to fire up the Mitsubishi and hit the road.

Leonard didn't hate the car anymore. It wasn't a Porsche, much less a Ferrari, but he was comfortable in it, and his cover story had held up pretty well—that he would just keep driving the Mitsubishi until the rioting and avalanche of crime began to subside, then he'd grab that limited edition V12 Ferrari he'd had his eye on. He often added that he'd probably pick up his new car at the Ferrari factory in Italy and spend a few months driving around Europe before shipping it back to the States.

Fielding hadn't said anything about taking the Mitsubishi back. Maybe he'd just forgotten the car. Or maybe he wanted the pleasure of seeing Leonard living in it.

The car scraped against the metal gate as Leonard drove out of the condo's garage. Then he took out a taillight on a car that had clearly parked too close to the driveway. People should learn how to park, Leonard thought as he tried to remember where the liquor store was.

Dennis watched as Lutz left the garage and tried to make his way down the street. He hoped that the police would stop Leonard before he killed somebody. It didn't take long.

The squad car pulled out of a side street just in time to watch the Mitsubishi graze a parked car and then veer wildly into oncoming traffic, recovering just in time to avoid a head-on crash.

The police hit their flashers, but didn't catch Leonard's attention. The siren did the trick, although the Mitsubishi didn't finally come to a halt for another half block.

Dennis parked as close as he dared and not be noticed. He rolled down his window to hear what the cops had to say.

Leonard didn't have a clue why the police had stopped him. He was pretty certain that his license tabs were up to date.

"Do you know why we stopped you, sir?" one of the cops asked.

Were these guys reading his mind?

"Did someone steal my license plate?"

"I need to see your license and registration," the cop said, ignoring what Leonard thought was a pretty damn good guess at why they might have stopped him.

Leonard was searching, unsuccessfully, for his driver's license when the other cop—who had sneaked around to the passenger's side—yelled and scared the hell out of him.

"Gun, partner!"

Suddenly, both cops were pointing guns at him.

"Sir, place both hands on the steering wheel and do not move them!" It was the first cop again, yelling much too loudly. Leonard wanted to tell him, I'm sitting right here. No need to scream at me.

The other cop opened the passenger-side door and Leonard watched him pull the gun out from between the seats. That's my gun, alright, Leonard thought, but what's it doing there? He couldn't remember bringing it with him tonight. He must have left it in the car the last time he took it with him. He was damn lucky it hadn't gotten stolen.

"Sir, step out of the vehicle slowly. No sudden moves. Keep your hands where we can see them!"

Why were these guys yelling at him?

Dennis watched as Leonard was handcuffed and searched, then he pulled carefully out of his parking spot and drove slowly by the cops as they maneuvered Leonard into the backseat of the squad car. No better time than the present to drop by Leonard's condo and retrieve the clean, never-been-fired gun he'd put in Leonard's little hidey-hole.

The next morning, Leonard awakened to a very different world. For one thing, he was sober, although he had the worst headache he'd ever had in his life. What he needed was a drink.

They'd offered him some indefinable goo that they'd called breakfast. He watched others wolf it down, but he figured he'd just throw it up. He forced himself to drink the coffee. They really needed to put a good bar in this place.

Around ten o'clock they'd brought him to this interrogation room. Some guy, Detective Something-or-Other, had read him his rights and had him sign a piece of paper. Leonard knew he was entitled to an attorney, but he had no idea what he was dealing with here. There were some pretty big gaps in his memory. So, he thought he'd just play along for a little while till he figured out what the deal was.

After he signed the paper, Leonard figured they'd just jump right in on him, maybe try one of those good-cop, bad-cop routines. But they hadn't done that. The detective just walked out and didn't come back. Leonard had been waiting for at least an hour with nothing to do but study the interrogation room. There wasn't much to study. There was a camera in the corner, pointed right at him. Leonard couldn't tell if it was recording or not. Then, finally, the door opened and in walked a female detective. She wasn't bad looking. Short blond hair. Nice rear end.

"I'm Detective Lancaster, Mr. Lutz. How are you feeling this morning?"

Lutz was thinking, Detective Lambchop. "I've got a little headache," he said, summoning his pleasant, dating tone.

"Do you know why you're here?" Getting right to it. No foreplay.

"I'm thinking drunk driving," Leonard said.

"That's part of it," Detective Lambchop said, "but, frankly, we're more interested in the gun."

What gun? Then he realized he hadn't said it out loud. "What gun? Did you search my condo? Did you have a warrant?"

"Do you have a gun in your condo?"

This was starting to get tricky. Leonard didn't say anything.

"I'm talking about the gun that was found, in plain view, when you were stopped last night."

Leonard was beginning to have a sinking feeling in the pit of his stomach. He kept silent.

"Why do you have the gun?"

"Personal protection," Leonard said, perhaps a bit too quickly. It seemed like a safe answer.

"Have you ever fired the gun?"

"Absolutely not."

"Who did?"

"No one, as far as I know."

"Someone did. It's been fired since the last time it was cleaned."

"Must have been before I got it."

"We don't have any record that you registered the gun."

"I was going to. I just forgot."

"Someone has removed the serial number from the gun. That's illegal."

"It wasn't me."

"The next thing we're going to do," Detective Lambchop said, "is turn the gun over to forensics, and they're going to test fire it into a water recovery tank. Then they're going to take the bullet details and run them through the national computer system. Each gun marks bullets in a unique way. The computer system is going to tell us if bullets fired from your gun were ever recovered at a crime scene. What I want to know from you is what we're going to find out. If you help us, we can help you."

Leonard knew that he could stall, but he also understood that his goose was cooked. He knew that his bullets had been recovered at the scene of the Deshawn Jackson shooting. If that were all, he could just claim that the gun must have been used before he got it. It was the 911 call that would finish him. He should never have done that. Now they had the gun in his possession, and his voice on the phone.

"I need an attorney," he said.

"Okay."

"When I get my attorney, I want to make a deal."

"What kind of a deal are we talking about?"

"Leniency for me in exchange for my giving you the guy who planned what you're going to find out happened—and a whole lot of other stuff," Leonard said. Then he thought, why not give her a little tease? "Stuff like, who burned down Congressman Sandstone's house. I can't tell you who lit the match, but I can tell you who paid for it."

"Well, Mr. Lutz, let me see what I can do for you."

"One other thing," Leonard said, "I'll need to be put into some kind of protective custody. The people I'm going to tell you about will try to kill me."

Detective Lancaster excused herself and found her partner

down the hall.

"We need to talk to the Chief and speed up the forensics on the Lutz gun. I think we've stumbled onto something really big."

41

The first night at the White House went remarkably well. There were additional speeches—more red meat for the crowd. Harley Bask, supportive as ever, brought his band and played for a couple of hours. The crowd kept calling for "Woke-Scam Blues" and "Mean Old Teleprompter Blues," which he played more than once, then did both again as an encore. The crowd, as they say, went wild.

Alex had expected that the first night would be easy. It was the next morning that worried him. Would the dawn find them encircled by federal troops? It was difficult to imagine troops attacking their peacefully protesting fellow citizens. On the other hand, it was difficult to imagine the FBI raiding the home of a former president at the behest of the National Archives. These were strange times indeed.

He also worried whether the protest would collapse. It was one thing to enjoy a long night of partying. It was quite another to hang on as the hours, or even days, dragged on and conditions grew increasingly uncomfortable. Would the crowd simply drift away?

But the dawn broke and the dreaded troops did not appear. Quite a different thing occurred. New protestors began to arrive—by the hundreds of thousands. The crowd engulfing the White House had swelled to over a million. Some, on their own initiative, had taken it into their heads to besiege the Capitol as well. Why the hell not?

Alex's delight at the hoard of new protestors quickly

turned to concern. How could they possibly provide food, drink, and all the other necessary support for so many people? Remarkably, the problem of too many protestors turned out to be self-solving. With a small protest, you had to husband your resources, hold everyone together. When you had over a million, people could come and go as they pleased. It didn't diminish the force of the protest. It was like removing one glassful of water from the ocean. If someone decided to leave a spot close to the White House, others immediately flowed into the void. Or, your friends could hold the spot while you were sent to bring back sandwiches. It wasn't an easy trek, but it was being done.

Now that the cat was out of the bag, so to speak, and they'd made it clear that they were here to protest, the signs came out.

CHAOS IS NOT AN ACCIDENT – IT IS THE PLAN

MAKE CRIME ILLEGAL AGAIN

AMERICA – GREAT WHILE IT LASTED

CHAOS IS THE GATEWAY TO TYRANNY

DON'T LET GRANDPA DRIVE THE CAR

IF GRANDPA ISN'T DRIVING, WHO IS?

MINIMUM JOB REQUIREMENT – YOU CAN READ
THE TELEPROMPTER

AMERICA IS IN ITS DEMOLITION PHASE

It was midafternoon when Alex caught sight of a military man working his way through the crowd toward him. He was wearing his field fatigues and had three stars on his shoulders. He was a big guy. His primary focus, at the moment, was trying not to step on anyone. When he had finally made it to Alex, he offered his hand.

"Travis Blake," he said

"Alex Walker."

"Well," Blake said, "I'm the guy who's supposed to be running this new military district around here that they've set up under martial law. I thought it was about time for me to come over here and meet the guy who's really in charge."

"We're not looking for any trouble, General."

"We can see that, and we're impressed. One of the reasons I wanted to meet you was to thank you for that. When people talk about a peaceful protest, this is what they hope for. Not this big, of course."

"Thank you," Alex said, "but something tells me you have something more on your mind."

"How long are you going to be here?"

"That's up to the president."

"I was afraid you would say that." He appeared thoughtful for a moment, then said, "I'm not going to stand here and pretend that I can move you out. My people estimate that there are something like 1,200,000 of you, and the number keeps growing. In this setting, no sane person would consider employing the amount of force that would be necessary to disperse a crowd this size. There are some people, political people, who disagree with that, but I don't take orders from them."

"I appreciate that, General," Alex said.

"What I can do, is try to help prevent a disaster from occurring. You've been lucky so far, but there is so much that could go wrong. That ranges from simple medical emergencies to full-blown panic and a human stampede. I'm sure you've thought of that."

"It's kept me up nights, but it's a problem I can't solve."

"I've gotten approval to help, with the clear understanding that we're not supporting what you're doing, we're only trying to prevent some tragedy from occurring. What I propose is to bring in unarmed soldiers to create corridors through the crowd so that people can more easily and more safely move. I can also bring in medical support to handle emergencies, including any necessary transporting of patients to hospitals. There are other things that we can discuss, but these are the two main issues on my mind right now. You have my word that neither I nor anyone under my command will in any way attempt to interfere with your protest. Obviously, aside from your permission, what I need most from you is for you to prepare the crowd for what will happen so that they understand that we are only here to help. Then we will need to proceed very slowly. We certainly don't want to cause the stampede we've come to prevent."

"Thank you, General. This is very generous of you. I will need to talk to others, but I don't have any doubt that we will accept your offer."

"Excuse me." It was Lucius St. John. He whispered in Alex's ear that Ham Hobart was on the phone.

"I apologize, General, but this is extremely important. Please forgive me. It'll only take a few minutes."

Alex moved over to the area they'd established for private communications. It wasn't perfect, but it was better than standing in the middle of the crowd.

"Hi, Ham, how's it going?"

"I have about twenty people," he said. He listed the names. The list included two serving governors, four retired senators, a number of men and women who had held senior leadership positions in the House, former cabinet members, and a couple of people who had made their careers managing presidential election campaigns. All were Democrats. Most were household names. They were people who the president knew and respected.

"They will be meeting with the president at 6:00 pm," Hobart said. "They will tell him that the time has come for

him to step down."
   "And if he doesn't step down?"
   "They will go public with their advice."

Made in the USA
Middletown, DE
28 August 2022